Matthew Skelton

ENDYMION SPRING

He shall have knowledge both Good and Evil

PUFFIN

For Mum, Dad and Lou

PUFFIN BOOKS

Published by the Penguin Group
Penguin Books Ltd, 80 Strand, London WC2R 0RL, England
Penguin Group (USA) Inc., 375 Hudson Street, New York, New York 10014, USA
Penguin Group (Canada), 90 Eglinton Avenue East, Suite 700, Toronto, Ontario, Canada M4P 2Y3
(a division of Pearson Penguin Canada Inc.)
Penguin Ireland, 25 St Stephen's Green, Dublin 2, Ireland (a division of Penguin Books Ltd)
Penguin Group (Australia), 250 Camberwell Road, Camberwell, Victoria 3124, Australia
(a division of Pearson Australia Group Pty Ltd)
Penguin Books India Pvt Ltd, 11 Community Centre, Panchsheel Park, New Delhi – 110 017, India
Penguin Group (NZ), cnr Airborne and Rosedale Roads, Albany, Auckland 1310, New Zealand
(a division of Pearson New Zealand Ltd)
Penguin Books (South Africa) (Pty) Ltd, 24 Sturdee Avenue, Rosebank, Johannesburg 2196, South Africa

Penguin Books Ltd, Registered Offices: 80 Strand, London WC2R 0RL, England

www.penguin.com

First published 2006
6

Text copyright © Matthew Skelton, 2006
Illustrations copyright © Bill Sanderson, 2006

The moral right of the author and illustrator has been asserted

This is a work of fiction. All characters and incidents,
including the depiction of historical figures and events,
are the product of the author's imagination

Set in Baskerville MT by Palimpsest Book Production Limited, Polmont, Stirlingshire
Made and printed in England by Clays Ltd, St Ives plc

British Library Cataloguing in Publication Data
A CIP catalogue record for this book is available from the British Library

ISBN-13: 987–0–141–32035–9
ISBN-10: 0–141–32035–4

St Jerome's College Library,
Oxford

What sort of book is this?

Blake turned over one page, and then another and another, looking for a way into the story, but he couldn't find one. There were no words to guide him – only a series of blank pages that led like a spiral staircase into the unknown. He let his mind follow them for a while, wondering where they would go, but they seemed to be leading nowhere, over and over again.

He felt disappointed and yet exhilarated too, as though he had embarked on a quest to find something. But what was he looking for? And how would he know when he found it? He was just a twelve-year-old boy who wasn't particularly good at reading. And yet he felt certain that the more he explored, the deeper he delved, the more likely he was to uncover something – some secret encoded in the paper perhaps – that would lead to an even greater discovery.

But how, he wondered, could anyone read a blank book?

In the end, he closed the volume and returned it to the shelf, little realizing that the story was already writing itself . . .

MAINZ,
Germany 1452

 ohann Fust arrived on a cold winter's night. While most of the city slept under a mantle of softly falling snow, he bribed the sentries to open the Iron Gate near the river and advanced, unobserved, through the streets. A young man hauled a heavy sledge behind him.

Even in the white-whirling darkness, Fust could see the bulk of the cathedral looming over the other buildings inside the city walls. The turrets, made from rich red sandstone, were an attractive rose colour by day, but by night they formed a vast mountain range, steeped in shadow. He glanced at them through narrowed eyes, but kept his distance, sticking to the walls of the half-timbered houses in which the noble patricians lived.

All around him were heaped-up smells: the fug of wood-smoke, the tang of straw, not to mention the stink of human sewage, which even the snow could not mask. Occasionally, pigs squealed as they wrestled for warmth in their pens, but otherwise there was just the slithering sledge behind him.

Fust waited for the boy to catch up.

Peter, dogging his Master's heels, paused to wipe the snow from his brow and mitten his hands under his armpits. He was so cold! Fust might have the luxury of a full-length cloak, thick gloves and laced boots, but his own leggings were too thin to withstand the severe pinch of winter. Worse, his low-cut shoes were no match for the mounting snowdrifts, which sent ice crystals avalanching down to his ankles. All he wanted was a fire to warm his body, food to fill his belly and a bed to rest his weary limbs.

He gazed at the wooden signs hanging above him in the gloom – the stuffed pigs and wheat sheaves sugges-tive of inns and bakeries – and longed for the journey to be over.

'Not far now, Peter,' said Fust, as if reading his thoughts. 'We're almost there.'

Letting out a long silver breath, Fust cut across an empty square towards the lanes and alleys that criss-crossed behind the market like fractured glass. His foot-steps scrunched the snow.

Peter did not move. Each of his muscles was mulishly

reliving the agonies of the trip. From Paris, they had tramped to Strasbourg and then, not finding what they sought, headed north-east towards Mainz, on the banks of the River Rhine: a journey of almost 400 miles. They had avoided the obvious river routes – the vineyards on the surrounding hills were too exposed, the towns too meddlesome – but kept to the hooded woods and vales, which were nearly impassable this winter. Peter did not believe in spooks or spectres, both of which were rumoured to dwell off the beaten track, but he was disturbed by Fust's constant need for secrecy. What was the man not telling him?

Peter cupped his hands over his mouth and blew into them, hoping to ignite a spark of feeling in his finger-tips. Surely they were meant for finer things than this! Little more than a month ago, he had been studying at one of the most distinguished libraries in Europe – the Library of St Victor in Paris – where he was learning the art of calligraphy from the best scribes. He had developed a fine, graceful penmanship and was proud of his achievements, copying missals and other religious books by hand. He liked to think that he wielded the quill with the finesse of a sword – drawing ink, if not blood.

But then Fust had arrived, changing everything.

A ghost from the past, Fust had promised Peter riches, power – anything – so long as he fulfilled a few simple tasks and chose to follow. He even pledged the hand of his daughter, Christina, in marriage in return for the boy's allegiance. How could he refuse?

Peter spat on the ground and scowled into the night, rubbing the spots where the blisters had formed on his hands. A rope had been looped around his waist and secured to the sledge behind him, which, like an ox, he had to drag through the snow. It was his yoke, his burden; his part of the agreement. Peter Schoeffer of Gernsheim was no better than a beast.

As if the provisions and blankets weren't heavy enough, there was a formidable chest to lug around. Loathsome monsters were engraved on its wooden panels, scaring away even his inquisitive fingers. Still more frightening were the two snakes, cast from black metal, which twisted round the lip of the lid. Their heads were entwined so as to form an ingenious lock. One false touch, Fust warned, and their fangs would release a poison so venomous it would paralyse him forever.

Peter shuddered. Could this be true?

Fust spoke mostly in riddles, partly to bewitch the boy, but also to safeguard his secret. Inside the chest was a material so rare, so exquisite, he suggested, that it would bring the whole world within the scope of their hands. It held an eye to the future and a tongue to the past. All they required was a means of harnessing it, a way of reading its prophecies in the form of a living, breathing book. That was why Fust needed Peter . . .

Peter shook his head. Now they were nearing the end of one journey, and beginning the next, he was having second thoughts. What if this book was a mistake – like Eve's decision to bite the apple, an attempt to gain forbidden knowledge? What if he was putting his very soul in jeopardy? Servitude in life was one thing, but eternal damnation another!

Sensing Fust waiting for him by the mouth of one of the alleys, Peter muttered an oath, strained against his harness and began once more to drag the heavy load behind him. He grunted like a workhorse. There was no turning back. His choice had been made.

The snow, falling more thickly now, swiftly and silently filled their tracks so that no one rising early the next morning could tell from which direction they had come or where they had gone. Instead, the citizens of Mainz opened their eyes to a pristine world: a glittering, snow-covered city that hid the mounds of dung from view. They were too dazzled by the spectacle, the surface of things, to sense the peril that had arrived under the cover of darkness.

Only I knew differently . . .

As usual I was peering up at the moon from the small casement window in the workshop on the corner of Christophstrasse. Despite the snow, its pocked face shone through the clouds and I watched, mesmerized, while snowflakes fluttered blackly against its luminescence before settling on the ground in drifts of perfect white – a stunning alchemy. Above the rooftops rose the shadow of the cathedral, as watchful as heaven.

My Master had not noticed the dip in temperature nor the diminishing light, but was absorbed in the finicky craft of invention. The other workmen had retired for the night to the dormitory at the top of the house, but he had pulled a stool closer to the fire and was busy tinkering with a complex piece of metal. Using a sharp tool, he scraped away tiny scrolls of brass from the edges of a mould.

A perfectionist, he was making ever more minute alterations to the equipment so that each piece of type he created would transfer exactly the right amount of ink to the paper he had imported from the mills upstream. Barrels of ordinary stock were stored beneath the stairs, while finer reams of rag paper from Italy, which he preferred, were kept alongside the expensive animal skins, which he was going to prepare as vellum.

Each night, he tried to convince me that we were one day closer to our dreams, but I was no longer so sure.

The money he had invested in the printing press – a much-guarded secret – was swiftly running out and what remained of his gold was turning to sand between his fingers. Besides, I was content the way things were. The room crackled with warmth, and the sounds of my Master's industry were all the company I needed. It was a far cry from my past.

Just then, I sensed a bundled-up figure lurking outside the church on the opposite side of the street and pressed my face closer to the glass, trying to distinguish its shape. A lump of shadow had detached itself from the main porch and was staring in my direction.

'Are you moon-gazing again, young Endymion?' said my Master, making me turn round. 'Come, I need your fingers.'

I nodded, then glanced back at the window. The figure had gone. Breathing on the thick swirl of glass, I drew a face in the moon of condensation and turned back to my Master before the smile could fade.

'My hands are too clumsy for this work,' he sighed as I crouched beside him. His fingers were scored with scars and his skin coated in a soft silvery sheen from the metals he used: lead, tin and just a touch of antimony – that most poisonous element, which gave his pieces of type their bite. Black inky blotches had settled on his knuckles like flies.

I took the magnifying lens from the table and held it out to him. His face was streaked with dirt and his beard had grown long and grizzled, but I loved him just the same. He studied the mould in his hand for a moment, his eye swimming behind the lens of beryl. Even now he was not satisfied. He held the apparatus closer to the fire and resumed his tinkering.

I liked to think that I could help Herr Gutenberg. He had taken me in as an apprentice two years before, when I was a starving waif on the street. It was the least I could do to repay his kindness – no, better yet, his confidence.

Mostly, I performed menial tasks in the print room. I rose early to stoke the fire, sweep the floor and dampen the sheets of paper prior to his daily experiments with the printing press: a machine he'd had specially adapted from the wine presses in the region. This latest model consisted of a sturdy, upright wooden frame with a lever and screw that lowered a heavy plate on to an artfully arranged tray of type, which he slid beneath. The inked letters then transferred their message to the paper he inserted, sheet by sheet. We could print multiple copies of a text for as long as the type lasted. Books would no longer have to be copied laboriously by hand; we could print them with this machine. The invention, Herr Gutenberg believed, would change the world.

Sometimes he allowed me to mix the inks. This was a messy business that involved blending the soot from our lamps with varnish, with just a splash of urine added in for good measure ('The secret ingredient,' he said with a smile); but what I really enjoyed was composing type. This was my special task – a job reserved for my fingers alone.

For a few hours each day, while the workmen operated the press, I would sit at a low trestle table with hundreds of bits of metal type – a broken alphabet – in front of me. Piece by piece, I would string the letters together to form words, sentences and finally whole passages of text, always mirror images of the examples my Master set before me. Backwards writing, he called it. I excelled at it. Even better, I was learning to read.

So far, we had experimented with basic Latin primers for the law students who thronged the city, but my Master had recently set his sights on greater, bolder initiatives: Bibles. This was where the real money lay. There were always people hungry for the Word of God. All we needed was additional backing from our investors and a chance to prove that our books were every bit as beautiful and accurate as those produced by the most accomplished scribes.

Unbeknownst to my Master, I was also practising the art of printing on my own. Already, I had put my name

on a little toolkit he had given me on my first anniversary: a soft leather pouch containing my picks, awls and
chisels. One by one, I added the letters in my composing
stick, and then punched them into the leather with the
utmost care, gradually assuming my new identity: E-n-
d-y-m-i-o-n S-p-r-i-n-g. The letters were a little crooked,
but the name stuck.

I knew that my skill impressed him. Herr Gutenberg
said that I had swift fingers, but an even swifter mind. I
was growing into a fine apprentice. 'A real printer's devil,'
he said half-jokingly, dislodging my cap and mussing my
hair.

I wanted to tell him that he was growing into a fine
father, too, but I didn't. I couldn't. My voice, like everything else, had been taken from me at birth.

At this moment the door downstairs blew open and I got
up to shut it.

No sooner had I reached the top stair than I stopped.
A figure had entered the house and was rapidly ascending
the steps towards me. A gust of snow raged in behind
him. I rushed back to rejoin my Master by the fire.

Within moments a bullish man had appeared on the
threshold of the room. Red welts streaked his cheeks,
where the frost had nipped him, and he breathed

through flared nostrils. His eyes roamed round the workshop, knocking over tables and equipment, until they settled on my Master, who had looked up in surprise.

'Fust,' he said, recognizing the stranger. There was little warmth in his voice.

The intruder bit back a smile. 'Gutenberg,' he replied.

Fust noticed my look of disapproval.

'And who is this urchin?' he asked, flicking the snow from his shoulders and advancing towards the fire. A short, round-shouldered man, he was dressed in a heavy, fur-trimmed cloak with chains and medallions draped across his chest – a sure sign of his wealth. The boards creaked under his weight.

He brought a surge of cold air into the room and I shivered.

'His name is Endymion,' said my Master. 'My apprentice.'

I glowed to hear those words, but Fust snorted derisively. He tore off his gloves and slapped them on the table, making me flinch. Then he reached out and grasped my chin between his ring-encrusted fingers. Turning my face from left to right, he inspected me with hard, flinty eyes, which flashed in the firelight. He had thick, reddish-brown hair and a fox-coloured beard that divided at the base to form two distinct points.

'Endymion, eh?' He tasted my name, then spat it out. 'What is he? A dreamer?'

My Master said nothing. He had often told me the legend of Endymion, the Greek shepherd boy who was loved by the moon and granted eternal youth. He said the name suited the way I gazed into the distance, dreaming of other things.

'Johann, what are you doing?' said Fust, finally letting me go. 'Just look at him. He's a runt! Too puny even to pick up a piece of type, let alone turn the screw. What use is he to you?'

I opened my mouth to protest, but no sound emerged.

'And a mute, too,' said Fust, amused, smothering me in a foul-smelling laugh. 'Tell me, Johann. Where did you find him?'

I willed my Master not to answer. I didn't want him mentioning the time I had reached for his purse in the crowded market-place, only to encounter a pouch full of type and a firm hand fettered round my wrist.

Luckily, he chose to ignore the insult.

'I see you have an apprentice of your own,' he said, glancing at the young man who had entered behind Fust. 'Peter Schoeffer, if I'm not mistaken, back in Mainz at last.'

I turned to stare at the newcomer, who stood at the top of the stairs, ill at ease. Dressed in rags that were hardly suited to the weather, Peter inched closer to the hearth, trying to steal whatever warmth he could from the room.

A furtive look from Fust warned him to remain still.

My Master, noticing the young man's discomfort, addressed him directly. 'Tell me, Peter, where have you been?'

'Never you mind,' snapped Fust, but Peter had already opened his mouth to speak.

'Paris,' he mumbled, looking down at his soiled shoes. His leggings were patched with mud and holes gaped in his jacket. 'The Library of St Victor.'

My Master's eyes widened with approval. 'The Library of St Victor! Why, move closer to the fire, boy, and tell me all about it! Is it as remarkable as they say?'

'It's wonderful,' said Peter, his face brightening for the first time. 'The library must contain a thousand volumes. I've read half the books in the world!'

Fust interrupted: 'Peter, aren't you forgetting something? In fact, why don't you take this opportunity to fetch my things and get this' – he eyed me up and down – '. . . boy . . . to help you? There's no point delaying the purpose of our visit.'

He pressed a hand to my back and shoved me towards the stairs. I checked with my Master to make sure I was not needed, but he was staring at the lens in his fingers, apparently under the impression that the meeting could not be avoided.

'Now then, let's talk business,' I heard Fust say as I followed Peter down the stairs.

Snow had drifted against the side of the house, nearly obliterating the sledge Peter had dragged up to the door. White peaks crowned the surrounding roofs and reared against the neighbouring buildings like a frozen sea, spangling timbers and frosting shutters.

I started bundling the heavy, snow-caked blankets into my hands, wondering how long our guests were planning to stay – it looked like a long time – when Peter stopped me.

'Not those,' he grumbled. 'This.'

With a flourish, he ripped off the remaining covers to reveal a monstrous chest buried beneath the mound of blankets. I stared at it, appalled. The casket seemed to suck the very night into it: it was laden with shadow. A chill wind whipped the loose snow round my legs and I hugged myself to keep warm.

'Here, take that end,' Peter bossed me, evidently in a hurry to return to the fireside, 'and be careful not to drop it.'

I took the iron handle in both hands and attempted to lift it. It was extremely heavy. Fortunately Peter bore the brunt of the weight in his strong arms and slowly, stopping every few steps, we managed to heave the chest into the house. The icy metal bit into my skin.

As we climbed the stairs, the light from the workshop began to pick out shapes from the sides of the box. Lumpy knobs revealed themselves as hideous beasts I had never seen before. Scaly monsters and frightening demons leered at me, as if from the pits of Hell. They had scabby cheeks and savage teeth and eyes like burnt umber. But it was only once we re-entered the room, half-kicking and half-sliding the chest across the floor, that I noticed the two snakes coiled tightly round the lid, their heads interlocked. Peter eyed them with obvious distrust, but I was fascinated. They seemed to draw me towards them.

'I wouldn't touch those if I were you,' Fust advised me suddenly, catching my hands straying closer to the snakes. 'They just might bite.'

My hands whipped back to my sides. Something about the way he said this made me believe him. Perhaps they were venomous? Fust was regarding me down the length of his nose, his dark eyes glinting. Obediently, I backed away.

Fust turned his attention to my Master, who was staring

at the fire, as though the future were held in its flames. He seemed to have aged in the interval.

'So, Gutenberg, what do you say?'

There was a heap of gold and silver next to the discarded lens on the table – more gulden than I had seen since the start of the year.

'I fear,' said my Master slowly, 'I shall have to sleep on it.'

'Pish! You know you cannot resist.'

'Yes, but what you propose is –'

My Master paused, unable to come up with an appropriate word.

'Perfectly reasonable,' suggested Fust.

'Preposterous,' retorted my Master.

Fust spat with scorn. 'Johann, you know not what you are saying! With your machine and my cunning, we can achieve . . . everything! There will be no end to our wealth or influence.'

'Yes, but at what cost?' asked my Master warily, rubbing his eyes and smearing a daub of ink across his face. 'It is not exactly the kind of influence I was hoping for. I will have none of it.'

'Come, where is the merciless desire that once fired your spirit?'

Fust surveyed the room. Surrounding the press were numerous benches and ink-splattered tables, covered with crucibles, iron frames and padded ink balls – the tools of our trade. Folded sheets of paper hung from the rafters like birds.

'I have put those times behind me,' said Herr Gutenberg moodily.

'Nonsense! I can see that even now you're engaged on some new enterprise.' Fust patted the handle of the press like a pack animal. 'What is it this time? Almanacs? Indulgences?'

Herr Gutenberg glanced up. 'Well, I was thinking of printing a Bible,' he said diffidently. 'A huge and potentially lucrative undertaking.'

Fust spotted his opportunity. He snaked his way behind my Master and laid a jewelled hand on his shoulder.

'Allow me, then, to fan the flames. Another 800 gulden, effective immediately, to help you launch this latest venture. Just think of what you'll achieve. Wealth befitting a patrician of the city! Books impressed with your name throughout the Empire! You will be spoken of with awe and adulation for generations to come!'

'And your demands?' said my Master, tasting temptation. He looked up into the other man's face like a captivated child.

'Why, an interest in your business, of course,' responded Fust, rubbing his hands together. 'And a right to use your equipment, if and when I see fit.'

Once again his eyes landed on me, as though I were one more of my Master's possessions. I squirmed.

'And that chest?' My Master nodded towards the wooden box, which lay hidden, but not forgotten, near the hearth. In the firelight, I could see the ugly faces jeering and scowling at me. Drops of melted snow, tinted red by the fire, glinted on the snakes' fangs.

'A special kind of paper, that is all,' said Fust, 'part of my own invention. As you say, it need not concern you. Peter, I am sure, will safeguard it in my absence.'

Peter and I exchanged looks.

'In fact, he may as well assist you by learning the tricks of your trade.'

A downward curl to Peter's lips suggested he was not altogether thrilled to have his services volunteered in this way. No doubt he had been looking forward to more salubrious accommodation at his Master's house. He clenched his swollen fingers, as though gripping an imaginary sword.

'So, Gutenberg, what do you say?' said Fust, indicating the time had come for a decision.

My Master glanced at the heap of coins on the table and then at me. Wearily and with misgivings, he nodded.

'Excellent!' said the visitor. He spat on his palm and extended it towards my Master, who took it rather more hesitantly in his own.

They shook.

'I shall get Helmasperger, the notary, to draft an agreement in the morning. Until then, I bid you farewell.'

Peter took a few steps to waylay him, but Fust was impatient to be off. 'I am sure that Gutenberg will have some bread and beer for you,' he snapped. 'After all, he is no longer quite the . . . pauper . . . he was.'

Peter appealed, but to no avail. Without another word, Fust swept out of the house, while my Master, overcome by sudden tiredness, asked me to see that our guest was fed and made to feel at home. There was not enough room in the dormitory upstairs, so Peter would have to make do, like me, by bedding down before the fire. Herr Gutenberg bade us both goodnight and retired to his private bedchamber, with the mound of gold stacked heavily in his hand.

While I prepared my cot, Peter strutted around the workshop, picking up pieces of equipment from the surrounding benches and testing their weights in his hand. He then gave the handle of the press a forcible yank, scraping the flat wooden plate against its marble bed.

Finally, he contented himself with the mirrors along the walls. Muttering to himself, he paced back and forth like a peacock, admiring his reflection. He had a handsome face – penetrating brown eyes, thick brows and the makings of a beard. He obviously took pride in his appearance, for among the hand-copied books and writing instruments we carried in from the sledge were several pouches and horns full of ointment and dried herbs. He ran a finger across his teeth with a paste of powdered sage and pinched a few spots before settling down on a bed of blankets by the fire. Almost immediately, he was asleep.

I watched and waited and then, when I was certain he would not stir, padded lightly over to the chest and knelt beside it. The remaining firelight picked out yet more ghoulish shapes from its sides. Red shadows flickered over the two snakes, which courted and kissed, coming together in a seductive embrace.

Detecting a vague rustling movement inside the box, I placed my head closer to the lid. Something was alive within it! A soft sound, like a breeze, whispered in my ears.

Cautiously, I ran my fingers along the bumps and warts of wood until my hands collided with the snakes. My heart, a cannon of excitement, drowned out Fust's previous warning and I coiled my fingers round the cool metal domes of their heads. Carefully, I tried to prise them apart – avoiding the fangs, which looked sharp enough to bite.

Nothing happened.

There were no catches or springs to release the locking mechanism. The lid was clamped shut. There was no way in.

All the same, I could hear the faint hissing sound inside, beckoning me closer.

The fire snapped suddenly beside me and I jumped.

The movement must have disturbed Peter, for he murmured in his sleep and reached out a slumbering hand to catch me . . . but it was the name 'Christina' on his lips and not mine, and he was quickly asleep again. His breathing deepened into a pig-like grunt.

Nevertheless, I could not risk incurring the wrath of Fust so soon. His presence seemed to linger in the house like a menacing shadow, a suspicion I couldn't shake off. Remembering the strange way he had looked at me, as though I and not Herr Gutenberg were now the object of his quest, I returned to my cot and lay for some hours awake, my mind full of restless, moving thoughts.

What, I wondered, lay inside the chest?

Finally, the thief of sleep overtook me and, like the snow falling outside, dreams began to settle.

St Jerome's College,
Oxford

One

Blake glanced at his watch and let out a small, exasperated sigh. What was taking her so long? His mother had promised to be ready more than half an hour ago. He started drumming his fingers along the books in the college library. What should he do now?

He had already climbed the rolling ladders in the Mandeville Room and used the metal tracks along the shelves to propel himself from one bookcase to another. Then he had taken down the largest, heaviest volumes he could find and placed them on a desk near the window so he could look through them properly. The letters in the stone-coloured paper had reminded him of fossils and he'd run his fingers over the vertebrae of words for a while before closing the covers. Most of the books were written in languages he couldn't understand and he'd given up trying.

Next, he'd spun the globe near the door and searched

for a sign of his home town. He couldn't find it anywhere. North America was just a featureless blob with a few rivers traversing its plains – like cracks in the varnish. Where the Great Lakes ought to be, the map-maker had planted a forest of tepees and drawn a solitary buffalo. This, he realized, was about as close to home as he would come for the next few months . . .

He sighed.

Leaving the room, he now tried to calculate the number of books in the library. There must be tens of thousands, he guessed, scanning the shelves around him: a lifetime's reading stacked from floor to ceiling, extending in both directions.

He trailed his fingers along the spines, expelling little clouds of dust in the air as he walked.

Passing the office door with 'PAULA RICHARDS, LIBRARIAN' stencilled neatly on its white surface, Blake paused to listen. He could just make out the rise and fall of his mother's voice on the other side. She wasn't angry, just forceful – used to getting her own way.

A visiting academic in Oxford for one term, she spent most of her time in the Bodleian Library, one of the largest collections of books in the world, and needed someone to keep an eye on her two children. She was busy negotiating a new arrangement with the librarian, who was fast becoming their babysitter.

Blake checked his watch – thirty-six minutes – and sighed.

He tried walking backwards now, tapping the books in reverse order, to see if this would help pass the time.

A series of stern-looking portraits glared down at him from the walls. Like magicians, they were dressed in dark capes and had sharp, pointy beards. Elaborate ruffs, like squashed chrysanthemums, burst from their collars. The older men had jaded eyes and tortoise-like skin, but there were also a few pale-faced boys like himself. He glanced at their nameplates: Thomas Sternhold (1587–1608); Jeremiah Wood (1534–1609); Isaac Wilkes (1616–37); Lucius St Boniface de la Croix (1599–1666). Each man was holding a small book and pointing to a relevant passage with a forefinger, as though reminding future generations to remain studious and well-behaved.

Blake disregarded their frowns of disapproval and continued running his fingers along the books, rapping the spines with the back of his knuckles.

All of a sudden, he stopped.

One of the volumes had struck him back! Like a cat, it had taken a playful swipe at his fingers and ducked back into hiding. He whisked his hand away, as though stung.

He looked at his fingers, but couldn't see anything unusual. They were smeared with dust, but there was no obvious mark or injury on his skin. Then he looked at the books to see which one had leaped out at him, but they all seemed pretty ordinary, too. Just row upon row of crumbly old volumes, like toy soldiers in leather uniforms standing to attention – except that one of them had tried to force its way into his hand.

He sucked on his finger thoughtfully. A thin trail of blood, like a paper cut, was forming where the book had nicked his knuckle.

All around him the library was sleeping in the hot, still afternoon. Shafts of sunlight hung in the air like dusty curtains and a clock ticked somewhere in the distance, a ponderous sound that seemed to slow down time. Small footsteps crept along the floorboards above. That was probably his sister, Duck, investigating upstairs. But no one else was around.

Only Mephistopheles, the college cat, a sinewy black shadow with claws as sharp as pins, was sunbathing on a strip of carpet near the window – and he only cared about one thing: himself.

As far as Blake could tell, he was entirely alone. Apart, that is, from whatever was lurking on the shelf.

Slowly, cautiously, he ran his fingers again along the books.

'Blake!' his mother hissed. Her face had appeared from

the office doorway. She was checking up on him – as usual, just when he was on the point of disobeying her.

Paula Richards, the librarian, stood behind her, smiling amiably.

'What did I tell you?' his mother scolded him. 'You're not to touch the books. They're fragile, rare and in some cases extremely valuable. Now pick up that book *carefully* and go find your sister. I won't be much longer.'

Blake looked down, surprised. There, in front of him, face down on the floor, was an unremarkable brown leather volume he hadn't noticed before. It seemed to be waiting for him to turn it over.

His mother apologized to the librarian. 'I'm sorry, Mrs Richards, but Blake's not what you'd call a natural reader.'

'Oh, I wouldn't say that, Dr Winters,' said Paula Richards, happily. 'I sometimes knock the books off the shelves myself.'

She winked at Blake and then pulled the door shut behind them, so he couldn't overhear the rest of their discussion.

Blake liked Mrs Richards. She was a boisterous woman who loved books and, even more, loved talking about them. Her thick glasses clattered against the desk whenever she took them off, and through them, Blake could see the words on the pages she showed him swimming back and forth like legs in a pool. Some letters bulged and curved more than others, but what fascinated him even more were the little indentations in the paper – like footprints in snow. They reminded him of polar expeditions.

Mrs Richards made books seem magical, almost fun, whereas his mother turned them into work. She used them to test his reading comprehension and often quizzed him about his results at school.

He'd not done very well last year, it's true; but she wouldn't believe him when he said it was not from lack of trying. Things just didn't make sense any more. It was as if the words started disintegrating the moment he looked at them. One minute they'd be sitting in a straight row like birds on a wire; the next, they'd take off like a flight of startled sparrows. He couldn't pay attention.

It was hoped that a short break in Oxford, tutored by his mother, would give him a renewed focus. 'A fresh perspective,' his home-room teacher had said, as though the phrase encapsulated everything; but his mother had simply passed him on to other college officials who were also busy, and so he spent most of his time working on his own in the library or looking after his little sister. His mother was researching a new book and didn't have time to be 'disturbed'.

Blake bent down to pick up the volume that had fallen to the floor, but then stopped. A ripple of anxiety passed through him. Was this the book that had attacked his finger?

But that's impossible, he thought. Books don't do that. Besides, the cover of this book was chipped and cracked, scabbed like an old leather glove. It looked perfectly harmless. He shook his head. He was just being silly.

Quickly, before he could change his mind, he reached down and scooped up the volume. Then something else happened: the book realigned itself in his fingers – just slightly. The movement was barely noticeable, yet Blake was certain he had felt it. The book sat in his hand, a perfect fit, as though that was exactly where it belonged.

His heart skipped a beat.

Looking closely, he could see that two small clasps, once holding the book together, had broken and the strips of leather hung down like unfastened watchstraps. A silver prong, like a snake's tooth, dangled from one of the bands. Obviously, it was this metal fang that had pricked his finger. His knuckle throbbed with the memory and he sucked on the wound, where another bead of blood was forming.

There was writing on the cover, too, but this had faded so that the title was barely visible. The words were as delicate as the strands of a spiderweb, and he blew on them softly to remove a fine layer of dust. A name or title, pressed into the leather in unusual rounded letters, appeared before his eyes:

ENDYMION SPRING

He opened the book.

His fingers were jittery, but even so the pages flickered of their own accord – as though an invisible hand had reached across time or space and was searching for the best place to begin.

He held his breath, amazed.

Some of the pages were stuck together, joined at the edges, unopened, while others unfolded like maps without obvious destinations. They reminded him of the origami birds he had once seen a Japanese lady making on television. There were no lines on the paper, unlike a notebook, and no sections to write in, unlike a diary; and yet there were no printed pages, so far as he could see, so it couldn't be a regular novel either. It was as if he had discovered a completely blank book. But what was a book without words doing in a library?

A faint tingling sensation, like the suggestion of a breeze, tickled his fingertips and he moved closer to the window to inspect the book more thoroughly. He thought he could detect minute ridges glowing inside the paper, as though the sun were shining through it, communicating something; but when he held the pages up to the light, hoping to find a secret message encoded inside, he couldn't see anything. The pages were like thin, frosty panes of glass. Unreadable.

Disappointed, he walked back to the shelf, stroking the paper absentmindedly. It felt softer than anything he had touched before. Like snowflakes before they melt, he thought – or, or, or what precisely? It was an elusive feeling, a sensation he couldn't quite grasp. Yet once he had opened the book, he didn't want to let go. It had cast its spell on him.

Obviously, this wasn't an ordinary book at all!

'What are you looking at?'

Duck had surprised him by sneaking down from the gallery upstairs. She clung, monkey-like, to the edge of a bookcase and studied him with a curious expression.

'Nothing,' he said, and abruptly turned his back so she couldn't see.

'You're lying.'

'I told you, it's nothing.'

'Since when do you like reading?'

'I don't, so go away.'

Duck rummaged through some of the other books on

the shelf. She selected a few of the fatter volumes and took them to a desk, where she skimmed through them. 'Typography?' she asked, wrinkling her nose. 'Since when have you been interested in that?'

She showed him the frontispiece of the first book she had chosen: *De Ortu et Progressu Artis Typographicae.* An illustration beneath the title portrayed a group of men in a vaulted chamber full of heavy machinery and sloping desks. They were printing books.

'I'm not,' he said. 'This book's different. It was just in the wrong section, that's all.'

'What's it about?'

He ignored her and continued leafing through the volume. It's as if I'm the first person to have discovered it, he thought; or else it's the first book to have discovered me . . .

But that was impossible! Mrs Richards must have looked through it when she catalogued it. He flipped through the volume for an index card or something to identify it, but there was nothing inside. Nor was there a label on the spine, where the librarian sometimes placed a number so that students could sign out books from the library. There didn't seem to be any record of this book at all. It was as though it didn't exist.

For a moment he considered slipping it inside his knapsack. Would it be stealing, he wondered, to keep a book that no one knew existed? It doesn't even have any words in it, so it can't be of much use, he thought. Or could it? Perhaps he could sign it out – but then he'd have to ask Mrs Richards for a call number, and how could he justify wanting to read a blank book?

He decided to put the volume back on the shelf. He'd had enough mystery for one day.

Then, just as he was about to close the covers, he noticed some words etched on the paper in front of him, in the very centre of the book. He had not even turned to the page. It just lay open there.

Where had they come from?

The name he had seen on the cover was repeated, but this time within a series of lines – or what looked like verses. They were written in such minuscule letters as to be almost invisible. Like the book, they appeared to make no sense.

He whispered the words to himself.

'What did you say?'

Duck again.

'Nothing. Mind your own business.'

'Well, it sounded weird to me. What book is that anyway?'

She got up to take a closer look.

Blocking her with his shoulder, Blake recited the words in an even softer voice, so she could not overhear:

'When Summer and Winter in Autumn divide
The Sun will uncover a Secret inside.
Should Winter from Summer irrevocably part
The Whole of the Book will fall quickly apart.
Yet if the Seasons join Hands together
The Order of Things will last forever.
These are the Words of Endymion Spring.
Bring only the Insight the Inside brings.'

Blake scratched his brow, confused. The sun might refer to the lines he had seen in the paper, and the last sentence seemed to confuse two similar sounding words, but who – or what – was Endymion Spring? And how could anyone read a blank book?

Obviously, he wasn't smart enough to figure it out, since he couldn't make head or tail of the poem, let alone the book's mysterious contents.

'Can I see it?' said Duck again.

'No, go away.'

'Well, from here it looks like a blank book.'

'That's because there's nothing in it,' he said automatically and then stopped, surprised she couldn't make out any of the words in front of him.

'Show me!' she insisted.

'No, don't touch it,' he said firmly, holding it away from her fingers. 'It's rare or valuable . . . or *something*.'

He glanced at her. As usual, she was wearing the bright yellow raincoat with the orange hood that she had been wearing since the Day of the Big Argument. That was the day their parents had been arguing so much that they had ended up crying. Duck had gone to her room to fetch her favourite raincoat and had startled them all when she got back. 'It's to protect me from your tears,' she'd said in a squeaky voice that was trying to sound like an adult's, but sounded so childish instead. Everyone had burst out laughing then – even Duck eventually – and there had been tears of laughter in their eyes, instead of pain.

And for a time that had done the trick. Their parents had been happier, if only for a while.

But since that day Duck had gone on wearing the coat, unwilling to take it off in case it undid the magic. Yet the effect, Blake knew, was rapidly wearing off. It had faded so much, in fact, that it was almost gone. That was partly why they were here in Oxford, when their dad was on the other side of the Atlantic.

He looked at her again. She seemed unhappy.

'It's nothing,' he said more gently. 'It's just an empty book.'

He let her hold it for a moment, then returned it to the shelf, where it disappeared between two thick volumes on printing history.

He put his arm around her. 'Come on. Let's wait for Mum over there.'

Two

Reaching the foyer, Blake went to sit on the marble steps leading up to the gallery. A grandfather clock ticked wearily beside him.

Above him, on a landing halfway up the stairs, was a glass cabinet containing the most treasured item in the library's collection: a thick manuscript belonging to the monks who had lived in the college more than 500 years before.

He got up to take a closer look.

The manuscript was decorated with elaborate vines of green and gold paint that blossomed into feathery leaves and beautiful peacock-coloured flowers. He breathed on the glass and watched as the twin columns of black hand-writing disappeared beneath a layer of ice.

From his vantage point he could see the foyer below – a hall lined with pillars and busts – but there was still no sign of his mother. Duck crouched by one of the tall card catalogues, stroking Mephistopheles. The cat curled like a comma round her feet.

Blake returned his attention to the manuscript.

As the mist slowly cleared, he saw a red oval letter regain some of its colour at the top of the left-hand column. Inside the large crimson O was a miniature painting: a monk in a black robe sat on a faldstool with a tiny puppet-like figure perched on his knee. The unusual character wore a distinctive mustard-coloured hood, a bit like a jester's cap, and a dull yellow garment that barely disguised his hunched back.

A typewritten note next to the manuscript explained:

Majuscule: Here, the scribe Theodoric receives words from an old man in a yellow cloak. Identity unknown. Mid-15th century.

Blake stared at the strange, emaciated figure. 'But he's a boy,' he murmured to himself, 'not an old man.'

'I'm afraid you're mistaken,' said a voice at the bottom of the stairs.

Blake tore his eyes from the manuscript to see Paula Richards, the librarian, bounding up the steps towards him. Readjusting her glasses, she leaned in for a closer inspection, her blouse crushing against the glass in an explosion of silk and lace – like a frilly airbag.

'See here,' she said, underlining part of the text with her finger and spouting something incomprehensible in Latin. 'Theodoric attributes great learning to this figure. How could a child know such things? Most scholars agree he is an old man, extolling the wisdom that comes with age and experience.'

Blake was about to object, when he noticed a string of words unfurling from the puppet's mouth like a square speech bubble.

'What does that mean?' he asked.

The librarian considered the motto for a moment and then translated it as: 'Wisdom speaks with a silent tongue.'

Blake frowned. 'I don't get it.'

'No, nor quite frankly do I,' said the librarian with a laugh, wiping away the smears his fingers had left on the glass.

'Oh no, not you too,' exclaimed his mother from downstairs. 'Come on, Blake. Don't take up any more of Mrs Richards' valuable time. I'm sure she has better things to do.'

Blake muttered something under his breath, but Paula Richards merely chuckled. She put her arm round his shoulders and gently guided him down the steps towards the door, where his mother was waiting, briefcase in hand.

'I think it means it's better to be seen, but not heard,' the librarian remarked privately in his ear.

Blake nodded, then glanced over his shoulder at the manuscript in its glass coffin. 'I still think it's a boy,' he murmured to himself.

The sun was shining brightly when at last they emerged from the library.

Paula Richards held the door open for Mephistopheles, who was undecided whether or not to go out. He stretched lazily, half in and half out of the door, although Blake noticed that she finally nudged him out with her foot.

'The library is no place for the likes of you,' she told the cat warningly.

Blake grinned. He remembered her telling him how Mephistopheles had once been trapped in the library overnight and left her a 'little present', which it wasn't part of her duty to clear up.

Juliet Winters led Duck and Blake down the steps and round a small circular lawn that faced the library. A warm breeze followed them through the trees and cast a shimmering pattern of light and shade on the path. Mephistopheles bounded ahead, leap-frogging over shadows.

They passed under a stone archway, thick with matted cobwebs, and continued along the side of an immense building with protruding diamond-paned windows: the dining hall. A stairwell led up to the main doors, which were stippled with carved roses, but they carried on, round the buttery, until they came to a long, covered passageway.

This was the oldest part of the college, dating back to the fourteenth century, when St Jerome's was home to an order of Benedictine monks. Back then, it had been a warren of stone buildings with neatly tended herb gardens and cloistered passages leading to the chapel; now, it was a good place to whoop and holler, since the low ceilings and colonnaded walkways rang out with echoes.

Blake raced ahead, disturbing centuries of peace and quiet.

To his right, dusty staircases spiralled up to what had once been the monks' dormitories, but were now book-lined offices, while, to his left, a series of stone arches gave way to a central plot of land, in which a giant plane tree was growing. A bench had been positioned beneath its lowest branches – 'for quiet contemplation', his mother had said, meaning it was not for him or Duck to clamber on.

Almost exactly opposite, just visible through a screen of ivy, was the Old Library. A series of jagged curves, like teeth, had been carved around its entrance, making it resemble a snarling lion. A low wooden door, slatted with iron bolts, barred the way in. Blake longed to see inside – he could imagine all sorts of treasures on its shelves – but like many things in Oxford it was closed to tourists, and especially children.

Blake did not wait for his mother to catch up, but stepped into an adjoining courtyard. He gazed up at the honey-coloured walls. As always, the college reminded him of a castle. Stone battlements crowned with square towers engulfed him on all sides. Gargoyles grinned at him from the gutters. They weren't drooling rainwater today, which was fortunate, but basking in the strong sunlight.

Blake closed his eyes and, like them, let the warm air cushion his cheeks.

'Come on, Quasimodo,' his mother called out, turning unexpectedly towards the Fellows' Garden. Duck giggled and screwed up her face at him, before following their mother. Blake charged after them.

The Fellows' Garden was a private area extending behind the chapel to the eastern edge of the college, where a tiny door opened on to a tree-lined boulevard that divided St Jerome's from its neighbours, St Guineforte's and Frideswide Hall. Thick walls guarded the flowerbeds from view, although Blake could detect a faint summery sweetness in the air.

'Aren't you going to the Porter's Lodge?' he asked, trying to redirect their steps towards the small building inside the main gate, where the post arrived. It was unlikely that a letter from his father would have been delivered since that morning, but he wanted to make sure.

'I thought we'd go for a short stroll instead,' answered his mother, shading her eyes with her hand. 'Then walk back to the house. It's such nice weather. It'd be a shame to waste it.'

She turned to unlock the gate.

Blake was happy to get some exercise – the previous weeks had been rainy and cold, and they'd travelled in on a bus each day – but he wasn't in a hurry to return to Millstone Lane. The house there didn't feel like home yet. It was damp and dreary, no matter what the weather, and there wasn't even a TV or computer to keep him company during the long evenings.

'Well, can I go and check?' he said. He knew he was pushing his luck and scraped a line in the gravel with the toe of his shoe.

The key grated in the lock.

'Oh, go on,' she said, 'but be quick. We'll wait for you over here.'

She indicated a stretch of grass just inside the wrought-iron gate, where a few late flowers were soaking up the sun. Blake nodded and dashed back the way he had come.

It was about time a letter reached them. They had

been in Oxford for almost two weeks now and he'd already written several postcards home. He'd not been able to say as much as he wanted to, since his large, loopy handwriting filled up the space too quickly. Worse, his words left a lot unsaid. He wasn't sure whether he ought to tell his father how he liked the college, Mrs Richards and the library – or how much he missed home. He hadn't many friends at Forest Heights School, so he wasn't particularly lonely, but it still felt kind of weird to be skipping the start of the new year. What if everyone thought he'd failed?

Yet even his dad had recommended the break. 'Oxford's a great place,' he'd said when the opportunity first came up. 'You never know, you might enjoy it. Think of it as an adventure.'

Duck had agreed. '*Alice in Wonderland*, *The Lord of the Rings*,' she'd said, listing her favourite titles. 'They were written there. I can't wait to go!'

Blake, however, was not so sure. Nor really, had he known it, was his father. The smile on his father's face that morning had been faraway and sad, and there was a quiver of doubt – or defeat – in his voice.

Blake tried to block out the memory. The lodge was a short distance ahead and he sprinted towards it.

A man with dark curly hair had arrived moments before him. Dressed in a black leather jacket that made a crunchy sound when he moved, he sauntered up to the main counter and deposited an iridescent green helmet, like a decapitated head, on its surface.

The porter was busy slipping letters into a number of pigeonholes on the wall behind him and signalled the motorcyclist to wait.

Drumming his fingers on the counter-top, the visitor turned to survey the room.

Blake, streaking past a pile of suitcases near the door, met the stranger's cool, confident gaze and skidded to a halt. He looked away in confusion and went over to check a laminated sign that had caught his eye. It had been erected on a special notice board in the corner.

The poster welcomed members of the Ex Libris Society to its annual conference, to be held conjointly at St Jerome's and All Souls Colleges throughout the week, and featured a prominent image of an enormous Bible on a fancy wooden desk. A caption at the bottom read: 'Notable speakers to include Sir Giles Bentley, *Whose Mortal Taste? First Editions & Forbidden Fruit* and Prosper Marchand, *Gutenberg's Dying Words: The E-book and the Virtual Library.*'

Blake was reminded of the blank book he had found in the college library and wondered whether this could be of any interest to the society. Probably not, he gathered, judging from the lavish tome on the poster: that book had a burnished silver binding, inlaid with rubies and pearls, whereas his own had a broken clasp and mouldering brown cover.

He was interrupted in his reverie by Bob Barrett, the porter, who had finished sorting through the post and turned to greet the visitors. 'Right,' he said. 'Sorry about the delay. And you, sir, are . . .?'

'Professor Prosper Marchand,' responded the man, as though he needed no introduction.

Blake whirled round. Sure enough, the man in the leather jacket matched the name on the poster. He had been watching Blake with an amused expression and now winked. Blake blushed.

'And this,' continued Prosper Marchand, indicating a tall, bird-like woman who had entered behind them, 'is Dr Adrienne de Jonghe of the Coster Institute in Holland. We're members of the Ex Libris Society.'

Dr de Jonghe waded on stork-thin legs in front of Blake and shook hands with the professor.

The porter, all smiles, asked the visitors to sign a register in front of them and then handed them each a clear plastic folder containing various conference materials and a guide to the college, on which he had marked the shortest routes to their rooms. Finally, he told them the access code to the library and other main buildings, before passing them their keys. The professors promptly gathered their things and left.

The porter let out a sigh as soon as the door was closed. 'Goodness, Blake, they've been arriving all day, they have. From all over the world. I've been run off my feet. Who'd have thought so many people would be interested in a few books?'

Blake was gazing out of the window. He could see the Dutch scholar bending down to stroke Mephistopheles, who curled seductively around her legs, but Prosper Marchand was nowhere to be seen. An engine soon revved in the street, however, and roared into the distance.

Bob was a short, stocky man in his mid-fifties, with just a smudge of a moustache beneath his nose. His shirt-sleeves had been rolled up to reveal a dragon tattoo on one wrist and a spinach-green anchor on the other. He rubbed his hands together and grinned at the boy. 'Now then, Blake, what can I do for you?'

Blake glanced wistfully at the pigeonholes behind the counter. 'Is there a letter for me?' he asked, suddenly feeling hesitant and shy.

Even though his dad made a point of calling them every evening, he wanted to receive a special letter – something personal, in writing – to help him make sense of their present situation. His parents were barely speaking to each other and he needed some assurance that everything would be all right.

The porter gave him a sympathetic smile. 'I don't think so, but you never know. It's always worth another look.'

While Bob bent down to check the slot that had been temporarily assigned to 'Dr Juliet Winters and Family', Blake busied himself by studying the tags on the suitcases near the door: Australia, India, Russia, Japan . . . People from all over the world were converging on the college for the conference, while his dad – the only person he really cared to see – was thousands of miles away. It wasn't fair. They would never be a family without him.

'Well, wouldn't you know it,' said Bob, springing up again like a puppet. 'There's something for you after all. How did it find its way in there?'

He winked at Blake, whose heart leaped at the discovery. The boy grabbed the letter.

Almost immediately, he knew it was not from home. There were no airmail stripes on the envelope and the handwriting was too fussy and feminine to be from his father. A graphic designer, Christopher Winters had distinctive lettering that reminded Blake of circus animals in a procession: his Js swung their trunks like elephants and his Qs sat like fat owls on branches. Everything he touched turned into a work of art.

Blake frowned. This letter was addressed to 'Dr Juliet

Somers & Child' and appeared to be an invitation to some formal engagement.

'Not what you wanted, eh?' said Bob, reading the look of disappointment on his face.

Blake didn't respond. He was having trouble swallowing. It didn't really surprise him that the envelope mentioned only one child – Duck was the obvious choice – but it upset him to think that his mother was using her maiden name here in Oxford. He wondered if there had been a mistake, but deep down he knew that she probably preferred it this way.

He glanced at the porter. 'No, not really. But maybe tomorrow,' he said, almost managing a smile.

Three

'It's a reminder about the dinner tonight,' said Juliet Winters, reading the letter. 'You two are invited and so, it seems, is Sir Giles Bentley. He's the guest of honour.'

Duck skipped ahead, pleased to know she would get a chance to show off to the college professors, but Blake lagged behind. He didn't want to go to a stuffy old dinner and meet yet more grown-ups who were either impressed with his mother's books or else astonished by Duck's intelligence. As usual, he would spend most of the time unnoticed. What's more, he didn't want to be introduced to anyone as Dr Somers' kid. It surprised him that his mother hadn't mentioned it.

'It says only one child on the envelope,' he tried. 'Do I have to go?'

'Of course you do. It's simply an oversight or a misprint; you know how these things happen.'

No, he didn't know how these things happened – but they seemed to happen to him an awful lot.

Juliet Winters noticed the sceptical expression on his face and waited for him to catch up. 'The college understands perfectly well that I have two children,' she said testily, putting an arm around him to speed him up. 'Everyone will be expecting you to come, just as I'll be expecting you to be on your best behaviour.'

'Who is Giles Bentley?' asked Duck, skipping back to join them.

'Sir Giles,' her mother corrected her, 'was Keeper of Books in the Bodleian Library for many years. He's retired now, but by all accounts is the same crotchety old curmudgeon he always was. I don't want you going anywhere near him.'

'Why?'

'Because I said so.'

Blake could tell that his mother didn't want to discuss the matter further, but Duck had already formed the next question on her lips.

'Why don't you like him so much?'

'Oh, Duck, if you really must know,' said her mother, fighting to control her temper, 'he interfered with some research your father and I were doing when we were students. He acquired an important manuscript we needed to consult, but refused to let us see it.'

They were walking along a shady path near the back of the Fellows' Garden. At the sound of her voice a few timorous birds flew out from the undergrowth, shrilling their displeasure.

'It was an important document,' she said more softly. 'It could have made our careers. Yet still he kept it from us.'

'Why?'

'Oh, I don't know!' She scowled at a fir tree leaning over the other plants. 'Power, perhaps. Or greed. Sir Giles learned long ago that it was possible to make more money by purchasing rare books for his own collection than by sharing them with others.'

Juliet Winters motioned them towards an old wooden door set into a mossy wall. Savage spikes jutted above it in an iron crown. She reached into her pocket and withdrew a set of keys.

'Sir Giles's decision set me back – who knows how long – years, probably,' she said irritably. 'It was all I could do to scrape my way back, but your father . . . well, he just gave up.'

Blake was stunned. He was having a hard time imagining his parents agreeing on anything, let alone a research project, but now he wanted to know what they had hoped to accomplish. It sounded important.

His mother stabbed a key in the lock and twisted it.

'I'd still like to get my hands on the manuscript,' she said, forcing the door open with her shoulder.

They passed through on to a wide boulevard lined with trees that were gradually losing their leaves. Some had knobbly trunks with bumps and warts of wood; others jigsaws of grey and green bark. An old black-framed bicycle had been propped against a nearby post and Duck raced towards it. She couldn't resist ringing its bell. It let out a dry, rusty croak.

'What book was it?' asked Blake tactfully. 'The book you wanted, I mean.'

'It wasn't a book,' said his mother, ushering them towards the end of the road, where Blake could see the dark silver dome of the Radcliffe Camera, another library, rising above the towers and spires of the city centre. 'It was a manuscript belonging to a monk who lived in Oxford during the Middle Ages.'

Blake stopped. 'A monk?' he asked, remembering the mysterious book he had found in the library. It had looked hundreds of years old too. Perhaps the two were related?

A tremor of excitement crept through him.

'What was his name?'

'Ignatius,' she said, much to his disappointment. His face fell. She regarded him curiously for a moment. 'Why the sudden interest?'

Blake pretended to study a leaf floating belly-up in a

puddle. He could still feel the weight of the blank book in his hands; the memory haunted him. 'No reason,' he said, unwilling to divulge his discovery to anyone just yet.

His mother shrugged. 'Well, it's a fascinating story. Ignatius claimed to have seen the Devil entering the city with a book of forbidden knowledge on his back. No one believed him, of course, and no one ever found the book. It's a piece of apocrypha really. But I was interested in it because of my research on Faust.'

'Who?' said Blake, looking up.

'Faust,' said Duck, showing off. 'He sold his soul to the Devil.'

'Did not,' muttered Blake and swung his knapsack in her direction. She ran off, squealing.

His mother gave him a warning glance. 'Duck's right. According to some, Faust was a German necromancer who craved all the knowledge and power in the world, made a pact with the Devil and was dragged down to everlasting hellfire by a legion of devils.'

Blake's eyes lit up. He didn't know what a necromancer was, but he could imagine a sorcerer dabbling with black magic and being consumed by a ring of fire.

'And Dad?' he asked. 'What did he think of the manuscript?'

'Your father had a much more speculative theory,' answered his mother, more evasively. 'He believed there was some truth to the legend and thought he could prove it.'

Blake's heart was pounding fiercely inside him. Perhaps his dad had hoped to find the forbidden book? Perhaps he knew where it was hidden?

'And did he?' he asked breathlessly.

'He never got the chance.' His mother snorted contemptuously. 'Sir Giles saw to that.'

Blake kicked at a twig that had fallen to the ground.

'It would have made his reputation had he been right,' his mother added regretfully, 'but . . .' Her voice broke off and she gazed at the scaly branches of an overhanging tree. 'But he was probably wrong.'

Blake blinked with surprise. He wanted to know much more about his father's ideas, but Duck was more interested in Sir Giles Bentley's collection of books.

'Like, how much do you think Sir Giles's books are worth?' she asked.

Her mother shook her head. 'No one knows precisely what Sir Giles paid for the Ignatius manuscript, nor even where he found it,' she said, 'but his private library is rumoured to be worth more than a million pounds.'

Duck whistled. 'What does he do with all his books?'

'He's a collector,' responded her mother. 'He doesn't necessarily do anything with them.'

Blake glanced at Duck, appalled.

'It's the thrill of the chase that excites him,' their mother continued. 'He hunts down rare books like endangered species and exhibits them on his shelves. They're like gold in the bank.'

Duck's eyes lit up greedily. 'Do you think we can see his books, if we ask nicely?' She was proud of her collection at home and probably wanted to compare notes.

'You can ask him whatever you like,' said Juliet Winters, glancing at the invitation in her hands. 'He's giving a special lecture this week. But I wouldn't waste your breath: he doesn't share his collection with anyone.'

They came to a broad street interspersed with stone-fronted colleges and tall tilting shops, all selling the same merchandise: Oxford jerseys, Oxford scarves and Oxford teddy bears. Tourists flocked from one to the other, shepherded by guides with colourful umbrellas.

Even though Blake knew his way around the city now, he still felt like a foreigner himself. His accent made him stand out like a flag. Nevertheless, he was beginning to appreciate life in Oxford. Inside each tawny college lay a forgotten world of libraries, chapels and dining halls. It was like stepping back in time. He kept expecting to bump into people like the figures in the paintings he had seen: scholars with powdered wigs, silk stockings and dark robes – like caped crusaders from long ago.

Unexpectedly, his mother stopped. She was standing next to a secondhand bookshop, staring at a display of fine leather books and novels in torn dust jackets. Before he could prevent her, she had gone inside, telling him to look after Duck. There was something she wanted to look at. 'I'll only be a minute,' she called out over her shoulder as the door jangled shut behind her.

Blake rolled his eyes. He'd heard that one before.

Annoyed, he wandered over to the kerb and started swinging round an old-fashioned lamp-post, letting the city swirl past him in a blur of sensations.

It felt liberating to be outside. During the previous weeks, he'd seen mostly dun-coloured museums and waterlogged statues from the misted heights of a double-decker bus. This afternoon, however, the city blazed with life: colleges glowed under an azure sky and pigeons spiralled round the towers on whistling wings. Golden clock faces, scattered around the streets, told a multitude of times.

And then he saw him.

The man was sitting close to the bookshop, reading what looked to be an old battered book. Blake slowed to a crawl – then stopped completely.

The stranger was dressed in a brown leather robe and had an unfashionably long, scraggy beard. Despite the heat, he was wearing a peculiar hat that looked sort of like a nightcap with a fur trim on it. Blake had never seen anything like it before. It was as if one of the many statues in the city had come to life and was resting unnoticed on the pavement. Was he homeless?

All the while the boy stared at him, the man didn't move, didn't even turn a page, but concentrated on his book. In fact, he could have been carved out of stone; he was motionless.

Most of the people passing by didn't pay him any attention, but those who did dropped a few coins at his feet and hurried on. The silver coins glistened like gobs of spit on the ground. The man, however, neither noticed their looks nor pocketed their change. He was lost in his own private world.

A wiry hound with perky ears lay on a tattered blanket beside him, a bright red bandanna wrapped around its neck. Duck walked straight up to it.

'I like your dog,' she said, bending down to stroke the animal, which thumped its tail lethargically.

Even then, the man didn't look up, but continued reading. He clutched the volume in grubby fingers that looked like gnarled tree roots.

'Duck!' hissed Blake, trying not to disturb or offend

the old man. The dog might have fleas, he thought, or, worse, might bite her; but neither possibility really worried him. He was much more concerned with what his mother would say if she found Duck talking to a stranger. He was supposed to be looking after her, after all.

'Duck!' he hissed again.

This time she heard him and looked up, smiling.

'What's your dog's name?' she said, but still the man ignored her.

Blake went to drag her away by the arm.

Then, suddenly, the man lifted his head. It was as if he had come to the end of a complex sentence or an extremely long paragraph. He looked at Blake with an expression that was not altogether hostile, but not entirely friendly either. It was a searching, penetrating gaze, as though he was surprised to find a young boy standing in front of him, casting a shadow over his book. He seemed to have woken from a deep sleep.

Blake felt uncomfortable and immediately turned away, pulling Duck after him.

Just then the shop door opened and Juliet Winters returned, without the book she had wanted. She gave the man a quick, dismissive glance and led the children away.

'What did he want?' she asked idly, as they drifted

towards the main shopping area and blended in with the crowds.

Blake didn't answer. He had looked back just once — as they were crossing a side street — and was alarmed to see that the man was following them with his eyes.

Four

Blake tried his best to ignore Duck. She had assumed that smug expression she sometimes got when she knew she had a secret he would want to hear, and which she was secretly dying to tell; but, as usual, she would wait for him to beg her for it first. He decided to ask his mother about the book she had wanted instead.

'Oh, it was a book I used to like when I was a girl,' she said vaguely, tucking a strand of hair behind her ear. 'A book about butterflies. I saw it in the shop window and it brought back some memories. Only, I don't have time to read such things now. I have more pressing things to do instead.'

'Well, I think you should have bought it,' he said simply, but firmly, thinking it wouldn't do her any harm to be a child again for a few hours.

'Perhaps you're right,' she answered, but he could tell

from the sound of her voice that she was already miles away.

Duck's eyes were now the size of marbles. Blake couldn't stand the suspense any longer and slowed his steps to fall in line with hers. 'Go on,' he growled. 'Tell me.'

She clutched him eagerly by the arm.

'Did you notice the strange man?' she squealed.

'Of course I did.' He disentangled himself from her grasp. 'I was standing right next to you, idiot.'

'No, I mean, did you notice *what* he was reading?'

Blake shook his head. 'It was just an old book, but it must have been exciting, cos he didn't look up once till he got to the end.'

'That's it!' she said triumphantly.

'What's it?'

'I noticed what he was reading.'

She skipped back and forth, trumpeting the air in her cheeks.

'Well?'

'Nothing!'

'What?'

'Nothing,' she said again.

'What do you mean, nothing?' he snapped, suspecting a trick. 'You're joking, right?'

His voice was louder than intended and his mother

turned round to make sure they weren't arguing. He smiled at her sheepishly and she continued on ahead.

'I'm serious,' said Duck. 'There were no words in his book. He was staring at a blank page – just like in your book.'

She watched to see how he took the remark.

He remained silent and thoughtful for a while. 'That doesn't mean anything,' he said finally. 'It could have been a notebook. Maybe he was going to write something in it when you interrupted him.'

'But he wasn't holding a pen,' she said quickly. Obviously, she had been thinking this through.

'Or maybe he'd just finished reading a novel and was thinking it over when you came along,' suggested Blake. 'Some books have blank pages at the end, you know.'

'Possibly,' she conceded, 'but I got a closer look at it than you, and I don't think it was a novel. Or even a notebook. Besides, he stared at you in such a funny way. That suggests there was definitely something fishy about the book – or about you.'

She gave him another look.

He grunted, unwilling to take the bait. 'He was just irritated because you interrupted him, that's all,' he answered and quickened his pace to catch up with his mother. Either Duck was being annoying or else she was mistaken. The man had certainly looked like he was reading *something*. The possibility that there could be two blank books in one day seemed too unlikely to be true.

They had arrived at a busy intersection. To their right stood an ancient stone tower with two gold-helmeted figures ready to strike the hour on the bells with their clubs, while several hundred metres away, beyond a college and its meadows, lay a low bridge, which crossed the river towards the neighbourhood in which they lived. Already Blake could sense the cramped row of houses in Millstone Lane growing nearer and shivered.

'Two blank books in one day,' Duck mused aloud. 'I think it's a mystery. And, if it is, then I'm going to be the one to solve it.'

'Oh yeah?' he retorted. 'You'll have to do so without me.'

'Good,' she said. 'I was planning to do just that.'

But Blake took no notice of her remark. He had already resolved to steal away from the dinner that night and return to the college library. He would find the blank book and this time read the riddle over and over again until he understood it.

Five

B
lake fingered the torch in his pocket apprehensively.

He had expected the dinner to take place in the cavernous dining hall, a room full of draughts and sputtering candles; but it had been relocated to the Master's Lodgings, a cosier, but no less opulent building tucked away in a far corner of the college. He wondered how, or if, he was going to be able to sneak away to the library.

Little lanterns lit their way, emitting a ghostly glow that barely illuminated the path. Plants with spiky fronds clutched at his clothes, while tangled shadows climbed the walls.

Ahead was a large house. Even now he could hear the din of voices breaking from the ground-floor rooms and felt tempted to run back to the peace and tranquillity of the library; but his mother put a hand on his shoulder and steered him onwards.

'Now, I want you two to behave,' she whispered, as they climbed the stone steps to the door, which was flanked on either side by stiff marble columns. 'There are important people present.'

The hallway was dominated by an enormous chandelier that descended from the ceiling in a fountain of frozen light. Duck danced beneath it, pirouetting on her heels, while Blake gazed at the paintings that once again graced the shot-silk walls. The largest was of an old man in a desert, with a disproportionately small lion at his feet. Wrapped in a scarlet cloak, he was scribbling feverishly in a book, although Blake couldn't decipher any of the words. They were gibberish to him. The saint-like figure, however, reminded him of the homeless man and he wondered again what he had been reading when Blake and Duck had stumbled upon him.

Juliet Winters did not pause to take in her surroundings, but guided them into a little cloakroom further down the corridor. A row of black robes had been strung up along the walls like dead birds. Blake noticed that his mother took one before putting her coat on the vacant peg. He placed his jacket over hers and was about to reach for a robe too, when she put out a hand to stop him.

'Gowns are for Fellows only,' she warned him, shrugging the black material on to her shoulders.

Blake didn't mind forgoing the formality – his mother looked like a dishevelled crow, he thought – but Duck was itching to try one on. She brushed her fingers along the embroidered sleeves and dreamed of being an Oxford scholar. She refused, however, to take off her raincoat.

Juliet Winters glanced at her reflection in a gold-framed mirror and then opened the door to an adjoining room. A multitude of people stood before them in conspiratorial circles, discussing books. Blake moved around the edge of the crowd, carefully avoiding conversation. An elbow jogged him once or twice and he apologized, but otherwise no one paid him attention.

Before long he found himself by a cabinet on which a cluster of glasses had been arranged like sparkling jewels. He couldn't resist. He reached for a glass of sherry as soon as his mother's back was turned. The amber liquid had a beguiling aroma and tasted warm and sweet when he tested it with his tongue. Not too horrible. He took a deeper sip and swallowed.

Immediately, a fire erupted in his throat and rushed up the sides of his face. He winced. Quickly, before his mother caught him, he put the sherry back on its tray and opted for a safer glass of orange juice instead.

Bleary-eyed, he looked around the room.

A series of marble busts perched like birds of prey atop the large chimneypiece that dominated one wall, while portraits of still more scholars jostled for space along the others. Everywhere he turned, resentful faces peered out at him from dark canvases, as if envious of the living. He turned away, unable to hold their stares.

His mother was clearly in her element. She was chatting easily with the other professors, a confident smile on her face. 'Mingling', his father had called it on the phone earlier that evening, although his mother preferred a more powerful word: 'networking'.

Duck, too, was making the most of the occasion. She was standing in front of a small semi-circle of people, all of whom seemed to be marvelling at the things she said. One goose-like lady, wearing a chintzy dress and reeking of gardenias, kept clucking her amazement. 'Yes, yes, oh very clever, yes,' she said, pulling at a pearl necklace. Later he overheard her telling his mother that Duck was 'an astonishing girl, so bright for her age – except for that coat. Most peculiar. And you have a son, you say?'

He dodged through the crowd to avoid detection.

He ended up by a large window and pulled back an edge of curtain to peer outside. It would be the perfect opportunity to escape. There were so many people in the room; no one would notice the disappearance of a small boy.

Just then, he became aware of a woman with silver

hair standing beside him. In a sensuous voice that made his skin shiver, she said, 'You must be Blake. I am Diana, Sir Giles Bentley's wife.'

The sound seemed to settle like snow on the back of his neck and he looked up, mesmerized by the feel of it. She wasn't wearing a gown like the other members of the college, but had draped a cream-coloured shawl across her shoulders instead. It was fastened together with a small silver clasp, fashioned into the shape of a delicate butterfly. Blake studied it admiringly. Its papery wings seemed so lifelike; they appeared to move.

She indicated a man in a special robe with gold embroidery on its sleeves, who was standing in the centre of the room, surrounded by a large number of people. Blake gulped. Sir Giles Bentley: he had a shock of white hair, glowering dark eyebrows and eyes as hard as gemstones. Arms folded across his chest, he was huffing and puffing in response to some other man – a cringing scholar in an ill-fitting, toad-coloured suit. Paula Richards, the librarian, stood between them, trying to keep them apart.

'They're disagreeing about editions of *Goblin Market*,' said Diana Bentley with a lisp that again seemed to tickle the back of Blake's neck.

'What market?' he asked, not understanding what she meant.

'*Goblin Market*,' she repeated. 'It's one of my favourite

poems, written by Christina Rossetti in 1862. It's about two sisters who are tempted to eat exotic fruit offered them by little goblin greengrocers. "Come buy, come buy," they sing to the girls, one of whom succumbs and then languishes from hunger. The language is wonderful. Lurid and alluring. Of course, it can be read on different levels.'

Blake understood even less of what she was saying and felt his attention begin to wander. While his ears listened faintly to what she told him, his eyes roamed the room.

Yet more members of the Ex Libris Society had arrived. All around him were murmurs about the future of books, which seemed to be threatened because of a new plan to digitalize the Bodleian Library's collection. As Blake watched, Prosper Marchand, one of the leaders of the digitization project, made a beeline for his mother, with two glasses of wine in his outstretched hands.

Suddenly Sir Giles roared with rage. 'Puce, I tell you! Christina's copy was puce! You, sir, are an ignoramus!'

Sputters of confusion circled the room. A short middle-aged woman with lank, brown hair, who appeared to have just stepped off her broom, jumped slightly and remarked to her companion in a voice like a squeaky balloon, 'I wish he wouldn't do that. He frightens me to death!'

Diana, however, seemed unfazed by the outbreak.

'Giles,' she continued softly, taking Blake's arm, 'believes that the first edition of *Goblin Market* is the only one scholars should refer to; but I prefer a later version, because the illustrations make the goblins appear more sinister, more beguiling, and therefore more dangerous.' She smiled and he nodded, thinking this was somehow an appropriate reaction.

Without his noticing, she had led him away from the window towards a large table spread with food. A butler was busily removing lids from plates crammed with lobster, monkfish and orange-glazed duck, accompanied by mountains of steaming vegetables.

What fascinated Blake even more, however, was the selection of fruit. Apart from the usual pineapples, plums and peaches were things he had never seen before: fruit shaped like stars and others like spiky sponges. There were also orange berries partially hidden inside leafy cages that looked like paper lanterns. He liked the look of these especially. It was just like the goblin market Diana Bentley had been describing.

As if confirming his thoughts, the woman hummed 'Come buy, come buy' while her eyes travelled up and down the table. 'It's a splendid feast,' she said to him, and then rejoined her husband near a tureen of pumpkin and coriander soup.

Blake piled his plate high with food and started to eat.

'I'm surprised she didn't offer you Turkish delight,' muttered Duck as soon as she joined him. 'I don't like her. She seems icy.'

Blake shrugged. 'You're just jealous because she didn't pay you any attention.'

'Yeah, right.'

'What is Turkish delight anyway?' he asked with his mouth full, to change the topic.

'That stuff,' said Duck, pointing to a plate covered with squares of orange and purplish jelly coated in icing sugar. 'Only evil characters in books like it.'

'Oh yeah?' he said, grinning. Unable to resist the temptation, he shovelled a large shivery portion into his mouth.

'Don't!' squealed Duck.

Immediately, he wished he hadn't. It tasted awful! The spicy sweetness of the jelly made his teeth twinge. He went to search for a glass of water to rinse his mouth. When he returned, he found Paula Richards deep in conversation with Duck, who was still keeping an eye on the Turkish delight.

To avoid them, he moved over to the selection of fruit. Even though the star-shaped fruit looked tempting, he took one of the lantern-like berries instead, wondering what it would taste like. He hesitated, then plopped it in his mouth.

An elderly gentleman behind him gasped.

Blake turned round, with the orange berry stuck like a gobstopper between his teeth. The man was holding his cheek as if he had a toothache. He looked at Blake and winked. 'I defy you to bite that,' he said. 'It tastes just like shampoo!'

Blake bit down and grimaced. The berry burst in a bubble of flesh that tasted first sweet, then sour, then slightly sweet again, before finally leaving a bitter residue in his mouth. Shampoo was a good word for it. He loved the sensation and immediately took another.

'They're known as winter cherries,' the man explained in a deep, benevolent voice. 'The appellation makes them sound sweet and appetizing, I find, but nothing prepares you for that ghastly taste! Never trust a euphemistically named fruit, that's what I say.'

'I like them,' said Blake dumbly, even though one side of his mouth felt curiously numb.

'You must be Juliet's son,' said the man, as though the contradictory remark had proved the point. 'My name is Jolyon. I used to teach your mother.'

He extended a hand so large and strong it seemed to engulf the boy's. Blake could feel the bones in his hand compressing like the quills of a fan and only barely managed to wriggle free. Without another word, the professor moved to a plump leather armchair in the corner of the room, away from the assembled members of the Ex Libris Society. Blake trailed after him, as if pulled by a gravitational force. He sat down next to him and gave the man a closer look.

Jolyon's gown was shabby and frayed, with long threads dangling from the armpits like untidy spiderwebs. Beneath this, he wore a tweed jacket with a checked shirt and stained tie. Apart from his coarse white hair, which stood up in crests and waves like an unruly sea, he looked just like an overgrown boy who had dressed up in layers of oversized clothing. Blake liked him.

The professor remained silent and thoughtful for a while, with his eyes closed. Blake knew he oughtn't to interrupt, but a question was rattling around inside his brain and gradually he built up the confidence to ask it.

'Um, was my mother a good student?' he asked, with a shy smile that broadened into a mischievous grin.

The professor opened one eye and said quizzically, 'It depends on how you define good.'

Blake shifted uncomfortably where he sat, and groaned. Like his parents, the professor was getting him to define his words more accurately. It was a game he didn't like much, since he wasn't very good at it.

The old man, noticing his distress, relented. 'I beg your pardon. It's a trick I play when I feel my students haven't formulated their questions properly. Sometimes it's more difficult to know the question than to find an answer.'

Blake gave him a puzzled look.

'Your mother was Juliet Somers then,' explained the man, unmindful of the boy's confusion. 'She was a capable, clever and highly motivated student, who finished her dissertation in good time, I believe, despite your father's efforts.'

Jolyon glanced at Blake to see if he understood the last remark and was confronted by two amazingly light blue eyes, as watchful as mirrors.

Taken aback, he continued in a softer voice, speaking more honestly than Blake had expected, 'She was, I dare say, even then, more conscious of her career than her vocation. I am not sure that she loved books, but she analysed what was in them very well. Still, without that passion, she was never, I fear, my best student.'

It felt odd to hear someone criticizing his mother and Blake looked around the room uneasily until he spotted her. There she was, still talking to Prosper Marchand, who was now offering her a glass of ruby-coloured port. They appeared to be on familiar terms. Too familiar, perhaps. Blake scowled.

'No, that distinction,' resumed Jolyon, 'goes to your father. He was my most promising student.'

Blake's eyes zipped back to the old man's face. 'My dad?' he asked, thinking he had misheard.

The professor eyed him astutely. 'Oh yes, your father

had a most remarkable imagination. Not always accurate, mind, but blessed with an insight I have rarely seen.'

Insight. The word resonated in Blake's mind, reminding him of the blank book he had found in the library. It had appeared in the final line of the poem.

Suddenly a grandfather clock started to chime the hour. It sounded so old and frail Blake thought it would expire before it reached the last toll. Seven, eight, nine o'clock . . . The numbers wheezed by, accompanied by a prolonged bronze echo.

Jolyon, following his gaze, seemed alarmed to notice the time. 'Good heavens,' he said. 'I had no idea.'

Blake was momentarily distracted.

'Huh?' he said. He had just caught sight of Duck tugging on Sir Giles Bentley's sleeve. The old man looked down at her with barely concealed contempt. His stare would have crushed a lesser opponent. Diana stood nearby, observing them both with mild detachment.

Jolyon staggered to his feet. 'You'll forgive me, I hope, if I make a hasty departure.' Once again, he extended a hand, which this time Blake noticed was spattered with ink. 'It's been a pleasure, my boy.'

'Um, yeah,' said Blake, sorry to see him go. There were still so many things he wanted to know about his parents.

The man clearly sensed his disappointment, for he said, 'You appear to have more questions in you yet. Why not come round to my office once you know precisely what you want to know.' He seemed to appreciate the riddle in the last part of this sentence and winked. Chortling softly to himself, he began to walk away.

For some reason, the question slipped out before Blake could prevent it. Immediately he wished the words unsaid, but there they were, out in the open, hovering in the space between them.

'What is Endymion Spring?'

What is Endymion Spring? The professor wheeled round sharply and stared at the boy, astonished. Evidently, this was *not* the question he had been expecting.

Blake backed away. For a moment he thought he could detect a glimmer of desire on the man's face – a lean, hungry look that reminded him of the homeless man outside the bookshop. Luckily, this was wiped clean almost instantly and replaced by a more affectionate expression.

'Who is *Endymion Spring?*' the man repeated, the name quivering on his lips. A hint of worry still troubled his brow.

Blake nodded.

Jolyon looked around the room apprehensively. 'Now is neither the time nor the place,' he whispered finally, scrunching his hands together and then plunging them deep into the folds of his gown. 'We must talk about him . . . later.'

With that, he rushed away, although Blake could tell that he was still agitated, since he almost forgot which way to go.

So Endymion Spring was a person and not a season, he thought to himself. He was probably the author of the book, then, and not the title. But how could anyone be the author of a blank book?

There was only one way to find out. Blake would have to go to the library, find the volume and figure out its riddle. It was now or never.

Checking to make sure that no one was watching, he moved towards the door. Just before he slipped out, he glanced at the plate of Turkish delight.

No one, it seemed, had touched it.

Six

It was colder outside than Blake had expected. After the warm glow of the Master's Lodgings the air felt chilly, almost like winter, and he hugged himself to keep warm.

Moonlight dusted the college paths and he stumbled clumsily, trying to negotiate his way in the silver-dark. Shadows clustered all around him. He didn't want to switch on his torch until he was safely concealed inside the library, just in case he got in trouble for sneaking out on his own.

The cloisters loomed ahead and he hurried towards them.

As he passed down the first dark-beamed passageway, he stopped. It was like a doubt tapping him on the back, making him turn round. Someone was following him.

He stood perfectly still, listening carefully.

Nothing. Not a whisper.

Then, peering stealthily around a column, he checked the doorway of the Old Library on the opposite side of the garden. Only the faint tooth-like striations in the stone were visible, taking a bite out of the night. Otherwise, there was nothing. No one was there. It must have been his imagination.

He carried on. Stairwells climbed into the darkness around him, while footsteps – his own – scratched the paving stones and rebounded off the walls, pursuing him as echoes. He started walking faster.

Reaching the next courtyard, he took a moment to steady himself. Buildings that were familiar in the daytime were now unrecognizable shadows. Trees shivered: black, bat-like rustlings. His heart was beating fast.

Spotting the library, a wall of darkness in the distance, he ran towards it.

As his feet tripped up the steps, he saw the illuminated keypad by the door, its numbers lit up like eyes. The college no longer used keys for the main buildings, but had installed a high-tech entry-code system instead. Rather foolishly, he thought, the code was the same for each building, since the students and absent-minded professors couldn't remember more than one number. In any case, he was lucky since his mother had made him memorize the sequence so that he and Duck could get in and out of the library on their own.

He entered the number – 6305XZ – and heard the door click open. With a sigh of relief, he slipped inside.

The library, as he had imagined, was totally dark.

The first thing he heard was the sound of the clock ticking softly. It reminded him of a slow, rhythmic heartbeat. He relaxed.

Dimming his torch so that it would not shine through any of the windows, he swept the beam across the hall. The light made the books on the shelves appear silver, ghostlike. The central staircase sloped away from him, up into total darkness, but he took the left-hand corridor instead, past the portraits of Thomas Sternhold and Jeremiah Wood. Eyes glinted at him briefly and then disappeared as he crept along the book-lined corridor, past other portraits, further into shadow.

Finally, he came to the bookcase where he had discovered the blank book – or, rather, where it had discovered him. The volume Duck had shown him earlier was still open on the desk: a small landmark indicating where he should look.

But where was the blank book?

He thought he had placed it right here, on the third shelf, between the two volumes that were now sloping towards each other slightly. A thin crack of shadow divided them. He wedged his fingers into the gap. Empty.

Fighting a wave of panic, he scanned the floor, but the book wasn't there either.

He bit his lip. Surely it couldn't have disappeared already!

Desperate, he trailed his fingers along the spines, just as he had done before, and whispered the words 'Endymion Spring' to himself, over and over again in a sort of mantra, willing the book to reappear . . . but nothing happened. It wasn't on the floor and it wasn't on the shelf. There was no sign of the blank book anywhere.

The library guarded its secret.

At that moment a book thwacked the floor near the front entrance and a sound skittered across the hall. Blake froze. Someone was in the library.

Instinctively, he switched off his torch and shrank back against the wall, creeping into the arms of a massive bookcase. The darkness crushed against him, pressing into his eyes, digging into his ribs. He could barely breathe.

Heart in mouth, he listened.

At any moment a footstep might betray itself, a whisper

of breath make itself known . . . but there was nothing. Only terrible, oppressive silence. The seconds weighed upon him.

Finally, when he could stand the suspense no longer, he switched on his torch and covered it instantly with his hand, so that the light flooded between his fingers like blood. Using its meagre light, he looked around him. Gloom stretched into the distance.

He edged out of his hiding place. Books lined the walls, perfectly still.

Taking tiny, shaky steps, he inched towards the entrance. A draught crept down the corridor towards him, sending a shiver up and down his spine.

At last he reached the front hall. With large, fearful eyes he peered into the shadows. The circulation desk was there, and the clock, and the tall card catalogue beside it, plus a trolley for returned books.

He stopped. Just below the bottom rung of the trolley was a book. It must have slipped off its shelf.

He moved towards it, then fell back, disappointed. It was just a dumb, boring textbook. Not Endymion Spring.

He bent down to put it back on the trolley – and nearly died from fright. Two metallic green spheres glinted at him from behind the corner of the cart. He jumped back.

Then, with a rush of relief, he realized what it was.

Mephistopheles!

'Oh no, not you,' he cried. 'You're not supposed to be in here! How did you . . .' he turned round '. . . get in here?' he mumbled, finishing the thought.

The door was closed. No one was there.

Making comforting kissing noises, he approached the cat and tried to lure it out of hiding, still uncertain how the shadowy feline had managed to elude him; but Mephistopheles simply retreated from his fingers and then, with a hiss that split the air like ripped fabric, bolted upstairs.

'Great,' exclaimed Blake, knowing Paula Richards would be furious if he let the cat stay in the library overnight.

Muttering to himself, he gave chase, sprinting up the wide marble stairs.

The gallery was divided into a series of deep, dark alcoves by rows of freestanding bookcases that were centuries old. They looked like a procession of monks in the dimness – hunched and round-shouldered.

Blake walked up the central aisle, creaking along the floorboards, hunting for Mephistopheles. He swept the beam of his torch across the shelves, illuminating hundreds of pale, spectral volumes that were bound to their desks with thick iron chains. Others were propped open – like moths – on foam pillows. Weighted necklace-like strings kept their pages from flickering.

He poked his light into corners and peered under benches, discovering a jumble of legs in the shadows.

'Come on, you stupid cat,' whispered Blake impatiently. 'I haven't got all night!' He could feel the seconds slipping away. Any moment now, his mother might notice his disappearance and then he'd be in trouble.

There he was!

Mephistopheles crouched behind a heavy wooden chest in the far corner of the room, under a gigantic portrait of a bearded man with a recriminating stare. Horatio Middleton (1503–89). His jewelled finger was tightly clasped round the spine of a worn leather volume.

'OK, out you come,' coaxed Blake, reaching down to pick up the cat. His shoulder brushed a bookcase, almost causing a book to fall.

At first, Mephistopheles refused to budge; then, deceived by Blake's false flattery, the cat relented and Blake seized him by the scruff of the neck. The cat yowled.

Struggling to maintain a hold on both his torch and the wriggling, squirming cat, Blake moved towards the stairs. 'Stop complaining,' he told the cat. 'There's nothing to be —'

Without warning, Mephistopheles raked his claws into Blake's shoulder and leaped free, arching high into the air. Trying not to cry out in pain, Blake watched help-lessly as the cat landed lithely on its feet by the glass cabinet and tore down the remaining steps . . . and out through the open door.

Blake's heart froze inside him. He could feel the night air sweeping into the library, wrapping itself round his legs, chilling him. The door was wide open.

'Who's there?' he called out anxiously, poking the torchlight into the gloom. Long stretches of darkness led away from him.

'Who's there?' he tried again, glimpsing a pale glimmer at the end of the corridor.

He moved towards it and nearly dropped his torch. For there, at the far end of the corridor, exactly where he had been standing before, a few volumes lay scattered on the floor. But they hadn't just slipped off the shelves: they'd been torn off, ransacked in a sudden fury. Scraps of paper littered the carpet like parts of a dismembered bird and at least one spine was dangling from its cover like a severed limb.

Blake gasped.

For a moment he stood rooted to the spot, unsure what to do, feeling the library swim around him; then, over-powered by a desire to escape, he lunged towards the door.

He scrambled down the steps and raced across the

lawn, nearly tripping over himself in his haste to get away.
So he had not been alone! Someone had followed him
to the library! These thoughts pursued him as he sprinted
wildly across the college, through the cloisters and up the
path towards the Master's Lodgings. Could someone else
know about Endymion Spring?

A glimmer of light, like a knife blade, shone through
a crack in one of the curtained windows, but by the time
Blake stumbled up the stone steps, the partition had
closed.

A man with owl-like glasses was helping himself to a slab
of crumbly cheese from a sideboard near the door and
Blake ducked behind him to take cover. He doubled over,
panting with exhaustion.

He checked his watch. Barely thirty minutes had gone
by. It was nothing . . . unless you happened to be waiting.

One look was enough. He was in trouble. Serious
trouble.

His mother, standing next to a group of quarrelling
scholars, was barely listening to the discussion. Arms
folded across her chest, she was staring fixedly ahead,
inwardly fuming. Her body language said it all.

He gulped.

Duck was eagerly on the lookout and got up as soon

as she had spotted him. 'Where have you been?' she snapped, pushing her way through the crowd.

'Out,' he said. Then, failing to come up with a better excuse, he added, 'It's really cold out there. It might even snow.'

He started rubbing his arms up and down, wondering if she would believe him. She didn't. He stopped his play-acting.

'How angry is she?' he asked, motioning towards his mother.

'Pretty angry,' said Duck. 'She's stopped talking to the other professors.'

That was a bad sign. It meant she was really angry – angry beyond words. The worst kind of angry.

'Where were you really?' asked Duck in a different voice, more curious.

'I told you. I went out for a walk.'

He watched as his mother went to fetch her coat. She met his apologetic grin with a steely expression. The smile died almost instantly on his face.

'No, you didn't,' said Duck. 'You went to the library.'

'Huh?'

Blake pretended not to listen, but his red cheeks were a dead giveaway.

'You went to the library,' she said. 'I know you did. You thought you could outsmart me by finding the blank book and solving the mystery all by yourself. You idiot! I saw you go.'

He frowned. 'What?'

'I saw you,' she crowed. 'You thought you were so sneaky, but I was watching the whole time. You're so stupid – it's a joke.'

Suddenly he turned on her. 'So you were the person in the library!' he cried. 'I could kill you, I really could!'

Several people turned, appalled by the vehemence of his words, but he couldn't control himself. The fear that had been growing inside him had found a release.

'Why did you do that?' he hollered. 'You scared me half to death!'

Something in Duck's eyes made him stop. They were suddenly large and fearful, on the verge of tears. She had no idea what he was talking about.

Immediately, he realized his mistake. She hadn't seen him leave; she'd merely said this to make him feel bad. She was probably jealous because he'd been able to evade her watchful gaze and sneak out without her.

She was about to add something when their mother returned, her coat folded over her arm. Without a word, she led them out.

'I'll deal with you later,' she told him icily as they followed her down the garden path. Her words hovered in the air like a frosty cloud.

Seven

That night, Blake awoke with a start. The book was summoning him.

Sitting up in bed, he switched on the light and blinked as the stripes on his bedroom wallpaper reappeared, one by one, like the bars of a prison. And then he remembered: the book was gone. He'd failed to find it. He let his head fall back against the pillow with a crushing sense of disappointment.

In his dream, the college library had been transformed into a magical forest. Tall trees lined the corridors, reaching up the walls, extending their brilliant canopies across the ceiling. Books filled the shelves, which were made from vast, interlocking branches. As he walked through the library, red, gold and vivid green scraps of paper drifted to the floor like autumn leaves.

Birds chattered noisily in the air above him, hopping from one branch to another; but then, in an explosion of wings, they suddenly shot off into the air, leaving the branches – the shelves – as silent and bare as winter. The building was cold and empty, apart from the blank book, which was once again lying on the floor, waiting for him to turn it over.

Mephistopheles sauntered along the corridor to meet him, a scrap of paper dangling from his mouth like a feather.

Blake shuddered at the recollection, convinced the book was trying to reach him. Then, realizing that the shiver had as much to do with the temperature of his room as his nerves, he crept to the foot of his bed to switch on the radiator beneath the window. It was freezing!

He turned the dial and waited for the primitive, fossil-like coils to heat up, unused to such antiquated devices at home. The pipes groaned and quivered for a moment and then slowly filled with warmth. It was like the ghost of heat, barely noticeable, but it was better than nothing.

To ease his mind, he peered out through a gap in the blinds. Street lamps spilled pools of yellow light on to Millstone Lane and a dog barked somewhere in a neighbouring yard. Otherwise, there was no sign of life. The houses were dark and deserted. Everyone was asleep.

It was the middle of the night.

Blake settled back in bed and stared at the cracks that crept along the ceiling like giant spiders. It unnerved him that the blank book had disappeared so soon after he had found it. The book had felt unusual, as though it might contain anything. The paper had an ability to make hidden words come alive, a magical power he couldn't begin to comprehend. It was as though it had contained a mind of its own – a djinn, perhaps. Some secret power. But how was that possible?

He let out a long sigh. The book was gone. He'd missed his chance to solve it.

He switched off the light and lay in the dark, a feeling of inadequacy settling over him like a blanket. And then, in the silence of his room, he became aware of a soft secretive sound spitting against the outside of his window. It might be snow, or it might be rain. But it was so nice and warm in his bed, and he felt so tired, that he didn't get up to see what it was.

His mind dissolved into the outer edges of another dream.

He was back in the library. Endymion Spring was waiting for him to pick it up.

Anxiously, before it could disappear, he curled his fingers round the worn leather spine and opened the covers. Automatically, the blank pages started riffling to reveal the riddle hidden at the heart of the book:

When Summer and Winter in Autumn divide
The Sun will uncover a Secret inside . . .

As Blake recited the words, he was instantly transported to a snowy scene, somewhere else, somewhere like home. White fields surrounded him like the pages of an open book and a frozen pond shone in the distance – a watermark dusted by a light sprinkling of snow.

Someone approached. Footsteps scrunched behind him. He turned round, just in time to see a clean-shaven man with a face like worn wood emerging from a fringe of frostbitten trees. The man was dressed in a fur-collared tunic with brown leggings and leather shoes that appeared to have no laces. He dragged a felled tree behind him.

Blake rubbed his eyes. The leaves were changing from blood-red to white as they passed over the snow.

On the man's shoulders sat a young girl with flaming auburn hair. She wore a filthy smock and had rust patches on her stockings. Tears clung to her cheeks. Her grim face softened into a smile when she saw Blake and she held out a grazed hand for him to hold, but her fingers passed through his like a ghost's, a whisper of contact, no more than a cobweb.

Blake took a step back and watched as the man trudged by without a word – without a glance in his direction. The pair disappeared over the brow of a hill.

Suddenly, his parents were on either side of him. Blake gripped them with his mittened hands, but they broke free and without a word moved off in opposite directions, fading into the snow. Blake wanted to run after them, to make them stop, but he was unable to choose which parent to follow and remained stuck in one spot. Tears welled in his eyes, icing his vision.

Then, through his misery, he glimpsed a gleam of yellow. Duck was there. Duck, as she had been since the Big Argument, her hood pulled up to hide her strange tomboy's haircut: a messy bob that no one could tame. She was peering at something in the snow, calling out for him to come and look, but her words were printed in clouds of breath and he read them rather than heard them.

He raced towards her, but no matter how hard he tried, he could not reach her. The snow was deep and his legs felt heavy. He was chained to the ground. Then she too vanished and he collapsed, too tired and lonely to go on.

The boundaries of his dream began to shift. A wind rose and Blake was suddenly lifted into the sky like a freed snow angel, watching as the field below him grew smaller and smaller. And then his heart lurched. For there, in the snow, ending exactly at the spot where Duck had disappeared, was a path of footprints.

They formed a giant question mark.

Immediately, his dream burst and he hurtled back towards the ground like a skydiver without a parachute. His head snowballed into his pillow.

Desperately, he clutched at the lines of Endymion Spring's poem, but the words faded and all he could remember was the snow.

He turned over and fell asleep again.

MAINZ
Spring 1453

he silence woke me. Something was wrong. I opened my eyes and peered into the gloom, trying to detect any sound, any movement, but there was none. Only a silver cusp of moonlight cut across the floor. The darkness pressed in all around me, as thick as velvet.

For months now, Peter had been my sleeping companion, keeping me awake with his twitching and scratching, tormented by the dreams he never shared and the fleabites he did. And yet I was grateful for his company. The bear-like warmth of his body had kept me from shivering through the long winter nights when snow capped the roofs of the city and icy draughts crept through the house.

Spring had finally arrived. Ploughmen and vintners began once more to prepare their fields and people picked their way through the thawed lanes with renewed vigour, the memory of fresh fruit revived on their tongues. At long last the frozen river relinquished its hold on the boats trading goods up and down the Rhine.

Since the start of the year, Herr Gutenberg had been pushing us to complete a trial section of the Bible for the upcoming fair in Frankfurt, now only a few days away. He had swiftly invested Fust's money in five additional presses and even more compositors who, together with the other apprentices, had relocated to the Humbrechthof, a more spacious abode where the majority of printing was taking place. Peter and I, however, remained his special charges, sharing a bed at the top of his house. Peter was fast becoming a talented printer, while my fingers were still the undisputed masters of the type.

Work was progressing on the new Bible, a mammoth undertaking for which we had prepared thousands of pieces of type and countless reams of paper. Even at this rate it would take us another two years to complete the massive tome. My Master had planned on printing 150 copies initially, including thirty on the finest parchment, but already there was a growing list of subscribers: clergymen and patricians all hungry to see how our fabulous machine compared with the work of the most industrious scribes. There was even talk of our being in league with the Devil, for how else could we achieve identical copies of the same text so quickly? Of course, it was all nonsense. It was simply down to our hard work.

Herr Gutenberg was busier than ever before. Each day, he refined the typeface a little bit more and resized the margins, experimenting with the number of lines he could fit on to each page. Everything had to be just so. He expected his Bible to be the most beautiful, legible book ever created: a tribute to his ingenuity, a testament to God's Holy Word and a profitable enterprise that would repay Fust's investment many times over.

Fust, for his part, was more often to be seen in Gutenberg's house, close to his mysterious chest, than in the workrooms. To him, the Bible was of only minor importance. Another project was occupying his thoughts. I wouldn't have been surprised to learn he was practising the Black Art, secretly hoping to uncover the laws of the universe, for I frequently saw him poring over old manuscripts belonging to the Barefoot Friars, trying to piece together fragments of ancient texts: strange lines, runes and symbols that befuddled most minds. His fingers were black from the pages he perused and a heavy shadow haunted his eyes. Often, while I bent over my table, arranging words, he watched me – holding out a hand to stop me, as if testing the quality of my work. I shrank from his touch.

He timed his visits, I noticed, according to the waxing and waning of the moon, staying longest on those nights of total darkness, when even the faintest glimmer of light failed to illumine the sky. Tonight, only a splinter of moon was visible through the window at the top of our bedchamber, snagging a few clouds on its pilgrimage over the city. Yet it was enough to show me that the room was empty. Peter was gone.

At first I presumed he was on another of his nocturnal missions to see Christina, Fust's dark-haired daughter. He had developed quite an infatuation for the modest, kind-hearted maiden. On religious days, when work was suspended on the press, he could be seen lingering outside the walls of Fust's house like an exiled lover – and by night, in our bed, he could be heard chattering about her beauty. But Peter was not with Christina tonight.

From somewhere deep in the house came voices. Whispers. Traces of movement scudded across the print room below, as though someone were dragging Fust's chest out of hiding and sliding it along the floor.

Wiping the drowsiness from my eyes, I crept towards the stairs. The candle in its iron holder had burned down to a tallow stub that gave off a fatty, rancid smell, but no light. I stumbled, trying to find my way in the dark. Shadows moved around me like quicksilver.

I descended slowly, careful not to make a sound. Even the slightest creak of wood might betray my eavesdropping ears.

The room below was aglow with red light. From the stairway, I could see that the fire was a riot of flame, a phoenix reborn from the ashes. Shapes dashed and flickered along the walls, dancing round the press like devilish minions.

I stepped nearer.

Fust was bent over the horrendous chest, which he had dragged towards the flames. Muttering an incantation I could not understand, he ran his fingers along the sides of the box. Then, in a deft movement, like a scribe replenishing his quill, he dipped them in a cup that Peter held out before him.

I nearly collapsed. The ink was dark and thick, like blood.

Quickly, Fust coiled his hands round the serpents' heads and fed them each a bubble of liquid from his fingertips. The fangs seemed to bite into his skin and then slide together at his bidding. The lid yawned open.

Had my eyes deceived me? Were the fangs not poisonous, as I had always believed?

I inched closer.

The press stood like a monster chained to the floor in the middle of the room and I ducked beneath its wooden belly, wedging myself between its protective legs.

From the top of the chest Fust now pulled out a pale silver-green animal skin. I caught my breath. He held it up to the light, where it immediately absorbed the glow of the fire and turned red like a sunset – a blood-soaked battlefield.

Amazed, Peter held out a hand to stroke it.

Fust batted him aside. 'Psst! Do not touch,' he hissed, as he draped the layers of skin on the floor and plunged his hands deep into the dark interior of the chest.

My eyes widened further as he withdrew a long billowing sheet of paper, which seemed to ripple and stir with life. I had never seen such a spectacle before. It was an enormous wing of parchment! The paper was as white as snow, but did not melt, not even in the blaze of the fire, which crackled and spat nearby. Instead, the enchanted skin seemed to suck the colour from the flames and burn with a more intense white-ness. Even my Master's best parchment looked dull in comparison.

My fingers squeezed the legs of the press. I longed to feel this amazing apparition for myself.

The chest contained other, similar sheets of paper – I could see them lapping in the box like a moonlit sea –

but even as I watched, this single leaf divided in Fust's hands into ever-finer, thinner membranes that were all nearly transparent, yet veined with a delicate silver light. There seemed to be no end to the number of pages emerging from this individual sheet alone. It was a miracle!

'Yet for all its fragility, it is virtually indestructible,' said Fust, dipping a corner of the skin into the fire.

I listened, astounded, as the paper emitted a soft hiss, but did not burst into flame as I had expected it would. Instead, it seemed to douse the fire, which turned from raging red to sullen grey and back again. Yet there wasn't so much as a scorch or a burn mark on the paper when Fust retrieved it from the fire.

I rubbed my eyes. Could this be real?

Peter peered over his Master's shoulder. 'How did you come upon this – this magic parchment?' he asked with an incredulous whisper.

Fust remained silent and thoughtful for a while. Then he smiled. The tip of his tongue protruded briefly between his teeth. 'You could say it was a gift from an especially pious fool in Haarlem.'

Breathlessly, I listened as he explained the origins of the paper.

Several years before, a Dutchman named Laurens Coster had been out walking near his home in the Low

Countries with his granddaughter, a girl of no more than five or six. Coming to the middle of a wood, they had chanced upon a magnificent tree he had never seen before. To his surprise, she had insisted she could see a dragon hiding in its leaves.

'And was there?' asked Peter, with bated breath.

'Patience!' said Fust, silencing him with a reproachful stare. 'I shall tell you.'

Coster's granddaughter was an imaginative girl, prone to dreams and fancies, and Coster did not believe her. The tree looked like a mighty beech to him. And so, to prove her wrong, he had stuck his knife deep into the heart of the trunk – in a whorl of bark that looked diseased – and challenged the dragon to reveal itself or be chopped into firewood. Nothing happened. The dragon failed to appear.

'In a rage, the girl stomped off,' continued Fust, seeming to delight in the young girl's distress. His eyes burned with a vicious light. 'She was so blinded by tears that she ran headlong into another tree and fell to the ground. Her cry brought her grandfather running.'

Peter was losing interest in the story, for he asked what this had to do with the paper.

'I am getting to it,' remarked Fust coldly. 'The little girl scraped an elbow or a knee, I cannot remember which, but the abrasion bled – enough to make her grand-father staunch the wound with a cloth.'

He held up a finger to silence Peter, who was about to interrupt.

'This is important,' he said severely. 'To cheer her up, Coster used part of the bark of the tree she had found to whittle a series of letters for her as a toy alphabet. He was a master craftsman, you see, used to designing wood-cuts. He wrapped the letters in the blood-soaked cloth and led her home, resolving to return as soon as she was asleep and chop down the tree – for it really would make splendid firewood.'

Fust paused to study Peter's face. 'Only, when he arrived back at his lodging,' he continued, lowering his voice, 'Coster found that the letters had transferred more than their sap to his bloody rag.'

Peter shook his head. 'What do you mean?'

'I mean, Peter,' said Fust, 'imprinted on the cloth were not just the outlines of the letters he had carved, but a whole word – a word strung together by some unseen, all-knowing hand. It really was as if the tree had possessed a dragon . . . or a spirit.'

Peter's mouth dropped open. 'But –'

'The letters,' said Fust, even more slowly, 'were addressing Coster's granddaughter by name.'

Peter tugged on his ear, as if he had misheard.

'But how can that be?'

Fust appeared to smile. A shiver crept up and down my spine.

'Open your eyes, boy. The answer lies before you.'

He spat into the fire.

Shielded from the flames, the dragon skin on the floor had turned back to its original greenish silver colour, like a mound of frosty leaves. Once again I found myself desiring to bury my hands in its tempting texture.

'You mean there was a dragon in that tree all along?' stammered Peter. 'It knew her?'

Fust jerked his wrist slightly and caused the expanding sheet of paper in his hand to fold shut again. 'When Coster returned to the forest,' he said, 'he found a mass of quivering leaves in the clearing, exactly where the tree had been. The creature was writhing in agony, tearing its bark-like hide across the ground, in the very throes of a burning death. Its last breath left the earth scorched and fallow.'

Fust paused to consider the fire in the hearth for a moment. The flames were fizzing and sighing.

'After the dragon's incineration,' he resumed, 'Coster found a mound of pure white paper and intact scales among the ash and debris – a perfect parchment. The temptation to gather it in his arms was too strong for him to resist.'

'And Coster showed you this?' Peter took up the story excitedly, pointing at the open chest. 'He gave you the dragon skin?'

Fust hesitated. 'Let's just say he opened his storeroom to me one Christmas Eve,' he said, evading the question.

Peter turned to his Master in horror. 'You mean you stole it? On Christmas Eve too! How could you?'

'Ah, Peter, foolish boy,' Fust cajoled him. 'Stop trying to be so honourable. Holiness does not become you. This paper will make you a rich man – a very rich, enviable man.'

I shook my head. Part of me wanted to flee from the room, to escape Fust's wicked ways; yet another was tempted to remain by the fireside and see what other wonders this paper could perform. The lure of the skin, its luminous sheen, enticed me still nearer.

The promise of money, however, seemed to have stayed Peter's mind. He fumbled with the rough ends of his tunic, which Christina had darned with patches of mismatched fabric.

'That's my boy,' said Fust craftily. 'Coster did not know what to make of his discovery, but I do.'

Peter gaped at him for a long moment.

'What do you propose to do?' he stammered at last. The words barely escaped his mouth.

Fust picked at the points of his bifurcated beard. 'What

I desire is to harness the power of the skin,' he responded calmly. 'To turn the parchment into a book that will outstrip even Gutenberg's most precious Bible.'

My heart jumped inside me. How could anyone dare to compete with my Master's sacred work?

Peter looked perplexed. 'I don't understand.'

'I have devoted many months of study to this skin,' said Fust. 'It belongs to the rarest, most mystical breed of dragon – a dragon fabled to have dwelled once within the walls of Eden and to carry the secrets of eternal wisdom within its skin. Everything Adam and Eve hungered for – but lost – is now within our grasp. Just imagine what the paper will reveal once we can read it!'

Peter bit his lip. 'But –'

'Why, everything!' cried Fust ecstatically, clapping his hands together and causing his gemstone rings to clack. 'All the secrets of the universe will be ours, all contained within one book!'

'But . . . but the paper is blank,' murmured Peter. 'How will you find the information you seek?'

Fust smiled cunningly and his eyes darted round the room. I cowered even lower in my hiding place, hoping he would not see me. His eyes were as restless as flies: they landed on each piece of equipment until they settled on the smudged, padded ink balls we used to wet the type.

'Ink,' said Fust finally. 'We need ink.'

He paused to rub the ends of his fingers, which were still smeared with the dusky ointment he had used to touch the silver fangs. Peter glanced uneasily at the table, where he had replaced the metal cup. Whatever it contained was slowly filling the room with a noxious odour – a metallic scent like blood.

'You remember that it was Coster's granddaughter who could see the dragon,' started Fust, raising a red eyebrow. 'Correct?'

Peter nodded.

'And her blood that brought the letters to life?'

Again Peter nodded, but this time with less conviction.

'Don't you see?' erupted Fust at last. 'This paper needs a special kind of ink to make its meaning known!'

I felt the colour drain from my skin. Peter, too, had turned pale.

'Blood?' he asked tremulously. 'Is blood the ink?'

Fust did not answer, but stared into the flames, which writhed and curled like snakes. His eyes were as red as hot coals.

'Just imagine,' he said. 'This little girl was so innocent, so naive, it borders on repellent. And yet she – *she!* – had the power to summon words from a dragon. A power even I do not possess. Yet.'

He snapped the final word with his teeth.

'What do you mean?'

'Coster was very crafty in the way he designed this chest,' explained Fust. 'As soon as he saw the dead creature, he was filled not with desire, but with regret. He realized he'd destroyed one of God's most sacred creatures, a beast invested with everlasting knowledge. Just one spiteful act – to crush his granddaughter's imagination – was enough to rob this fabled creature of its life. And so he made this chest so frightening, so hideous and horrifying, he hoped no man would dare open it. And he topped it off with these perfidious snakes, right from the Garden of Eden.'

Peter's mouth hung open. 'But how . . . how did you . . .' He pointed at the gaping lid of the chest.

Once again, I felt my eyes drawn to that frightful box. Ferocious monsters scowled at me from the engraved panels, while hellish demons wept tears of amber in the firelight. There was cruelty in its construction, but also guilt and remorse, a sadness that touched my heart.

'Up until now, I have attempted to purify my blood with that,' said Fust, indicating the cup on the table. 'It was enough to deceive the lock, but something is not yet right. Even monksbane is not potent enough to release the words from the parchment. For that I need something stronger.'

He waved a blackened finger in the air and, at last, I recognized the smell wafting towards me. Monksbane. One of the metals my Master used to create his special typeface, an element so powerful monks were believed to drink whole quantities of it to purify their souls. Yet, as my Master frequently warned me, in even minimal doses it could be lethal.

Fust shook his head. 'No, this paper responds to something else entirely. Something virtuous, honest and true . . .'

I felt tempted to run upstairs, to crawl beneath my blankets, for I knew what terrible truth was coming.

'This paper,' said Fust finally, 'feeds on children.'

Unable to control myself, I recoiled in horror. My head bumped against the frame of the press and the noise thudded in the dim room. With the swiftness of a fox, Fust turned away from the chest and swept his eyes round the furniture, hoping to flush out any unwanted quarry.

I remained where I was, perfectly still, too afraid even to breathe.

As Fust's eyes neared my hiding place, I pressed myself even deeper into its shadow. I feared he was going to drag me out by my heels and feed me to the paper; yet he seemed to shrug off the suspicion and turned back to the fire. He shuddered, as if cold.

It was then that I noticed my toolkit lying on a nearby bench. As inconspicuously as I could, I reached out to grab it and unrolled its soft leather lining. Inside was a row of shiny metal implements and I selected a sharp gouge to defend myself if either Fust or Peter came too near. Concealed beneath the press, I watched and waited.

Fust had gripped Peter now by the shoulders and was whispering something in his ear. I could not tell what he said, but was startled by Peter's reaction.

'Master! What's wrong?' he cried, for Fust had slipped to the floor. An ashen complexion had come over his face and he had started to shiver, as if seized by a fever.

The man clutched his stomach and made an agonizing retching sound. 'It's the monksbane,' he gasped. 'It disagrees with me.'

'What should I do?'

'Take me home. Close the chest and take me home. Christina will know the cure.'

The mention of Christina's name seemed to spur Peter into action. He rammed the dragon skin into the chest, kicked the lid to, and rushed to his Master's aid. Bending down, he managed to lift Fust awkwardly to his feet and guided him gently towards the stairs. The man reeled like a drunkard.

Just before he left, Peter allowed himself a quick glance in the mirrors lining the walls and checked his reflection. For the first time that night, I saw a genuine smile pass his lips. And then, remembering the monksbane in the cup, he rushed back to toss the remains in the fire. The flames emitted a choking white cloud and went out.

The room was plunged into darkness.

I remained where I was and listened. When I was certain they would not reappear, I hurried over to the chest.

The room was dark and cold, and I could barely see what I was doing. Only a glimmer of heat still seethed inside the fire. Like a hibernating beast, its red eye glinted at me from a cavern of ash.

The leather toolkit was bunched in my hands and I laid it out beside me. Desperate to see inside the chest, I worked my fingers round the carved panels of the box until I could feel the domed heads of the snakes protecting the lid. My fingers were jittery, but I fought hard to control them. I knew what I must do.

Taking a deep breath, I let my hands slide down the sleek curves of the silver fangs until they reached the tips of the teeth. The points felt sharp, cold to the touch, and I winced as they bit hard into my skin.

Despite all I had seen, I half-expected a rush of venom to seep into me, to lull my senses to sleep, but nothing happened. After the first stab of pain, there was only a strangely cool, comforting sensation as the fangs sipped from my fingers.

Would I be judged pure enough, I wondered, to see inside?

It did not take long for the flow of blood to subside. Following Fust's example, I then slid the teeth together and watched as the snakes' heads magically disentwined and the lid opened.

The fire sprang to life, and I jumped.

Almost immediately I discovered that the fangs I had feared for so long did not belong to the snakes, but were parts of the dragon – talons that pierced the front of the lid and protruded from the serpents' mouths. The snakes were merely a facade, a deterrent; it was the dragon itself that guarded the chest and all it contained. Its claws had read my fingers – and allowed me to enter.

Emboldened, I dipped my hands into the chest. The top layer of dragon skin felt like a covering of frost-hardened leaves. Tinged green and silver, they were forged together like an invincible plate of armour. I had to remind myself that these were neither leaves nor chain mail, but actual scales! Dragon scales!

My heart knocked against my ribs. How could this be true?

The parchment beneath was glowing softly and I immersed my hands in the billowing sea of material. My fingers dissolved in a pile of paper as cold and soft as snow, yet without its icy sting. My skin tingled. A feeling of overwhelming security flooded into me.

Greedily, I brought up several leaves of parchment and watched as the air buffeted and breathed within them, filling each separate layer with life. I could barely contain my excitement. The membranes were as thin as moth's wings, yet illumined from within by some strange source of light. I was captivated, spellbound.

And then something else caught my eye. A glimmer of words, in silver strands of gossamer, appeared before me like an oracle. Where had they come from? I read them quickly, hungry to glean their knowledge:

> The Child may see what the Man does not
> A future Time which Time forgot:
> Books yet to be and Books already written
> Within these Pages lie dormant and hidden.
> Yet Darkness seeks what Light reveals
> A Shadow grows: these Truths conceal.
> These are my Words, Endymion Spring,
> Bring only the Insight the Inside brings . . .

My skin shuddered with recognition. That was my name! The dragon was addressing me personally, just as it had appealed to Coster's granddaughter several years before. My hands began to shake.

Even now, I could see other words, other messages, appearing in the sheets of paper that were unfolding in my fingers. Pockets of parchment opened at random, each disclosing a hidden doorway to wisdom, a minia- ture book. It was more wonderful than anything I had imagined – much faster than Herr Gutenberg's press. Whole kingdoms rose and fell within a few pages, leaving behind their legacies of words. I wanted to follow each new path, each staircase of paper, to find out where they would lead, but all of a sudden my elation turned to fear.

Like a shadow passing into the room behind me, a suspi- cion entered my mind. Wasn't this exactly what Fust had wanted all along? The answers to the world's mysteries laid out before him like an open book? Still more words were appearing on the magic parchment, bleeding through the skin, spreading into the contents of the chest. They were unstoppable!

Instantly, I recognized the error of my ways. I had opened a vast florilegium of knowledge – a book of books without any conceivable end. How could I close it again?

A breath of night air stole into the room and brushed against the back of my neck. The door downstairs had opened and two sets of footsteps – not one – approached. Peter was not alone. Fust had returned with him.

Terrified, I tightened my grip on the paper. As if in response, the expanding sheet in my hand began to diminish rapidly in size, folding itself into smaller and smaller compartments. The immense wing of paper was soon no more than a booklet – a section of paper that fitted easily in the palm of my hand.

Grabbing my toolkit, I hastily removed its contents and stuffed the wad of paper inside, wrapping the leather straps around it as quickly and tightly as possible to form a secure bundle, hoping to keep at least these top layers of enchanted dragon skin from Fust's possession.

Miraculously, the words in the rest of the paper began to halt, as if frozen. Like shadows beneath ice, they were just visible against the whiteness of the paper, but virtually indecipherable. Perhaps these lower reams of paper would be incapable of releasing their power without the top layers to complete them? Perhaps I could still put things right? I had to hope so.

Fust had almost arrived.

Quickly, I closed the lid of the chest, leaving it as I had found it, and then as quietly as possible picked up the loose tools from the floor and trotted across the room towards the stairs, the booklet of paper concealed beneath my linen nightshirt. The fire had died to a red glow.

I could feel Fust's eyes hunting for me in the dark, but I was already on the stairs, hurrying back to the dormitory and my fate – a thief, once again.

OXFORD

Eight

Blake rubbed his brow and reached for his watch, wondering what time it was. He knew he'd over-slept; he just wasn't sure for how long.

His heart rang out in alarm. It was more than two hours after he was supposed to get up! His mother would be furious.

Jolted awake, he scurried into the clothes he had left on the floor and tried desperately to think of an excuse to tell her.

He'd had so many strange dreams. He couldn't remember them all, but weird images had flitted through his mind all night like a nightmarish picture book come to life. In one, voracious goblins had escaped from their pages and were attempting to devour books in a library he had never seen before. They had greedy, gluttonous faces with beastly teeth – like sharp, red pomegranate seeds – which they used to shred paper and pulverize words. He shivered at the recollection, wondering where they had come from.

The house seemed disconcertingly quiet and he crept down the stairs like an intruder, careful not to make a sound. There was no sign of his mother or sister anywhere. The kitchen was empty and even the regular clutter of cereal boxes on the dining-room table, which he and Duck used to build a wall so they didn't have to look at each other, had been cleared away. A note on the table confirmed his suspicions.

9.25 a.m.

Gone to college. meet us for lunch (if you're up).

m.

Duck had added her own postscript in lopsided writing:

PS Sleepyhead. We NEED to talk.

Blake tore the note into tiny strips and tossed them in a bin under the kitchen sink. He wasn't going to talk to his sister about anything. She was just being nosy as usual. But it was harder to know how to deal with his mother. There was no 'Good morning, Blake', or 'I love you, Mum' to lift his spirits. It was the shortest possible note

– a continuation of the silent treatment from the night before. He would have to make sure he arrived early for lunch to avoid further trouble.

At that moment, the letter box in the front door slapped open and shut.

Blake looked behind him, surprised. Apart from a few flyers, mostly for Indian takeaways, nothing had been sent to them at Millstone Lane before.

He stepped into the hall, wondering if his father had finally written him a letter, and came to an abrupt halt. A piece of bright red cloth lay on the mat just inside the door. It had been tied so as to form a small pouch, the ends drawn together and secured with a tight knot. Attached to it was a little note, written in wobbly letters on a piece of torn paper, which read: 'To the Boy of the House'.

Blake gulped. Immediately, he glanced at the door, but all he could see was a tiny moon of glass shining above the latch: a peephole. He checked it. No one was there.

Just to make sure, he unlocked the door and stepped outside.

An oily drizzle was falling, turning the leaves on the path to a slippery mulch. A damp autumnal smell filled the air. But apart from a hardy jogger crossing the road towards the river, a few blocks away, Millstone Lane was deserted. It was a regular September morning.

Blake rubbed his arms to ward off the chill, then closed the door and bolted it firmly behind him.

He tapped the cloth lightly with his foot. Nothing stirred inside it.

A funny smell had now reached him: a muddy, furry scent that made the insides of his nose twinge. The beginnings of a sneeze teased his nostrils. It smelled like a wild animal.

And then the answer struck him. The cloth belonged to the dog he had seen outside the bookshop. It was its red bandanna!

Quickly, he bent down to pick it up. It was incredibly light. In fact, he wondered if there was anything wrapped up in the cloth at all. The bandanna felt suspiciously empty.

Handling the package carefully, as though it were a bomb, he tiptoed through the kitchen and laid it out on the dining-room table. Cautiously, he loosened the knot and peered inside. Instinctively, he jumped back.

What was it?

At first glance, it resembled a large grasshopper or a cadaverous insect. A ghostly exoskeleton covered in hundredsof horned ridges, like scales, cowered at the bottom ofthe pouch. He half-expected the creature to leap into the air or spring out at him, but nothing happened. The creature was dead.

With his heart aflutter, Blake edged back to the table and this time untied the package properly.

It wasn't a grasshopper, but a lizard with a long tail snaking behind it, barely larger than his hand. Each of its reptilian legs ended in a sharp set of claws, ready to rip any unsuspecting prey to shreds. He prodded it gently with his finger. It rocked back and forth, perfectly harmless. Despite the scales plating its body like armour, it felt soft and light – like a husk. Picking it up, he realized that it was made from folded paper.

A strange sensual ripple travelled through him, setting off sparks in his mind. His heart began to thud. He knew exactly where the paper had come from . . . Endymion Spring!

He studied the scaly creature more closely, cradling it in his jittery fingers. It had to be the most intricate piece of origami he had ever seen.

For a moment, he considered unfolding it to see if the paper contained any extra information. And yet he didn't have the heart to destroy the lovely lizard. There was no sign of ink leaching through the scales and he doubted anything would be inside if he dismantled it. It was as if the object itself was the message: a greeting or invitation or even a clue. But what did it mean?

Turning the lizard over in his hands, he unexpectedly triggered a mechanism that unleashed two scrolls of paper on either side of the animal's body. Near-invisible wings of parchment unfolded in his fingers. They were smoother and stronger than silk, yet virtually transparent. He held them up to the light. A network of fine veins glowed from within – just like the book he had found in the library yesterday.

He swallowed hard, his breathing coming in rapid, shallow bursts.

The creature wasn't a lizard, but a paper dragon: a dragon made from the most marvellous paper he had ever seen; paper that seemed to communicate with him directly; paper that could possibly connect him to Endymion Spring himself.

But that didn't explain anything.

Nine

B lake was so engrossed in his discovery that he
almost forgot about the time. Luckily, his stomach
intervened and a rumble of hunger, like distant
thunder, reminded him of his rendezvous with his
mother. She would be furious if he missed lunch as well
as breakfast.

Grabbing an apple from the kitchen, he charged
upstairs to get ready. As he passed his sister's bedroom,
he felt a faint tugging motion in his right hand, as though
the dragon were struggling to escape. A quiver of scales
brushed against his skin.

He looked from the origami dragon to the closed
wooden door. 'Hey, you're mine, not hers,' he told the
creature firmly. 'I'm not sharing you with anyone.'

He placed the dragon on his bedside table.

Once he had eaten his apple and brushed his teeth, he
snatched his jacket from the back of a chair and shrugged

his knapsack on to his shoulders. Then, remembering the dog's bandanna, he rushed back downstairs to retrieve it. He stuffed the cloth next to the overlooked worksheets his teacher had given him to work on in his absence and finally placed the dragon carefully on top. Wondering what he would say to the homeless man if he saw him, he took the spare key from its hook in the hall and let himself out.

The rain had stopped, but the air was damp and fresh. A cool wind tugged at the clouds, pulling them apart like fleece. He thrust his hands into his pockets and turned towards the river.

Twenty minutes later, he passed the bookshop where he had spotted the homeless man the previous afternoon. Apart from tourists wrapped in colourful windcheaters, the street was deserted. There was no sign of the man or his dog.

Disappointed, Blake watched idly as a young man rearranged a pile of books in the cluttered shop window. He was suddenly struck by an idea. Perhaps he could find the book his mother had liked as a child and buy it for her as a present – as a way of apologizing for last night. He knew a serious confrontation with her was coming, but surely this would help her to forgive him. He smiled at his own brilliance.

Glancing at his watch, he reckoned he had just enough time to locate the book, which he knew was about butterflies, and then sprint to the dining hall to meet his mother for lunch. Without another moment's thought, he went inside.

A little bell jingled above him and he stood awkwardly in the doorway for a moment, uncertain where to go. The shop was longer and narrower than he'd expected and the walls were crammed with books. Mismatched volumes spilled from the shelves on to the floor, where stacks of oversized hardbacks grew like primitive rock formations. Apart from the man rearranging bruised paperbacks in the window, the shop appeared to be empty.

'Excuse me,' Blake murmured, 'where –'

'Fiction in front; Literature behind; History round the corner,' the man started, without looking up, 'Nature, Crafts and all that Granny Stuff, not that you'd be inter-ested, to the left; First Editions locked behind glass, away from grubby little fingers like yours; Modern Languages, Classics *and* Children's Literature upstairs.'

Blake listened in astonishment as the man recited all this in one long, short-tempered breath. With each new addition, his eyes bulged a little bit more and travelled along the rows of disorderly shelves. He still did not know where to go.

'What, you still there?' asked the man, sensing the boy's confusion. This time, he stood up. Not much taller than Blake, he had thick, bristly eyebrows that met in the middle like warring caterpillars and was wearing a faded T-shirt with the name of a rock band Blake had never heard of before: the Plastic Dinosaurs. A hand-knitted scarf straddled his neck like a lazy python, its rainbow-coloured ends trailing down to the ground.

Blake stepped back, feeling as though he had stumbled into a scene from *Alice's Adventures in Wonderland*, Duck's favourite book.

The man, sensing his apprehension, softened his approach. 'How can I help you?' he asked more reasonably. His mouth cracked into a grin and Blake realized that he was only pretending to be grumpy and troll-like.

Remembering what his mother had told him about the book she had liked, Blake tried his best to describe it.

'I don't recall a children's book being there,' replied the man seriously, scratching the back of his neck. 'Of course, it might have been sold since then – books in the window tend to go fast – but I put everything that was there this morning under the New Acquisitions. I didn't pay much attention to them myself. Science fiction is the way to go.'

As if to prove his point, he pointed to a pyramid of cloned silver novels he had built in the window.

'Um, thanks,' said Blake, wandering over to the section the man had indicated.

He put his head down and got to work. It was going to be more difficult than he'd expected. A tower of brown books reached high above him, almost to the ceiling. Some had detached covers, held together with elastic bands; others mottled pages that either reeked of tobacco or ponged of damp churches the moment he opened them. Still more had fancy covers and gilt edges, like the finest strands of hair. And then, nearer the floor, were books in brightly coloured dust jackets. These looked more promising and he knelt down to study them more closely.

Gradually, he became aware of a man standing close beside him, almost pressing into his back. A pair of dark trousers leaned against him and an expensive watch ticked above his ear. Blake felt uncomfortable and shifted his knapsack in front of him, guarding it with his body, just in case the man crushed the paper dragon he had placed inside.

Slowly but surely, the man picked his way down the stack of books, selecting a few volumes and then replacing them on the shelves with a dissatisfied grunt. He clearly knew what he was looking for.

Then, like birds of prey, his hands swooped past Blake's shoulders and grabbed a volume he was about to look at.

'Hey!' grumbled Blake. 'I was just about to –'

Glancing up, he realized with a start that it was Sir Giles Bentley. The man glared down at him coldly, his eyebrows as dark as thunderheads.

Blake immediately went quiet and shielded the remaining books from view. With a disdainful snort, Sir Giles continued flipping through the book, almost ripping the pages, his eyes ploughing through the text.

Blake reached for the next volume.

A faint rustling movement inside his knapsack stopped him in his tracks. He looked down. The top of his bag twitched. He was about to open the compartment to risk a look inside, when he noticed a half-hidden volume at the back of the shelf nearest him. Sir Giles's careless motion must have caused it to slip behind the others. It had become wedged between shelves. Trapped.

With small fingers, he reached in and tweezed it free.

Immediately, the paper dragon in his bag went still and a chill crept over him. Unlike Endymion Spring, this book didn't feel warm, comforting or inviting. Thin, bruised and bound in black leather, it seemed as ominous as a tombstone. A few specks of mould mottled its cover like lichen and a faint symbol, like a dagger, had been pressed into its surface: the shadow of a shadow.

Frightened, Blake opened the book. A vicious *F* slashed across his vision like a knife blade and his blood went cold. Printed in red ink, the initial went on to form a word in sharp, seriffed letters:

FAUSTBUCH

The *F* matched the design on the cover.

Blake recognized the first part of the title. *Faust.* Wasn't he the person his mother had mentioned the previous day, the sorcerer who had sold his soul to the Devil? Hadn't she believed that he was somehow linked to the legend of the lost book of knowledge, the book his father had longed to find and which Sir Giles had ensured was beyond his reach?

Blake's fingers shook. What had he unearthed?

On the facing endpaper, smeared with dirt, was a list of names in faded brown ink, the colour of dried blood. H. Middleton, L. de la Croix, J. Fell, N. Hart . . . the book's previous owners. Judging from one of the inscribed dates – MDCLXVI – he guessed the book must be hundreds of years old.

Blake's mouth felt dry and he shivered involuntarily as he leafed through the volume.

The book itself was in bad shape. Many of the pages had been torn and only a few jagged strips of paper survived in their place, coated in shady spots that spread through the volume like a pox. The bumped covers smelled earthy and damp, as though someone had once tried to bury it.

Occasionally, his eyes alighted on broken strands of text, which he tried to sew together to form a story. It was difficult. The sentences were punctuated by rips and tears. One passage, however, grabbed his attention:

> *In his simplicitie the boy has founde a marv*
> *booke which though blank does contayne*
> *elusive knowledge. Methinks it is tha*
> *which Ignatius claims did enter O*
> *Devil's back. The quiet boy fears*
> *I have found a way to see inside*

Blake's heart began to gallop. His mind was racing. Wasn't Ignatius the monk his parents had been researching? The one who believed a book of forbidden knowledge had actually found its way to Oxford? Could this terrifying volume *really* be part of the puzzle?

He wanted to read on, but became aware of Sir Giles peering over his shoulder.

'Hey, I was here first,' he snapped. 'Go find your own book.'

Sir Giles, however, did not apologize; nor did he move.

Blake held on to the *Faustbuch* fiercely. He was

unwilling to let *this* book go. Even though it filled him with trepidation, he sensed that it must be important. He could feel it in his bones. The paper dragon had drawn him towards it and now that it was in his possession the creature was dead still.

Slowly, Blake flipped through the volume and eventually found a price pencilled lightly on the inside cover. His heart sank. It cost more than he had. A note beneath indicated that the book was 'sold as seen'. He frowned.

Sir Giles was hovering behind him like a wasp, ready to seize the volume as soon as he put it back on the shelf. His hands clutched the air.

Deciding to haggle, Blake walked up to the counter, where the Plastic Dinosaurs man was now supervising the shop. 'I'd like to buy this book,' he said, 'but –'

'But what?' said the man sharply, suspecting a catch.

'But I don't have enough money to buy it right now,' confessed Blake. 'This is all I have.'

He emptied the contents of his pockets on to the counter. The foreign coins, which still felt heavy and unusual to his North American fingers, danced and spun for a moment and then collapsed in a paltry heap. They didn't amount to much.

'What's it say inside?' said the man, disinclined to be generous.

'£20.00.'

'And what've you got?'

Blake performed some quick mental arithmetic. '£9.83,' he said weakly, scrunching his nose.

The man pursed his lips.

'But it's falling apart!' exclaimed Blake. 'It's probably worth nothing at all! Please, it's important.'

The shop assistant looked sceptical. He made little suction motions with his mouth and started to scratch the back of his neck, where the python scarf was slipping. Finally, he opened the cover of the book and read the title. An involuntary laugh escaped his lips.

'"*A True Historie of the Faustbuch, as witnessed by one of Gods owne servants...*" That's pretty sophisticated reading, isn't it?' he said.

'Maybe,' said Blake, unwilling to give up. His mind fished rapidly for alternatives. 'Of course, if you're willing to wait, I could –'

'– pay you £20.00 for it right now,' Sir Giles finished the sentence and slapped a freshly folded banknote on the counter. 'For me,' he added, 'and not the boy.'

'But that's not fair!' shouted Blake.

'Sir, the boy was here first,' said the man responsibly, although Blake could tell that the money tempted him. He licked the corner of his lips and his eyes returned to the banknote again like a frog targeting a fly.

'That may be,' said Sir Giles, pushing Blake aside,

'but the boy can't afford to buy it . . . unless he means to *steal* it.'

A lethal glare from Sir Giles warned Blake not to make a sound. Perhaps he did recognize him from the college dinner, after all . . .

Blake clenched his hands into fists, but remained silent.

'Here, I'll tell you what I'll do,' said Sir Giles, taking control of the situation. He withdrew another banknote from his wallet. 'I'll double your asking price. That's my final offer. As the boy said, it really is in appalling condition.'

'But –' appealed Blake mutely.

'There, there,' said Diana Bentley, suddenly appearing from behind her husband and placing a comforting hand on Blake's shoulder. 'You shouldn't concern yourself with grubby old books. It's probably contagious.'

'It was . . . it was for my mum,' lied Blake, hoping to appeal to her emotions. 'I was going to surprise her with it.'

She gave him a compassionate look. 'How sweet,' she murmured. 'But really, Blake, I should think your mother would prefer a less contaminated sort of book. Why not flowers, perhaps?'

A playful smile teased her lips.

'But I think it could be important,' said Blake helplessly.

'This decrepit thing?' She brushed the cover with a gloved fingertip, as though disdaining to get her skin dirty. 'Surely not. Giles likes repairing old books. He'll rebind it and give it a fresh lease on life.'

Sir Giles let out a humph of protest. 'For heaven's sake, woman, stop humouring the child.' He turned his attention back to the man behind the till. 'Well?'

The shop assistant, weakening under the assault of Sir Giles's black eyebrows, looked from the man to the boy and back again. 'I'll take it,' he said finally, snatching the notes and entering them in the till before he could change his mind.

He shrugged at Blake and then said, 'Sorry, mate, but books nowadays are a business.'

'Don't fret,' said Diana mildly, helping Blake on with his knapsack and escorting him away from the shop. 'You can always come to our house if you'd like to see the book again.' She smiled at the idea. 'Yes, Giles has a magnificent collection. You must come by.'

Ten

Blake walked the rest of the way to college with slumped shoulders. Not only had he slept in, but he'd lost the blank book – and now another potentially important one. Nothing was going right!

He kicked at the stray leaves that had fallen overnight and didn't look up once, not even when he ducked through the small wooden door set into the massive gate guarding St Jerome's and from habit marched straight into the Porter's Lodge.

'Why, there's a message for you,' said Bob Barrett hurriedly, bending down to retrieve it. 'With your name on it, too!'

'Thanks,' said Blake gloomily, taking the envelope without looking at it.

'Come on, it can't be that bad. What's the –'

Just then the telephone rang and Bob paused to answer it. Blake took the opportunity to leave without another word. He didn't feel like talking to anyone right now.

He waved a hand in a half-hearted farewell and headed towards the library, where Mephistopheles immediately pounced on his feet, hoping to exact revenge on him for last night.

'Stupid cat,' he growled as the animal leaped away. He stooped to retie his laces.

Out of the corner of his eye, he could see Paula Richards bustling around the interior of the library, fetching things from shelves, a whirling dervish of activity. He didn't want to face her either, just in case she suspected him of damaging the books last night, and decided to redirect his steps to a bench under a tree on the far side of the lawn, where he could wait for his mother and sister in private.

He sat down on the bench, which was beaded with raindrops, and turned the letter over in his hands, careful not to let it get wet. A few more spiteful spots of rain shimmied through the leaves and landed on the back of his neck, but it was the driest place he could find.

The envelope bore the college coat of arms on its crisp, white paper: a ring of stars surrounding a knight's glove, which clutched a sharpened quill instead of a sword. Sure enough, his name was written on the front in a flourish of swirling letters:

Blake Winters, Esq.

He wondered what an Esq. was, but whatever it meant, the title made him feel distinguished and important, rather like a knight himself. He sat up a little straighter.

He opened the envelope. Inside was an abbreviated message in the same ornate writing:

Questions!

He glanced up, suspecting the anonymous author had read his mind. His head was teeming with questions.

He turned over the invitation, where he encountered further instructions.

Answers await you in the Old Library. Two o'clock, if convenient.

Hope to see you then.

Professor Jolyon Fall

A smile grew on Blake's face. Not only would he get a chance to see inside the Old Library, but he might be able to learn the secret of the blank book, too! Things were definitely looking up.

He craned his neck to see if he could see the Old

Library from where he was seated, but only the tip of the tower above the cloisters was visible, partially hidden behind a screen of leaves. Nevertheless, a quiver of excitement – a bit like a slide whistle of pleasure – passed through him.

The sound of his sister's voice on the other side of the lawn brought him crashing back to reality. His first obstacle: obtaining his mother's permission. Would she let him go? Judging from the way she was clutching her briefcase in her hand, she was going to spend the whole afternoon in the Bodleian Library. That could mean only one thing. He would be the obligated babysitter.

He sighed and, as if in sympathy, a volley of raindrops slid through the leaves and landed on his invitation, causing the ink to smear.

'Mum's got email access,' Duck announced as soon as they were within shouting distance. 'Isn't that great?'

'Yeah, great,' he replied, unconvinced. He got up to find a damp, heart-shaped patch on the seat of his jeans. Duck snickered.

Blake knew that his mother had found an elusive manuscript in the Bodleian Library and was eager to contact Professor Morgan, the Chair of her Department, for permission to prolong her trip. Secretly, he had hoped the college would ignore her request to install an Internet connection in her office, since then she couldn't apply for an extension so easily; but now it seemed a distinct possibility.

'Now we can email Dad every day,' said Duck cheerfully. 'I've already written to ask if he's finished any of his new drawings yet. He could be reading my message right now. It's like he's here with us!'

'No, it's not,' sulked Blake. 'He's on the other side of the world, in case you hadn't noticed.'

Duck had skipped happily ahead and not heard; his mother, however, had. She gave him a sharp look – like a pinprick – and he winced. He could sense that she had not forgotten about the trouble he had caused last night and decided to walk on ahead. He wandered towards the dining hall.

Blake's dad had been working from home for several months, ever since tiring of the rat race and leaving the firm he had worked for in the city. Blake preferred it this way: he enjoyed his dad's company and the extra attention he and Duck received while their mother focused on her career. Just before they'd departed for England, however, Blake had heard his dad despairing that his designs would give a whole new definition to the term 'blank canvas'. He wondered if Duck's email would only make him feel worse.

He was debating whether to send a message of his own, when he noticed his mother looking at the card in his hand. He showed her the name on the envelope.

'It's from Professor Jolyon,' he said, deciding to speak first. 'He wants to see me this afternoon.'

'Really? What for?'

She sounded sceptical.

'I'm not sure,' he lied.

His mother didn't look convinced.

'Can I see Professor Jolyon too?' piped in Duck suddenly. 'Please!'

'No!' snapped Blake.

His mother gave him a reproachful look.

'But it's none of her business!' he protested. 'She's always butting in.' He reached out to pinch her.

'Ow! Quit it!'

'I barely even touched you!'

'Yes, you did!' Duck sobbed petulantly and batted his hand away.

His mother cuffed him by the wrist and brought him to a sudden halt. 'That's enough,' she said. 'I don't want any more trouble from you!'

Blake could detect a serious recrimination behind her words and wriggled free from her grasp. He dodged up the steps to the dining hall.

He twisted the heavy iron handle of the arched

wooden door and entered an immense, oak-panelled room lined with benches and long wooden tables that generations of banqueting scholars had worn smooth. Little lamps with brass stands and red shades, like toadstools, sprung up at intervals, emitting weak coronas of light. A warm meaty aroma oozed through the air like gravy.

On a raised platform at the front of the hall, surrounded by dazzling diamond-paned windows, was a luxurious table spread with bottled water, silver cutlery and bowls of fresh fruit. A stained-glass crest shone above it like an incandescent sun, dabbing the tablecloth with splashes of colour. This was where the professors sat, although not Juliet Winters. It was one of the concessions she'd had to make to have her children with her.

She looked longingly at the High Table, while Duck and Blake bickered.

'But she can't come,' Blake was still complaining. 'Professor Jolyon invited me. It's my name on the invitation, not hers.' He knew he was whining, but couldn't stop himself.

'I know it is,' said his mother wearily, 'but it's the least you can do after last night. I need to finish some work in the Bodleian Library and it would be convenient — kind — if you looked after Duck for a few hours. After all, I was hardly able to stick to my normal routine this morning . . .'

Blake shook his head and groaned. It was like this every day. He was always taking care of his little sister – even when he wasn't guilty of sleeping in or sneaking away at night.

They queued in silence to receive servings of steak and kidney pie from a hatch near the kitchen and then followed Duck to a table she had chosen in the middle of the room, next to a section that had been roped off for members of the Ex Libris Society. A gallery of wasp-waisted women in bejewelled dresses and Puritanical men in dark robes with wan, preacher-like complexions stared at them from the walls.

His mother poured them each some water from a jug on the table. All of the glasses were stained and scratchy, but she chose the cleanest ones.

Blake could tell that something was troubling her, some-thing even more significant than his behaviour, for she swirled the water in her glass for a moment, blending her thoughts in its vortex of reflections. Then, in a slow, serious voice that was more solemn than any tone she had used before, she said, 'This morning Mrs Richards told me that someone had disturbed a number of books in the library last night. Not just disturbed them – attacked them, ripped them to shreds.'

She settled the glass on the table and fixed him with her eyes. 'Blake, please tell me you don't have anything to do with this.'

Duck was watching him closely, chewing with her mouth open.

Blake was appalled by the insinuation. 'Of course not!' he spluttered, his face flaming with anger and humiliation. He glanced at a painting of Nathaniel Hart (1723–1804), a lugubrious man in a clerical coat with a woolly wig on his head. His portrait seemed to be hanging over him in judgement.

'Blake, look at me.'

Blake forced his eyes back to the table. 'No, I don't know anything about it,' he said more forcefully.

'This is serious, Blake,' she said, tapping her tray with her finger. 'Are you sure you didn't see anything on your walk last night?'

He could hear suspicion lurking just behind her words and turned away. 'No, I swear I don't know who did that,' he said, fighting to keep his voice under control. 'I didn't see anyone downstairs in the library, OK?'

At once he realized his mistake. He'd admitted to being in the library. The truth had slipped out before he could prevent it, and he took a swig of water to hide his confusion.

His mother closed her eyes in despair. 'Oh, Blake,' she

said. 'I sincerely hoped you wouldn't be caught up in this.'

He looked up, surprised. What did she mean?

He glanced at Duck, who had discovered a piece of kidney on her fork and was picking it off with fussy fingers.

His mother shook her head.

'Look,' he said, feeling flustered. His temples were throbbing and his face turning a brighter shade of scarlet. 'I'm sorry I worried you, OK, but I honestly don't know what happened to the books! I was upstairs at the time. I was trying to fetch the cat, which had slipped in after me.'

Duck looked at both of them expectantly.

His mother sat silently for a while. 'Well, just in case,' she said after a long, pregnant pause, 'I think it would be better if Duck accompanies you this afternoon. Perhaps she can teach you a thing or two about responsibility.'

Duck cheered happily, but Blake groaned inwardly and stabbed at his food with his fork. A ring of gravy had congealed around the edges of his plate and the forest of overcooked broccoli had wilted and turned cold. He bashed at the brain of puff pastry covering his pie.

When at last he looked up, he was annoyed to find Prosper Marchand swaggering towards them. A silver skull dangled from one of his earlobes.

'So these are your two?' said the professor with a

specious grin, patting Duck familiarly on the head. Instinctively, she raised the hood of her coat and turned her face away, scowling. 'They look like quite a handful.'

The curly-haired professor, still in his leather jacket, winked at Blake. Coldly, Blake slid his tray across the table, his appetite gone.

Juliet Winters ignored the remark.

'He really is the spitting image of his father, you know,' continued the professor, unfazed. 'So how is Christopher, anyway?'

Blake stiffened.

'Fine,' responded Juliet Winters tersely, her shoulders tense. 'The same.'

'Ah, I see,' said the professor. Without warning, he crouched down beside her and whispered something in her ear that Blake couldn't quite catch. His leather jacket flexed its slippery muscles. As Juliet Winters listened, she flicked a strand of grey hair away from her eyes. The unconscious, girl-like gesture irritated Blake and he coughed.

Like a vampire interrupted mid-bite, Prosper Marchand glanced up. 'Don't worry, I'm simply inviting your mother to coffee.' His smile gleamed with polished teeth. 'It's perfectly innocent. You're welcome to come, too, if you like.'

Blake tried to outstare the professor, but lost.

'So how about it then?' continued the man, victorious,

turning towards Blake's mother. 'Three o'clock, the old place?'

Blake felt a sudden swell of anger and resentment inside him. He opened his mouth to protest, but caught his mother checking her watch. She looked at both children and then quickly away. Duck stared back at them from behind the rim of her hood, her face inscrutable.

'OK,' she agreed. 'Just coffee.'

'I wouldn't dream of anything else,' remarked the professor suavely and strutted across to the section that had been cordoned off for the members of the Ex Libris Society.

More than sixty scholars, of varying age and nationality, were now assembled there, avidly discussing books. Blake could hear the rumble of voices in the air. Dressed in almost identical turtlenecks and khakis, they resembled hunters preparing for an expedition – although they were armed with bifocal glasses and catalogues of rare books, instead of guns. Still, Blake didn't trust them. He knew from his mother the lengths scholars would go to to protect their interests.

He looked daggers at the professor's back. 'But what about –'

'I'm sure Jolyon won't mind looking after you for a little longer,' answered his mother calmly. 'If not, I'll meet you as usual in the college library.'

Eleven

Blake paced up and down the long passageway outside the Old Library. A cold rain pattered softly against the leaves of the plane tree growing in the enclosed garden beside him, and a chill breeze roamed the stairwells like a ghost. Hunched wooden doors led at intervals into secret rooms all along the cloisters.

There had been no response when he'd hammered on the solid oak door just a few minutes ago and he was beginning to despair that Jolyon had forgotten his invitation. Restlessly, he began to trace his fingers along the rows of jagged teeth carved around the entrance, glancing idly at the monk-faced figures hunched in the corners of the dark, beamed ceiling.

At that moment, a rush of footsteps rounded the corner and Jolyon appeared, stooped and out of breath. He wore the same scruffy jacket and soup-stained tie as the night before.

'I'm sorry I'm late,' he panted, towering over the children. 'There was an incident in the library last night and Paula Richards asked me to assess the damage.' His voice came out in stops and starts. 'Another visit from our nocturnal book-breaker, I fear.'

'Book-breaker?' asked Blake, alarmed.

He peered up into the man's face, which was as craggy as a cliff, but softened by tufted outcrops of hair. Deep, cuneiform lines surrounded his eyes.

'Scoundrels who tear books apart,' wheezed the professor. 'They rip maps and illustrations from old books and sell them for profit.' He took another deep breath. 'St Jerome's, I'm afraid, has had its fair share of book-breakers through the years.'

Blake averted his face. Unlike the professor, he suspected he knew exactly what the culprit had been looking for.

If the man noticed his agitation, he didn't care to comment on it. 'Never mind that now,' he said lightly. 'We have other things to discuss. More important things.'

A charge of excitement, like electricity, flashed through Blake, riveting him to the spot.

Jolyon beamed down at him. 'I'm delighted you could make it, my boy. And this, unless I am mistaken, must be your sister –'

'Duck,' said Blake, introducing her. She was standing

a little way off, gazing up at the glowering sky, her thoughts elsewhere. She had been strangely subdued since lunch. 'But that's not her real name. Everyone calls her that because of the coat.'

The old man acted as though the name and yellow raincoat made all the sense in the world. 'I see, I see,' he said happily. 'I'm pleased to meet you, Duck.'

She gave him a shy smile, as if uncertain whether or not to trust his jovial nature.

'I would have come alone,' said Blake quickly, 'only my mother told me to look after her. I hope you don't mind.'

'It's quite all right, my boy, quite all right,' said the professor agreeably. He rested a reassuring hand on Blake's shoulder, which sagged slightly under its gentle pressure. 'Duck may have a part to play in this uncanny mystery of ours. She looks like an exceptional character.'

Blake was grateful for the way Jolyon treated him like an equal, but was displeased to hear how his sister had already impressed him with her intelligence. She hadn't even said anything yet!

Before he could protest, the professor took an old-fashioned key from his trouser pocket and inserted it in the lock of the iron-slatted door. 'Shall we?' he commenced.

Blake watched as the heavy wooden door creaked open. His face fell. In front of him was a short narrow passage, ending in a dusty, disused cupboard. A mop and bucket stood like sentries before it.

'I'm afraid the Old Library doesn't get much use nowadays, except as a sort of glorified broom closet,' said the professor sadly, sensing the boy's disappointment, 'but I'm pleased to say that my office is still one of the best-kept secrets in the college.' He tapped the side of his nose and winked. 'This way.'

Hidden in the shadows was a faded tapestry that parted in the middle to reveal a concealed staircase that curled up the wall to the top of the square tower. Already, the professor's legs were disappearing round the first bend, receding into darkness.

'It's quite a climb,' he called down from above, 'but well worth it, I think you'll find. It used to be the chapter house, where the monks held their official meetings.' His voice died to a whisper.

Blake didn't need a second invitation. He bounded up the stone stairs, taking them two at a time, feeling like a rock climber scrambling into the interior of a shell. Duck followed more cautiously, running her fingers along the uneven walls. She didn't like confined spaces and there was no rope or handrail to hold on to. She negotiated the slippery, timeworn steps with care.

Blake took a moment at the top to catch his breath and then let it out in an amazed gasp. It had to be the most magical room in Oxford! 'Wow!' he exclaimed, gazing around him in wonder.

A single fluted column opened like an umbrella in the centre of the room to support a low vaulted ceiling, which hung above them like an ornate spiderweb spun from golden stone. Small rounded windows provided aerial views of the college: a gargoyle-inhabited landscape of spires, battlements and slate roofs, capped by gathering storm clouds.

Like the man, the room was wonderfully shambolic. Books were everywhere: piled on desks, propped against table legs, placed under lamps and perched on stools. There were even books on the armchairs, like sleeping cats, and Blake wondered whether he was supposed to sit on them or push them politely aside. But where was he supposed to put them? There wasn't an inch of available space anywhere. Books lay strewn across the floor, as though they'd been hurled there in a whirlwind of reading.

Blake looked around for a place to hang his coat, but couldn't find one. Instead, he folded it neatly over his arm and clutched his knapsack close to his side. The paper dragon inside was still.

Jolyon volunteered to take Duck's raincoat, but she refused.

'She never takes it off,' explained Blake, joining his

sister on the sofa least obscured by books. He removed one or two volumes that were in his way and added them to a precarious pile on the floor. Jolyon sat opposite, on a wooden chair with clawed feet, rather like a throne, which made him look like a storyteller or a benevolent king. A stray spear of light from the window behind him silvered the edges of his body and made some of the books on the shelves gleam like gold.

'So what can you tell me about Endymion Spring?' asked Blake immediately, eager to learn the secret of the blank book he had found.

Here, in the study, the professor didn't seem nearly so agitated to hear the name. Yet if Blake was expecting a straightforward answer, he didn't get one. The old man held up an ink-stained finger.

'Patience, my boy,' he stalled him. 'What I would like to know, first, is how *you* came to know of him. Did you overhear someone talking about him – your mother, perhaps?'

Blake shook his head. 'No, she's never mentioned him before.'

Jolyon seemed surprised. 'Are you sure?'

Blake considered the question thoughtfully. 'No . . . at least, I don't think so,' he said, less certainly.

'How about at the dinner last night?' resumed the professor. 'Someone there?' He asked this more carefully, as though the college might be full of interlopers, all plotting to get their hands on the book.

'No,' said Blake, frowning and shifting slightly on his seat. He wondered why the man was asking so many strange questions. Perhaps he doubted a boy his age could find a book like Endymion Spring? He decided to cut to the chase. 'No, I found a book with his name on it in the library yesterday; but it wasn't an ordinary book, cos it didn't have any words in it. So I thought I'd ask you about it last night.'

'Oh,' said the professor. His voice was soft, barely audible. An evasive look crossed his face.

Confused by the man's reaction, Blake asked tentatively, 'Is the book important, Professor Jolyon?'

The man observed him steadily for a long, silent moment and then nodded. 'Yes, Blake, it is very important indeed.'

Blake felt his skin shrink with foreboding.

Duck, impressed by the portentousness of the professor's tone, finally spoke up. 'It had a magic spell inside.'

'No, it didn't,' Blake corrected her quickly. Then, under his breath, he added, 'It wasn't a spell.'

'More like a riddle, was it?' suggested Jolyon, raising a squirrelly eyebrow.

'How did you know?' Blake gazed at him in wonder,

but the man was watching him earnestly, unwilling to divulge his secret.

'First, tell me how you found the book,' he said, leaning forwards to make sure he missed none of the details.

Slowly, Blake began to tell him about the previous afternoon. He decided not to mention that he had been running his fingers along the shelves at the time, just in case the professor, like his mother, disapproved. He might even accuse him of damaging the books in the library last night – and he didn't want to get into more trouble.

'And could you read what was inside?' asked the professor, as soon as Blake had finished his story. He studied the boy carefully. Blake's light blue eyes were as pale as ice.

'Well, sure,' said Blake, thinking the answer was obvious. 'I mean, I thought the book was blank at first, you know, but then I found some words in the middle of it, almost where you wouldn't expect to find any.'

The professor leaned even closer. 'And what did the message say?' he asked, with bated breath.

Blake bit his lip. He could feel the man's eyes boring into him. Seated on his throne, the professor reminded him of the scholars he had seen in the portraits all over college. Everything hinged on his next response. Yet, despite his best efforts, Blake couldn't remember the exact phrasing of Endymion Spring's poem. The words eluded him.

'I don't know,' he said at last. He pulled at his collar, which seemed to be growing tighter. 'I can't remember it very well. It had something to do with the seasons. The book was going to fall apart if something didn't happen.' He scrunched up his face with the effort of concentration. 'Only, I don't know what was supposed to take place. I can't remember the words precisely. They didn't make sense.'

'And I didn't see them,' said Duck, feeling this was important to mention.

'What, haven't you read the riddle again?' asked Jolyon anxiously. 'Have the words already disappeared?'

Blake glanced down at his empty fingers. 'I don't have the book any more,' he confessed. 'It's gone.'

'Oh dear.'

The man's voice dropped so low, it seemed to sink through the floor. Blake could feel the air of expectancy rush out of the room as though a book they had been enjoying together had been snapped shut, the story cut off in mid-sentence. Rain began to patter against the roof, increasing his sense of discomfort. The professor's office was clouded with gloom.

'I'm sorry,' he started to say, as thunder rumbled in the distance, but the man merely brushed his apology aside. Blake couldn't tell whether he was angry or just concerned. 'I didn't know what to do,' he resumed miserably, 'so I put the book back on the shelf. I didn't think I was supposed to take it from the library.'

'No, no, you were quite right,' admitted the professor, staring at the book-strewn rug as though something of immense value had slipped through his fingers and he was searching for where it lay. He twisted and untwisted his long legs, broodingly.

Another thought suddenly occurred to Blake. 'But I did go back to look for it after I spoke to you last night,' he said. 'Your reaction made it seem important.'

The professor instantly raised his head, alert.

'And?'

Blake gazed at the shadowy figure opposite him. He dropped his eyes. 'Only, I couldn't find it again,' he muttered gloomily. 'I went back to the shelf where I had found it earlier, but the book wasn't there. It had gone. Someone must have taken it.'

A troubled silence, deeper and darker than before, settled over them. In the half-light, Duck glanced uneasily at her brother. She sat on the edge of her seat, squirming uncomfortably.

But Blake was more concerned by the professor's next question: 'Blake, are you quite certain that the book was missing when you returned to the library last night?' he asked seriously, his chair creaking slightly as he leaned forward to emphasize his point.

Blake opened his mouth to speak, but the professor held up a finger to forestall him. 'Think carefully now. This is important.'

His voice sounded worried.

Blake closed his eyes and tried to re-imagine the scene. He could see the beam from his torch wavering in the darkness, illuminating the rows of silent, watchful books. He visualized the two volumes tilting towards each other on the shelf at the end of the corridor and the crack of shadow in between . . .

'Yeah, quite sure,' he said. 'It was gone.'

'And did anyone follow you?'

The question caused a shiver of fear to creep up and down his spine. 'Well, that's the thing,' said Blake nervously. 'Someone else *was* there.'

The professor's eyes were on him in an instant.

'Who?'

Duck was breathing rapidly beside him, open-mouthed.

'I don't know,' answered Blake, despairingly. 'It was dark. I couldn't see. The cat sneaked in after me, so I had to fetch him from upstairs. That's when it happened.'

'The books downstairs?' the man prompted him gently.

Blake nodded. A lump had formed in his throat and

he swallowed it painfully. 'The books were already on
the floor when I came down,' he said. 'Ripped pages
were everywhere . . . exactly where I had found Endymion
Spring earlier. It was like someone had been hunting for
the blank book. But I didn't hang around, you know? I
just wanted to get out of there. I ran back to the dinner.'

'No, no, that was advisable,' admitted the professor,
with a sigh. 'Did you report what you'd seen to the
librarian?'

'No. I didn't want to get into trouble. Besides, my mum
was already pretty mad.'

'I see.' Jolyon was silent for a while. Blake could tell
that he was privately wishing he had been only a bit
braver, or waited a moment longer, to catch the culprit
red-handed. The man steepled his fingers against his lips
pensively.

Blake didn't want to interrupt, but found himself apologizing anyway. 'I'm really sorry, Professor Jolyon. I didn't
mean for this to happen. Honest. I just wanted to find
out about the blank book, that's all.' His voice wobbled.

The man's expression, however, softened into a smile.
'No one's blaming you, my child,' he said kindly, his
wrinkles losing their stern edges. 'You're not the sort of
boy to damage books. I know that. You've simply stumbled into something, something . . .' – he searched for
a word – 'something much larger than you can possibly

imagine. Endymion Spring must have chosen you for a reason.'

Blake gaped at him in disbelief. 'A reason?' he mouthed to himself, but Duck was quicker off the mark.

'It chose him?' she burst out, incredulously.

'Yes, I believe it did,' said Jolyon seriously.

'But how can that be?' she cried. 'It's just a book.'

'No, Duck, Endymion Spring is not just a book,' said Jolyon severely.

'What do you mean?'

'It just so happens to be one of the most legendary, sought-after books in the world and could be incredibly dangerous if it falls into the wrong hands.'

Blake looked up from his lap, feeling as though a huge weight had suddenly fallen on his shoulders.

'Dangerous?' he asked, crushed by a new sense of responsibility.

'Oh yes. Books are powerful things,' said Jolyon. 'And, as you know, this book is not without its special *abilities*.'

'But Blake was making up that stuff,' objected Duck. 'I was standing right next to him when he found it. The book had no words in it, I'm sure.'

'It did so,' retaliated Blake. 'I swear, Professor Jolyon. I saw something inside it.'

'Yes, I believe you,' remarked the man. 'And if what you say is true, that the blank book threatened to fall apart if something didn't happen, then I fear the destruction of the volume – and all it stands for – could be imminent. Which is disastrous, considering it has only now decided to reappear.'

'Reappear?' both children asked simultaneously.

'Oh yes,' replied Jolyon soberly. 'You are not the first to be chosen. There have been others before you, Blake. And many more who have searched in vain . . .'

'Was it you?' said Duck quickly. 'Did you find the book?'

The professor gave her a rueful smile. 'No, I'm sorry to disappoint you, Duck. It wasn't me.' For the first time his face revealed a real depth of sadness. 'I did glimpse it a few times,' he said softly, 'but fortunately it didn't select me.'

He let his words settle for a moment, before adding: 'It nearly destroyed the person it did.'

Twelve

Blake didn't trust himself to speak. He felt sick with horror. What exactly had he found? And what, for that matter, had he lost?

He sat back and listened as Duck asked the question that had died on his lips. 'What happened?'

'It's a long story,' said Jolyon, and both children feared he was not going to tell them. They fidgeted on the sofa. *It's a long story* was a way of not explaining something to them, an excuse for not telling them about the past. That's how their parents often handled awkward or difficult questions.

Yet the professor was merely considering what he could – or could not – say. For a moment his face darkened with misgivings and then, as though the incident were still painful to recall, he began to tell his tale.

'It was a long time ago,' he said in a deep, unhurried voice, rubbing the corners of his eyes. 'I was a member of a society devoted to the study and appreciation of books. The Libris Society, it was called.'

'Isn't that the society that's here now?' asked Duck. 'The one in the dining hall today?'

A flicker of a smile passed his lips. 'That's perceptive of you, young lady,' he congratulated her. 'The *Ex* Libris Society, as it is now known, is a highly regarded community of scholars, librarians and book collectors from all over the world who are devoted to the preservation of books. All, that is, except for Prosper Marchand, who is at the cutting edge of a new technology threatening to make printed material obsolete. Digitization.'

He said the word as though it were one of his personal bugbears. 'But at first there were only a few of us, united by our passion for books,' he recollected more fondly.

'What kind of books?' said Duck.

'Oh, the best kind. The earliest, hand-printed books by the true Masters of the press: Johann Gutenberg, Peter Schoeffer and Aldus Manutius.'

Blake's eyes glazed over. He wanted the professor to fast-forward the discussion, to say what happened next, but Jolyon was speaking slowly, with great emphasis, as though each word was impressed with meaning.

'And then one day,' he remarked, 'the shyest member among us, a real daydreamer, found a book unlike any other.'

'Endymion Spring,' breathed Blake excitedly.

The professor nodded. 'Exactly. *Endymion Spring*. A legendary book we had never believed in before. He was the only person who could see inside it. To the rest of us, it was a closed volume, a dummy, its secrets locked between twoapparently keyless clasps that only his touch could open. The book, of course, was selective about its ownership; it needed to be. After all, it led to something much more powerful . . .'

Blake's mouth dropped. 'But – but the clasps were broken when I found the book,' he interrupted. 'That means someone else must have looked at it since then.'

The professor did not comment. His eyes had receded into shadow, like two small, dark caves. When he resumed his story, his voice sounded older, further away.

'For a while, we gathered to listen to the sayings of Endymion Spring,' he recollected. 'Yet the tone of our meetings soon changed. The book started to warn us of a shadow, a force that threatened to consume not only the book, but the whole world.'

Duck rolled her eyes, but Blake was absorbed in the tale. This was like a ghost story now, getting scarier by the minute. He hung on every word.

'The boy who had found the book had a strange voice, like a candle flame,' Jolyon remembered. It trembled and flickered as though he knew the darkness his words were bringing to light. He began to warn us of the Person in Shadow.'

'The Person in Shadow?' asked Blake, his voice quavering.

Jolyon nodded. 'What we didn't realize then,' he said ominously, 'is that the shadow belonged to one of us. There was a traitor in our midst, a person whose heart was already black.'

He stopped, as if haunted by the past.

Blake shivered, wondering if this was the person who had followed him to the library last night.

'For a while the book brought us together,' resumed the professor sadly. 'Then, one day, it ripped us apart. Endymion Spring, like its owner, disappeared and we heard no more.'

His words, like the smoke rising from a snuffed candle, began to fade.

'But how does it end?' asked Blake anxiously, peering round the room, which was suddenly full of eavesdropping shadows. 'What happens next?'

'I don't know,' answered the professor bleakly. 'The rest remains to be seen. The story, it appears, is still writing itself.'

Blake shook his head, confused. 'I don't get it. What does the blank book want from me? I'm just a kid. What am I supposed to do with it – *supposing* I find it again?

Can't you help me, Professor Jolyon? Can't you tell me what to do?'

The man considered him for a moment, then said: 'Endymion Spring believes in you, Blake. You will know what to do.'

Once again Blake felt a rush of excitement streak through him – just like the elation he had experienced when he first handled the book in the library and the paper dragon that morning – but then a new worry consumed him. He wasn't special. Duck was the extra-ordinary one; everyone thought so.

'What I don't get is why this book is so dangerous,' she objected, right on cue. 'It makes no sense.'

The professor peered at her with wise, owl-like eyes.

'Endymion Spring is a remarkable volume,' he said carefully. 'It is full of insights and prophecies that threaten to undo everything we know – or think we know – about the world. It not only foretells the future, but retells the past. It even claims to lead to a legendary book of know-ledge: the Last Book.'

'The Last Book?' asked Blake doubtfully.

The professor nodded.

'Don't listen to him,' said Duck. 'He's just making up stuff to tease us. I've never even heard of a Last Book.'

Jolyon regarded her stoically for a moment and then said, 'The Last Book is known by many names, Duck:

the Book of Sand, the Mirror of Infinities, the Eternity Codex. Perhaps you've heard of one of these?

Duck shook her head, still not convinced.

'It's a book that has eluded capture and defied definition for centuries: a book that predates all others and yet outlives them all; a book that contains whole libraries within its pages; a book that even has the power to bring words to life.' The professor was clearly fond of the subject, for his hazel eyes burned with a barely disguised passion. 'Literature is full of references to it and veiled allusions to its whereabouts.'

Blake's heart pumped wildly inside him. 'The Last Book,' he said excitedly. 'Is this the book I found in the library yesterday?'

The professor smiled sadly. 'No, Blake, Endymion Spring merely leads to it. It is like a key or a map; a piece of the puzzle. *The guide.* Its message, however, is visible only to a select few.'

'Like me,' said Blake weakly, hardly able to believe his own ears.

'Yes, Blake, like you,' said Jolyon, much to Duck's annoyance.

'The book should have chosen me,' she murmured under her breath. 'I'd have known what to do with it.'

'But why me?' asked Blake again. 'Why would the book want to contact me? I didn't even want it!'

Jolyon studied him judiciously for a moment. 'Perhaps that is a reason in itself,' he said cryptically.

Duck interjected, 'But who is Endymion Spring? He could be a fraud or a trickster for all we know.'

'Ah,' intoned the professor. 'Now that is a good question.'

Blake, who had been cradling his head in his hands, looked up at him through a web of fingers. 'Don't you know?' he asked despondently.

Once again the professor threw up a screen of words. 'Endymion Spring is more of a shadow than an actual person,' he said, 'a whisper rather than a voice. Some scholars doubt he even existed at all.' Then, seeing Blake's look of desperation, he added, 'Personally, I believe he was a printer's devil.'

Blake gulped, hoping he had misheard. 'A devil?' he asked, barely able to get his tongue around the word.

Jolyon grinned. 'Not the kind you're imagining, Blake; trust me. Printers' devils were often young apprentices – boys, even – who worked in the earliest print rooms in Europe in the fifteenth century. They were trainees, learning the art of printing books when it was still considered a Black Art.'

'What about girls?' Duck challenged him quickly.

'I'm afraid I don't know of any,' said Jolyon good-naturedly.

'You mean Endymion Spring was a boy like me?' piped in Blake with renewed enthusiasm, feeling an instant kinship to that mysterious figure all those hundreds of years ago. He and Endymion Spring were bonded by age, even if they lived centuries apart.

'Yes, I believe Endymion Spring was a boy just like you, working in the first and most famous print room: Johann Gutenberg's.'

'Gutenberg?'

'Here, let me show you,' said the professor. Getting up from his chair he bounded across the room in three quick strides. Within seconds, he had returned with a large brown volume, which he propped open for the children to see.

'Johann Gutenberg was the first man to print books with movable type,' he explained, pointing to an engraving of a man with a walrus-like moustache and long beard. 'He divided the alphabet into a series of metal letters, much like pieces of a broken typewriter, which he arranged in a wooden printing press, like this, to print books.'

While the professor explained how Gutenberg's press worked, Blake studied the portrait in front of him. Dressed in a heavy robe with square buckles up the side, Gutenberg looked just like the homeless man he had seen outside the bookshop.

The professor now turned to a different page with another man's face on it.

'Who's that?' asked Blake, disliking the dark knitted eyebrows and forked beard that looked out at him.

'That,' said Jolyon, following the direction of his eyes, 'is Johann Fust, Gutenberg's investor. He was a ruthless man, by all accounts.'

A shiver crept up and down Blake's spine. Fust's stern, defiant expression seemed to glare at him from across the centuries. For some reason the paper dragon started to move inside his knapsack. He tried to muffle it with his foot, squeezing the bag between his legs, but luckily the professor seemed to suspect nothing.

'It was a wretched business,' Jolyon explained forlornly. 'Just when Gutenberg had perfected his press and produced one of the most exquisite books the world has ever known, the 42-line Bible, Fust dissolved his partnership with the inventor. He sued Gutenberg for all he was worth and effectively left him penniless and destitute.'

'But why?' asked Blake.

'Nobody knows for certain,' remarked the professor, reticently, 'although for several centuries there was a rumour . . .'

He closed the book and the dragon in Blake's bag went still. Blake could tell that there was a darker side to the story than the old man was admitting, for he remained silent and thoughtful for a while.

Finally, in a soft, serious voice, Jolyon said, 'Have you heard of Faust?'

Blake shuddered, remembering the chilling book he had found in the bookshop – and then lost to Sir Giles. 'My mum's studying him,' he said. 'He's a sorcerer or something who sold his soul to the Devil.'

Jolyon nodded, then fixed the boy with his eyes. 'Some people believe that Fust was the original Faust,' he resumed warily, 'that he made a contract with the Devil at the time Gutenberg was experimenting with his printing press. And if you consider the power and know-ledge Endymion Spring is thought to have witnessed in the Last Book, it might not be a coincidence.'

Blake gawped at the professor, a cold fear curdling in his stomach. 'So it really is important that we find the blank book,' he said, his voice barely more than a whisper.

'Absolutely,' said Jolyon. 'Not everyone believes in Endymion Spring, but those who do – and the Ex Libris Society is certainly full of them – will stop at nothing to obtain it. If they knew you had held the book, Blake, or even believed you had seen it, Duck, your lives could be in danger.'

At that moment there was a loud banging on the door downstairs and all three of them jumped.

Jolyon was the first to recover. He pressed a fingertip to his mouth to signal that the conversation was now at an end and called out that the door was open.

Together, they listened as heavy footsteps climbed the spiral staircase towards them. Before long, a shadow entered.

'I wasn't sure what had happened to the kids,' said Juliet Winters brightly, 'so I thought I'd look for them here. I hope they haven't been a nuisance.'

Then, seeing their startled faces, she asked, 'What's got into you? You look like you've seen a ghost.'

Thirteen

Blake sat back in the professor's book-filled office, lost in thought.

While he pondered all of the things he'd learned, his mother perched on the arm of the sofa, talking vibrantly about her work. She seemed in a surprisingly good mood, as though everything was back to normal, but he couldn't help wondering privately whether anything would ever be the same again.

'I see your office hasn't changed one bit,' she told Jolyon idly as she played with the trim on Duck's hood. She then explained to both her children how she used to have tutorials in this very room many years ago.

Blake watched her with a curious expression, pleased to hear her sounding so relaxed and happy, and yet uncertain what had caused the change.

She caught him staring at her and suddenly snapped her fingers.

'That reminds me,' she said, reaching into the front pocket of her briefcase. 'I picked this up for you on my way here.'

She handed him a small plastic bag with the words 'LIVE LIFE BUY THE BOOK' printed on it in large white letters. Inside was a thick paperback novel.

'I hope you like it,' she said. It's about a boy who has an amazing adventure in Oxford. The shop assistant recommended it. I thought that this way you might be less inclined to get into trouble on your own.'

Blake ran his fingers over the cover and fanned through the pages, enjoying the dusty, papery, new-book smell. He allowed his eyes to stop at random on different paragraphs. Almost immediately sentences tugged at his imagination, pulling him in.

He didn't know what to say. She surprised him by apologizing first.

'I'm sorry I upset you last night,' she said. I panicked when I couldn't see you at the dinner. Just because I spend a lot of my time working doesn't mean I don't keep my eye on you. Understand?'

A playful, grateful smirk crossed his face and he nodded.

She smiled. 'Just promise me not to disappear again, OK?' she said, planting a coffee-scented kiss on his forehead.

'OK, I promise,' he said automatically. 'Thanks for the book.'

'You're welcome.'

Duck was straining to see the cover, but stuck out her tongue when he showed her the title. 'I've already read it,' she said. 'I could ruin the ending for you, if I wanted.'

His mother was now telling Jolyon about her time in the library. 'I thought Oxford would have progressed into the twenty-first century,' she said lightly, 'but I see it still takes days for the books you most want to read to reach you from the stacks. At least they have CD-ROMs and email terminals in the reading rooms.'

The way she described it, the Bodleian sounded like an enormous labyrinth of books. Built hundreds of years ago, the library housed millions upon millions of volumes, many of which were stored on miles of shelving below the ground. He could imagine tunnels worming beneath the city streets like tree roots, each full of rare, dust-covered books.

'Can we go down there one day and take a look?' he asked excitedly. 'I'd love to see where the books are stored.'

'Absolutely not,' she answered with mock severity. 'They'd be furious if someone entered the stacks without permission. Especially a young boy without a reader's ticket. It's strictly off-limits.'

She glanced at him and he smiled shyly back. It really was as if things were back to normal: not just the way they were before last night, but before the Big Argument. She hadn't seemed so relaxed, so young, in a long time.

For a moment even the thought of the Last Book slipped his mind and he yawned. His jaw stretched open like a rubber band . . . and then snapped shut again.

Without warning, he remembered her rendezvous with Prosper Marchand. Suddenly he felt anxious and suspicious. Was this the reason for her good mood?

Duck was swinging her legs like restless pendulums, eager to be off. Her mother noticed and glanced at her watch.

'Well, I suppose it's time we headed back,' she excused herself. 'Thanks again for looking after them, Jolyon. I know they can be quite a handful.'

'No, no,' said the professor. 'We've had a most interesting time. Most enlightening.'

Duck got up quickly and hurried down the stairs, but Jolyon reached out a hand and patted Blake once on the shoulder in farewell: a silent communication, which Blake understood well. It was an invitation to return to the Old Library, if or when he needed help. He wasn't alone in this mystery.

He nodded tacitly in response.

Before they left the college, his mother stopped at her

office to print an article she was writing: 'The Faust Conspiracy'. While the printer churned out endless reams of paper, Blake took the opportunity to send an email to his father. He wasn't sure what to say. There weren't enough words to describe everything that had happened. Too many thoughts crowded his mind. At last he wrote:

Things OK. Mum bought me a book. I geuss I'm in her good books again ;-) I miss you. Write soon. LOve, Blake.

His fingers stiffened as he felt his mother reading over his shoulder. He was considering whether to mention anything about Endymion Spring, just in case his father had heard of him, but decided for now to keep the secret to himself.

'It's g-u-e-s-s,' she pointed out, correcting his spelling.

'I know,' he lied and backspaced over his typo to change it. Annoyed, he thought about adding a note about Prosper Marchand, but decided against it. No one liked a tattletale.

As soon as his mother's back was turned, he entered a hasty postscript: 'I wish you were here.'

It was no better than a postcard, but at least his father would know he was thinking of him. He clicked the send icon and imagined the message arriving almost simultaneously on a computer screen thousands of miles away. Somehow, it only made the distance seem greater.

Blake discovered the reason for his mother's good mood once they returned to Millstone Lane. The university had accepted her proposal to prolong her research trip. She would be remaining in Oxford for an extra term after Christmas.

'Now I can finish researching my book,' she said excitedly. 'This will really boost my career.'

Blake didn't respond. He ran upstairs and barricaded himself in his room, slamming the door behind him and sitting on his bed with his back pressed firmly against the wall. He stared at the bars of his prison. Where did this leave him? Was he supposed to go back to his father or stay in England with his mother?

Home . . . the word didn't seem to mean much any more.

He wondered how Duck felt, but she'd retreated to her own room almost as soon as they'd got in, too. She was probably sulking about the present he'd been given. Well, let her sulk, he thought. The book now seemed like a bribe, a trick, an attempt to make him forget about missing his dad. He didn't want to read it any more. Ruthlessly, he flung it across the room and watched as it crash-landed near the bin. Its cover bent backwards like a broken wing and some of the pages crumpled. He stared at it through a wall of tears.

How could he have been so stupid? He should have known better than to trust his mother. She only cared about one thing: her work.

Everything *was* back to normal.

For a second night in a row, Blake could not sleep. Arms folded across his chest, he sat on his bed, brooding.

Outside, rain lashed against the window and he watched while the trees rocked and buffeted in the wind, bullied by the storm. Each gust sent a fresh marathon of fallen leaves scudding across the street. Large, angry shadows swept across the walls of the room, across the ceiling, occasionally slapping him on the face. Hot tears streamed down his cheeks.

It was past midnight. An hour ago, he had heard his mother creeping along the landing to Duck's door, which she'd opened briefly, and then across to his own. Blake had mapped her movements in his head. He could sense her standing on the opposite side of the door, only a few feet away, but a whole world apart.

'Go away!' he'd wanted to shout, willing her not to enter, but at the same time he yearned for her to check on him, to comfort him and tuck him in like a little boy. In the end she had withdrawn to her own room, making him feel even more isolated and miserable than before.

There had been only one other occasion like this. The Day of the Big Argument. It had been a Friday, the start of a long weekend, and he had planned to spend it gloriously, doing nothing; but both his parents had arrived home hours before him and were standing in the kitchen, glaring at each other. He could sense an unspoken hostility in the air between them – like a storm about to break.

And then, all of a sudden, it had started.

With a thunderous roar, his mother had snarled at his father, spitting an obscenity he had never heard her use before, her mouth ripped open with rage. Accusations flew across the room like bullets, ricocheting off the walls, landing in the furniture. He and Duck had dived for cover. The air had seemed fragile, like glass. Breakable.

Some of his friends had single parents and for a while he had wondered whether this was it: his parents' own D-Day. He'd plugged his fingers in his ears, trying to block out the possibility. He couldn't bring himself to think the word: divorce sounded almost as final, as fatal, as Death.

And then there had been the eerie silence afterwards, when his parents had run out of things to say. They'd walked around the house, their eyes swollen, as though they had been boxing, not shouting; but it was Blake who had felt bruised and battered all over.

Finally, the telephone rang, exploding into the silence. That's when Duck had got up to fetch her raincoat, the one she hadn't taken off since.

He glanced at the door of his dark Oxford bedroom. He ought to check on her. He couldn't remember the last time he'd asked her how she felt. Perhaps she was asleep, unaware that the world was falling apart?

Out of the corner of his eye, he glimpsed the paper dragon on his bedside table, where he'd placed it for safe-keeping. He'd almost forgotten about it. But there it was: reminding him of his mission. He had to find Endymion Spring.

But really, he didn't know where to begin.

Once again, he felt the inclination to unfold the dragon, to see if it contained any secret information; but it was too lovely to destroy. Besides, he was too tired. He could barely keep his eyes open. His head was full of drowsy thoughts, none of which seemed to make sense.

He reached out a heavy hand and switched off his bedside light, then slowly settled back in bed. The sound of the storm lashing outside the window began to lull him to sleep.

Through half-closed eyes, he peered at the window. He

could hear rain tapping against the glass like restive fingers and saw a tree swaying rhythmically in the wind at the foot of the garden. He watched it for a while, mesmerized by its movements. Gilded by street lamps, the leaves shook and shimmered – like a golden dragon preening itself in the wind.

He smiled to himself. Yes, there could be a dragon in that tree, he thought sleepily, his eyes closing still further. He could see its outline beginning to take shape: pointy leaf-like ears; horny snout; strong black wings, furled back like branches. Each leaf could be a scale and that black space, there, an eye. There was even a thin, plated tail descending from the lowest branches like a sprig of ivy.

Yes, there could be a dragon in that tree, preparing to spread its wings and fly away. It stretched and tossed and groomed itself in the wind. At any moment, it might breathe a jet of autumnal fire and soar into the sky . . .

But before he knew for certain, he was asleep.

MAINZ
Spring 1453

awoke from an uneasy slumber.

Peter lay on his back beside me, his hands cupped thoughtfully across his chest. Sculpted by the moonlight, he resembled one of the figures entombed in the cathedral on the opposite side of the city, a model of calm and repose. Yet, despite his outward composure, his mind was a hive of activity, busily concocting a plan to get me – and the dragon skin – as far away from Mainz as possible.

We could hear Fust prowling like an animal down-stairs, riffling through the contents of the chest, which I had opened a short time earlier. I wondered if he'd found the dormant words written in my blood.

'You don't realize what you've done,' grumbled Peter at last, filling the room with a menacing rumble of words like thunder.

I pretended to sleep, but he thumped me in the small

of the back. I turned over and was surprised to find that his eyes were moist with tears. He was genuinely afraid, but whether for my well-being or his own, I could not tell.

'There'll be no stopping him. You – the paper, whatever you've done to it – you've ruined everything. You're not safe.'

I looked at him, frightened.

'Fust knows,' he said. 'He can't see the words properly yet, but they're there; he's sure of it. He says you've done something to prevent the skin from unleashing its potential. But he'll figure it out soon, believe you me. And then you'll be in danger. We all will.'

He was silent for a moment, as if considering the awful truth he had to say. 'It's not only the knowledge he's after, but the power. He wants to be like God and will side with the Devil until he gets there. Nothing will stand in his way. Not even me.'

I could hear the hurt and disillusionment in his voice and realized that he, too, had been duped. Fust had used him. He had feigned his sudden fit of fever to get Peter out of the room, so that I would creep out of my hiding place and unlock the chest. He had known that I was there all along and had carefully shown me what to do. It had been a test and I had walked right into it – like a fool!

'You'll have to leave,' said Peter then, using the words I least wanted to hear. I cringed at the thought. I didn't want to be orphaned yet again.

Peter could read the helpless appeal in my eyes. 'You have no idea what Fust will do,' he tried to convince me. 'He'll use other children – not just you – to release the words in the paper . . . if that's what it takes. Anything to achieve power. You must go and take the whole damned skin with you! It's the only solution.'

I was trembling now – and not just from cold.

Unable to lie still, I got up and crept over to the dormitory window, which was set high in the wall. I stood on a stool and gazed out over the peaceful, sleeping city. Even though spring had arrived, a trace of winter still silvered the tops of the surrounding houses at night. Roofs sloped towards the cathedral like frosty waves rearing against a cliff. Mainz, I realized, had always been my home. I had no desire to leave it.

'The dragon skin can be neither burned nor destroyed,' said Peter, musing aloud. 'He's shown us that much already. So we need to hide it somewhere Fust will never go, somewhere he can't follow. But where?'

I glanced back at Peter, who was staring up at the joists of the ceiling. He noticed me watching him, shivering in my nightshirt, and in sympathy lifted the covers to allow me close. I tiptoed back to the bed and huddled next to his warm, protective body. He had become a brother to me.

'I'll help Herr Gutenberg with the Bible,' he promised, pulling the blanket up around my shoulders and rolling on to his side, 'but you must leave, the sooner the better. We'll figure out where. Perhaps after Frankfurt . . . Until then, I'll protect you.'

He yawned. Despite my predicament, he could not keep his eyes open and was soon asleep, leaving me even more worried and desolate than before. I listened to the sound of his breathing, which rose and fell in steady waves. Even now, he was drifting into another world, a land of dreams, where I could not follow.

Peter had Christina. Herr Gutenberg had the press. Where, I wondered, did this leave me?

To comfort myself, I reached out to make sure that the toolkit was safe beneath the straw mattress, where I had concealed it a short while ago. A judder passed through me as my fingers once again brushed against the snow-soft sheets of dragon skin. I was soothed by a momentary feeling of calm.

What I didn't realize was that the skin was already preparing itself for the long journey ahead. The paper was slowly stitching itself into the leather cover of my toolkit and another set of dragon's claws was magically coiling round the front edges of the bundle like a lock, guarding its precious secret.

I had opened a book that could not be closed, started a story that had no obvious conclusion. It was a tale in which I wanted to play no part. Yet Peter was right: I had to go.

The only question was . . . where?

The answer came a few days later.

Frankfurt was teeming with people. Heavy boats lay at anchor in the choppy river, bringing merchants from far abroad, while traders and journeymen thronged the muddy roads leading to the city walls and blocked the gates with their wagons and carts. Weighed down with bundles of wood and straw, peasants and artisans trudged across the bridge from the surrounding countryside to set up stalls in the cobbled squares. Oblivious to it all, clergymen and patricians waded through the streets like dainty birds among the common sparrows, showing off their finery.

Peter gazed at them longingly. 'One day, I shall be able to afford a cloak like that,' he whispered, as a wealthy nobleman strolled past in a bright green robe trimmed with rabbit's fur.

Everywhere, people flocked towards the Town Hall –

a string of tall gabled buildings in the old quarter, close to the market. Banners and pennants flapped from the walls and bells clanged in the spires in a joyous celebration, summoning pilgrims to church before letting them loose on the fair.

Downstairs, in the large stone hall, goldsmiths, silversmiths and craftsmen of every description were preparing their booths. Among the displays of Bohemian glass, Italian oils and Flemish cloth were brooches, rings and salt cellars wrought from the finest metals. The selection was astounding. I had never seen such riches.

Peter loitered by the drapers' stalls, looking like a smitten lover as he trailed his fingers along the bales of linen, brocade and silk. A purse of crushed crimson velvet eventually took his fancy – a present for Christina – and he stroked it like an exotic animal before finally parting with the coins to buy it. It cost nearly everything he had.

'That must prove I love her,' he remarked as I strolled past.

I preferred the aromas wafting from the far reaches of the hall and wandered over to the savoury corner where bronze-skinned merchants had set up a foreign coastline of fruits and fragrances. Horns, sacks and pouches full of ginger, saffron, aniseed and almonds lay next to the stickiest dates from northern Africa, which clung to the roof of my mouth as I chewed them.

I had just sniffed a flame-coloured powder that ignited a fire in each nostril when Peter tapped me on the shoulder and waved several silver coins before my eyes.

'Herr Gutenberg says we are to enjoy ourselves,' he said with a grin. 'I know how we can spend it.' His eyebrows performed a mischievous jig on his brow and he steered me towards the door.

I glanced back at my Master's stall, which he had erected near a man in a preposterous cockerel-coloured outfit, who was selling rolls of leather for binding books. Beside him, a heavy-set man with a warty nose flogged gory prints of martyred saints to pilgrims, who devoured such things in their devotion.

The Bible had been attracting a large amount of interest since the opening of the fair. Fust, in fact, was having to fend off merchants, all clamouring like pigs at a trough to see the quality of the print.

'Why, this is neater than a scribe's hand,' I heard one say. 'I do not need my lenses!' He waved a pair of pointy bone spectacles in the air as though my Master had performed a minor miracle.

'How do you obtain such results?' asked another, laying his hands on a sample of paper and holding it up to the light streaming in from the narrow windows.

Fust swatted away his fingers. 'You may admire, but not touch,' he hissed. His eyes caught mine from across the room and I flinched. All the way from Mainz, he had been breathing down my neck, trying to determine why he could not yet read from the magical paper in his chest. I was afraid that he would soon discover the pages in my toolkit, which I now carried on my person at all times, and throttle me.

'But the words are written back to front,' objected a third, dour-looking man with ashen lips. He was examining a tray of type I had set up specifically for the exhibit. 'What manner of devilry is this? The Word of God must not be interfered with in this way!'

I did not get to hear more. Peter grabbed me by the elbow and tugged me up the stairs.

I had to shield my eyes against the pandemonium outside. Acrobats tumbled and rolled in the square, dentists and quacks extracted teeth and coins from the vulnerable and weak, and vendors called attention to wild and wonderful beasts brought in just for the occasion: flightless birds with ungainly necks and massive pack animals with enormous ears and hides like wrinkled men. The air was full of smells and noise, chaos and confusion.

Away from the hall, Peter reverted to a little boy. He bobbed in and out of the crowds, swiping small rounded loaves from the street-sellers and juggling them in his hands before biting into them hungrily and running away from their catcalls of abuse.

For a while, we amused ourselves by leaping over barrels and coils of rope in the coopers' district – just one of five tiny lanes abutting the main square like the fingers of a hand – and ended up, breathless with exhaustion, outside a house the colour of dried ox blood. It stood on several wooden plinths like a fussy woman trying not to get her skirts dirty.

Nearby was the Plague House, a darkened building marked by iron crosses above the shuttered windows. We dared each other to stand outside its ominous facade for a count of ten while hopping on one foot to ward off the evil eye of the gorgon carved into the wooden pediment above the door. A bailiff, however, chased us off, telling us to be more respectful of the dead.

Stonemasons were busy extending the tower of the cathedral in the distance, and we moved closer to investigate. The city reverberated with the sounds of chisels and hammers, tap-tap-tapping in the air. The sky snowed chipped stone. Tall ladders, lashed together with ropes, zigzagged up the side of the building and an intricate system of pulleys and wheels spun in mid-air, hoisting baskets of stone bricks up to the masons, who stood on thin walkways high above the earth to receive them.

Labourers loaded with mortar scurried up and down the ladders like ants.

Just looking at them made me dizzy. One foot wrong and the whole structure would come tumbling down faster than the Tower of Babel. I much preferred the safety of the press . . .

The thought reminded me of the dragon skin and the need to get as far away from Fust as possible and I felt the city crumble around me. It was no good standing still, enjoying myself.

Peter grabbed me by the elbow. Lured back by the smell of food, we returned to the market. Spoiled for choice, we each selected a steaming frankfurter from the sausage stands and spent a long time licking the fatty juice from our wrists. A discordant blast from a trumpeter atop St Nikolai's Church alerted us to an important arrival by river and so, still chomping on our sausages, we headed the short distance to the quay, just in time to see a three-masted boat from the Low Countries glide like a wicker swan towards the customs tower.

A rotund man disembarked, followed by a retinue of servants, all carrying chests full of cloth. He cut a grand, distinguished figure.

Peter sucked in his breath and looked forlornly at the small velvet purse he had purchased for Christina. 'It's not very much, is it?' he said. It was all I could do to prevent him from tossing it in the waves.

A hoary old gentleman stood on the quayside to greet the newcomer. He bowed so low I feared he would kiss the ground beneath the stranger's feet. Together, they marched across the road to one of the finest residences in Frankfurt: the Saalhof, where the most important dignitaries were housed – unlike the communal inn where Peter and I would spend the night.

Tiring of the spectacle, we worked our way back towards the old quarter, losing ourselves in a maze of tight, twisting lanes. By now we were thirsty and the gleam of the remaining coins in Peter's hand had rekindled a spark in his eye.

'Follow me,' he said, as he spotted a nearby alehouse.

The Little Lamb was not as innocuous as its name suggested.

A dark hovel, it shrank into the corner of an overgrown courtyard, surrounded by tottering houses that blocked out the sun. A well in the middle of the yard had long ago dried and was now choked with filth.

Like a mongrel with its tail between its legs, Peter sidled up to the tavern door and pushed his way inside.

The room was thick with smoke. People played at dice

and draughts over large, upended barrels and the floor was slick with straw. I did not care to look down, but followed Peter as he threaded his way through the crowd and ordered two flagons of apple-wine from the innkeeper, a boar-like man with tusks for teeth.

Clutching our sour-smelling drinks, we dived into a back room, away from the noise and commotion out front.

The room was empty, apart from a slovenly individual lying in a pool of vomit in the corner. Peter paid him scant attention, but walked over to a bench and started speaking on his favourite subject: Christina. His voice swooned whenever he mentioned her and I stared moodily into my drink, letting the smell of rotting apples fester in my nostrils. I did not like to admit that I was jealous.

'Ah, young love,' murmured the man in the corner, looking up at us with two unfocused eyes. 'You can never trust the heart of another.'

Peter paused in his description of Christina's beauty and frowned.

'*Amor vincit omnia*,' the stranger continued in a voice that hinted of too much drink. 'It's a load of tripe, if you ask me.' His words had a foreign lilt to them and I could not understand them clearly.

Peter, however, detected something in the accent and

studied the man more intently. Huge continents of dirt had drifted down his clothes and his face was streaked with grime. It looked as though he had spent a lot of time sleeping in fields . . . or else on taproom floors.

'Love speaks with a false tongue,' the drunkard lamented aloud, continuing his bitter soliloquy. 'It kisses you in one ear, then turns with a hiss to bite the other . . .'

'Enough!' Peter slapped his iron flagon on the table before us. 'What do you know of love, friend?' His voice was venomous.

'Plenty,' replied the man, with a simpering smile that revealed several missing teeth. 'My heart has been broken more times than years you've been alive . . . boy.'

Peter did not rise to the insult, but leaned closer to whisper something in my ear. Then I noticed what he had. In his hands, the man clutched a small brown leather book. A thin ribbon, like a lock of hair or a rat's tail, slipped out from between its pages, marking his place.

This was a rare sight. Not many people could read books, let alone afford to buy them. Either this man was a thief or an impoverished scholar, down on his luck. They were often the poorest sort.

He glanced up at us, feeling the weight of our eyes on him.

'It's the tale of two lovers,' he said, indicating the

volume in his fingers. 'Piccolomini's latest. Scurrilous, rude and guaranteed to put the colour back in your young friend's cheek.'

He nodded in my direction and I blushed, despite myself. The man took no notice. A sour belch, like a toad, escaped his throat.

'May I?' Peter took the book from the man and leafed expertly through its pages, perusing the words and assessing the quality of the penmanship. 'Where do you come from, friend?' he asked in a different voice.

'Here and there,' came the answer. 'London once, Oxford before that.'

Peter pricked up his ears. 'Where?'

'Oxford.' The man made a vague sketching movement in the dirt with his blunt fingers, mapping his travels. A series of towers and spires grew around him.

'Never heard of it,' said Peter.

'I'm not surprised. You're just a young popinjay.'

Peter stiffened, stung by the insult. 'That may be, but this town you mention, where exactly is it?'

'To the north, across the water. No easy journey, I assure you.'

'Is it a place of learning?'

'Second only to Paris.'

'And does it have a library?'

The man looked up, aware he had an audience. I

gripped my apple-wine more tensely, sensing where the argument was headed. The stranger noticed my uneasiness and stumbled to his feet.

He wedged himself between us. 'Buy me another drink and I shall tell you all you wish to know.' He waved his empty mug at Peter. 'William's my name.'

I glanced at Peter, who was clutching the remaining coins in his sweaty palm. He could not resist the urge to learn more. He marched into the adjoining room and soon returned with three more flagons of apple-wine.

I could already feel the first mug clouding my judgement and slid my second to William, who guzzled it in one go. He smeared his sleeve over his mouth and then began to tell us about the university town of Oxford. Words streamed from his lips almost as freely as the wine entered them.

He had been a student of theology, he said, living a virtuous life in virtual poverty, when a girl named Moll ignited a passion in his heart – and a fire in his loins. For some reason this did not sit well with the proctors who prowled the town by night, maintaining order and discipline, and he had been cast out from the university in disgrace. Then, when Moll's family got wind of the affair, William had fled for his life, pursued by a rabble of drunken townies, as he called them. Ever since, he had been driven to distraction, moving from library to library, working as a scribe. Those books he could not copy he carried with him in his head.

'If life has taught me one thing,' he said, 'there is nothing so loyal or true as the written word.'

'And this library in Oxford,' Peter prompted him. 'Is it large?'

William's eyes took on a dreamy appearance. 'Chests full of books; colleges crowded with manuscripts; book-binders forever preparing new ones . . . Nothing can compare!' he said. 'Even now a new library is being built to accommodate the collection of Humfrey, Duke of Gloucester, God rest his soul.' He made a clumsy attempt at signing the cross on his stained doublet. 'It will surely be a new Alexandria, the greatest seat of learning this side of Rome!'

'Will it?' said Peter dubiously.

I, too, was disinclined to believe him. The library of Alexandria, I knew, had been built by the Greeks to accommodate all the scrolls and manuscripts in the world. It had been the most impressive, exalted depository of books in history. Yet what had taken its devoted librarians hundreds of years to acquire from passing travellers had been lost in a blazing inferno. Many of the greatest works known to man had gone up in smoke, the victims of that most avaricious reader: fire. Even now, I supposed, there was a chance the dragon skin could revive them.

'And if we should attempt to find this library?' asked Peter, filling me with trepidation.

'Just follow the banks of the River Thames from that great eyesore, London, and you cannot miss it,' said William. 'I have travelled far and wide, but I have yet to meet its match.'

With that, William reached the end of his story. With a last apologetic belch, he sank to his knees and collapsed in a heap on the floor, leaving Peter and me to ponder his information alone.

Outside, the noise of the fair reminded us of our duties and we reluctantly left the alehouse to join Herr Gutenberg and Fust in the Town Hall.

That evening, in the dormitory of the inn where we were lodging, Peter turned to me.

'This place William spoke of,' he whispered. 'That is where you must go.'

The words stabbed at my heart. I knew Peter could not easily come with me, but the prospect that I was to leave Mainz – and travel alone – was too much to bear. For a moment, my eyes pricked with tears and I rolled over to face the pale, snoring stranger by my side to keep him from noticing. The long communal bed was full of rank, unwashed bodies.

Fust and Herr Gutenberg, like many of the richer merchants, had opted for finer accommodation a few streets away, leaving us to fend for ourselves.

'It's the only way,' continued Peter. 'I've been thinking. When I was copying books in Paris, I came across an old saying: "The safest place to hide a leaf is in a forest." How could anyone find a solitary leaf among so many trees?'

I shut my eyes and tried to imagine the scene. Each time I came close to counting all those leaves, the wind shifted slightly and rearranged the branches. It was a fool's task – an undertaking to last all eternity.

Peter put his hand on my shoulder. 'Don't you see? The best place to lose the dragon skin is in a library. The paper would be lost in a labyrinth of words, a forest of books. Fust would never be able to find it.'

Begrudgingly, I nodded. My toolkit had already completed its magical transformation into a small book, as though it knew its destiny. The brown leather covers, with my name printed on it, were guarded by two dragon-claw clasps that kept the paper inside from stirring and revealing their secrets. Perhaps the sheets in the chest would do the same?

'The Library of St Victor is too near,' said Peter, refer-ring to the abbey in Paris where he had trained as a scribe. 'Fust would follow you there too easily and discover the book in no time. He knows it too well. But this library in Oxford is unknown. It could be even larger . . . It's certainly far enough away; Fust would never find you.'

The thought ripped at my heart. I started shaking. Then, recalling the way Fust had been creeping closer to me ever since I had opened the chest, as if I held the key to everything he wanted, I knew that Peter was right. I must go. I had no choice but to sacrifice my own happiness to save the skin.

OXFORD

Fourteen

The sound of scratching woke him. Something was trying to get in!

Blake opened his eyes and tore the covers from his body in a panic, remembering the camouflaged dragon he had glimpsed in the tree a few hours earlier. His legs were tangled in a bed sheet, but he managed to scramble free and backed against the wall, breathing hard. He gripped his pillow like a shield and stared at the window.

Nothing was there. Nobody was trying to get in.

He rubbed his eyes. The branches of the nearest tree had been stripped of their leaves by the storm last night and the dragon, if there had been one, had flown away. His imagination must have been playing tricks on him.

He listened carefully, straining to hear anything over the sound of blood galloping in his ears. Then, from somewhere outside, came the soft, scratching noise again.

He edged closer to the window and peered outside.

There, by the garden gate, stood a dog. A scruffy grey dog with a wiry tail. It was scratching at the post, as if beckoning him to come down. Blake raked his hand through his hair, wondering what to do.

And then, out of the corner of his eye, he glimpsed a flash of yellow, streaking from the front of the house to the gate. Duck! What was she doing up so early?

He blinked in astonishment. The dog wagged its tail, as if it had been expecting her all along, and then licked her face as she bent down to stroke it.

And then he remembered. The dog belonged to the homeless man he had seen outside the bookshop. He scanned the pavement for a sign of the strangely dressed figure, but couldn't see him anywhere.

What should he do? It was too early to wake his mother and he knew he oughtn't to leave the house without her permission; yet surely a dog couldn't be dangerous . . .

'Duck!' he hissed, watching helplessly as she started following the dog towards the main road, as if they had planned this little excursion together. She didn't look back once.

'Oh, Duck!' he moaned and dashed away from the window.

There was no time to lose. He pulled on the same

scruffy jeans, hooded sweatshirt and smelly socks from the day before and quickly tied his shoelaces, his fingers in knots. Grabbing his coat from the back of a chair, he raced across the landing; then, remembering the dog's bandanna, he rushed back to retrieve it.

He glanced once more out of the window. Duck was almost at the street corner. Soon she would be out of sight.

'Damn, damn, damn,' he muttered as he darted down the stairs. He snatched the spare key from its hook – Duck had failed to take it – and ran outside.

The morning was frosty and cold, suffused with a soft white light like the milk bottles he almost tripped over on the doorstep. Duck was visible a short distance ahead, a bright yellow sun battling her way through the mist. Blake rushed after her, cursing her under his breath. She showed no sign of letting up.

'Duck!' he yelled as she crossed the main road and followed the dog down a short slope towards the river, her little legs motoring quickly. He braked sharply to avoid an oncoming bus that kicked up a spray of water against the kerb and then, nerves buzzing, charged after her.

'What do you think you're doing?' he snarled when he finally caught up with her by the river. The current was strong, flowing fast. 'Are you deaf or something?'

He clutched her fiercely by the arm and swung her

round. Her eyes were dark and puffy, ringed with shadow, as though she had been crying.

'What's wrong?' he said, taken aback.

'Let me go,' she said weakly and struggled against his grasp. She managed to wriggle free.

'Look, I don't have time for this,' he protested. 'You've got to get back before Mum wakes up.'

'I'm not going anywhere,' she said petulantly and dug in her heels. The dog whimpered and wagged its tail, confused.

Blake shook his head and kicked at the ground. 'Come on, Mum's going to be real mad if she finds out you're missing.'

He tugged on her coat, but she wormed her arm free and left the sleeve dangling. He let go.

'Fine, suit yourself,' he said, changing his mind. He took two large strides back towards the road and then checked behind him. Normally, that worked; normally, his sister lost her nerve and followed. But this time she headed in the opposite direction.

'Oh, for goodness sake,' he cried out, exasperated, and rushed back to join her.

'Who's the baby now?' she sneered.

'I'm not a baby,' he defended himself, 'but Mum's going to be furious if you're not home by the time she gets up.' He glanced over his shoulder at a dark, creeper-covered house that was just visible through a gap in the trees. It straddled a small brook that threaded away from the river. An old wooden rowing boat had been moored alongside it.

Duck didn't say anything.

'Are you sure you're all right?'

'I'm fine.'

She sounded anything but fine. He looked at her again, concerned.

'OK, I couldn't sleep very well,' she confided at last. 'I was thinking about the blank book and everything Professor Jolyon told us and then I heard the dog scratching at the door and I thought that . . . well, maybe . . . it could be important. The homeless man could be in trouble.'

The dog regarded them hopefully, its tail set on autopilot. Without its red bandanna, it looked older and scruffier than Blake remembered and he felt sorry for it. It was probably hungry, poor thing.

'Well, do you think we should tell Mum where we're going?' he asked, trying to maintain some semblance of responsibility.

'And where exactly is that?' she scoffed.

He looked around helplessly and shrugged. On the north side of the river loomed a series of boxy boathouses, shrouded in mist, while an empty playing field stretched into the distance to his right. 'I don't know,' he said at last, 'but at least we could tell her about the dog – and maybe about the homeless man. She might be able to help . . . if he really is in trouble.'

Duck shook her head. 'Are you crazy? She'd never let us go. This is our only chance.'

Blake bit his lip. She had a point. Their mother would never agree to an early morning expedition, no matter how important.

'But what if it's a trap?' he asked, replaying Jolyon's warning in his mind. They could both be in danger.

'Yeah, right. A dog is trying to kidnap us! Just tell Mum you were trying to stop me,' said Duck, marching after the dog, which once again led the way.

Blake remained where he was. He was convinced the homeless man knew something about Endymion Spring. Perhaps he could even help them find it? And yet his methods were more than a little unorthodox and Blake wasn't sure he could trust him.

'Well, let's just make this quick, OK?' he said, breaking into a trot to catch up. He didn't want to admit that he was frightened – especially to his sister – but he wasn't going to turn back without her. At the very least, he could defend her if something went wrong.

'Sure, whatever,' she said and wandered on ahead.

Against his better judgement, he followed.

The mist was thicker away from the city and swans glided towards them along the water in silver Vs, like ghostly ballerinas. It was too early for rowers or joggers, and they were alone on the muddy path. They meandered past boggy fields and yet more boathouses, where the colleges kept their long racing boats and sculls.

Blake could see the shadowy outline of the city's buildings growing ever more distant behind an avenue of trees on the far side of the river. Its spires and domes dissolved in the dim light. Yet hidden somewhere inside that impressive backdrop, he was convinced, lay the secret to Endymion Spring, and he was determined to find it – no matter what it took. Even if it meant opening every book and following every clue until he tracked it down.

The mud squelched underfoot and spattered against his jeans as he walked. Duck had been sensible enough to put on boots, but she was cold. The morning chill penetrated her thin raincoat and she shivered.

To be kind, he offered her his jacket, which she accepted with a small, grateful smile. She didn't say anything, but kept her eyes fixed ahead, her thoughts far away.

Was she envious because Endymion Spring had singled him out for attention? Or had she, too, heard what his mother had said last night – that they weren't going to be a family together after Christmas – and wanted to get her own back by disappearing?

He wasn't sure what to think; yet he was grateful for her company, a feeling that surprised him, even though he didn't mention it to her.

They trudged on in silence.

Behind them, a chorus of bells began to strike the hour. Four, five . . . six o'clock. A medley of bangs and bongs circled the city like a flock of iron birds. Blake raised the hood of his top and squirrelled his hands into its pockets, hunching his shoulders.

The world seemed strangely unreal to him this early in the morning – like a dream. Mist clung to the trees on either side of the river like fragments of sleep, draping their silvery fronds in the murky water. The sun, he noticed, was struggling to burn through the haze, but it was too weak. Only a ring of dim gold leaked through the cloud. Clumps of mud stuck to the soles of his shoes like hoofs.

Just when he was beginning to tire of walking, he spotted a small village on the brow of a hill overlooking a narrow waterway in the distance and heard a rush of water spilling through a weir. It sounded like a waterfall. A sign indicated they were entering Iffley Lock and that cyclists should dismount and dogs be kept on short leads.

The homeless man's dog paid no attention to the sign, but guided them over a stone bridge towards a strip of tarmac with neatly tended flowerbeds planted along its sides. The children looked around them. The water flowing into the lock was deep, black and flecked with leaves and litter. Further along the river, a brightly painted longboat chugged upstream, leaving traces of coal-like smoke in the air.

And then they saw him.

The homeless man was seated at the bottom of a series of stone steps leading right down to the water's edge. Several ducks squabbled for the bits of bread he tossed into the current. He noticed the children, but did not get up.

'What do we do now?' whispered Blake.

'Join him, I guess.'

'I'm not going down there,' he answered, glancing at the man's stooped form. 'It could be dangerous. If he wants to speak to us, he can come up.'

They waited uneasily while the man continued feeding the birds. Blake was relieved to see another figure on the opposite side of the lock: a lock-keeper inspecting the moorings and other pieces of equipment, a coil of rope slung across his shoulder. He noticed them and raised a hand in greeting.

'You needn't worry about her,' he yelled across the

water, indicating the dog. 'She doesn't need a leash. She's a real softie, she is.'

As he said this, the homeless man got up rather stiffly and mounted the steps towards the children. Blake felt a splinter of fear run under his skin and pushed Duck behind him, to protect her. The man was wearing the same mangy robe and furry nightcap as the other day. Tall and gaunt, he carried a staff – a bit like a wizard.

The man and boy exchanged silent looks for a long, tremulous moment and then the stranger led them towards a small clearing behind a cluster of trees close to the lock: a private place where they could talk. Blake checked to make sure that the lock-keeper was keeping an eye on them, just in case they needed help.

The man waved.

Duck, too, seemed to have lost some of her initial bravado. Like Blake, she was probably wondering why they weren't safely tucked up in bed, fast asleep. Anything could happen to them out here and no one would know. Warily, they followed the man through the thin, nearly leafless trees.

There were remnants of a bonfire in the middle of the clearing and Blake sat down on one of the logs that had been placed nearby. The mound of twigs resembled a large, smouldering porcupine and he inched closer, grateful for its warmth. A scratchy, smoky scent prickled his nose.

The dog sidled up to him and placed a grizzled muzzle on his knee, looking up at him with doleful eyes.

The boy stroked its head, while the man selected some more wood for the fire. A tarpaulin had been spread across a pile of twigs on the far side of the clearing and Blake guessed that the man probably camped here often. There were a few tins and discarded blankets weighed down with bricks on the leaf-littered ground.

The stranger approached and pressed an armful of sticks on to the remains of the fire. The mound hissed and crackled slightly, but did not burst into flame. Shrugging, he sat down opposite the children, but not too close. He apparently didn't want to alarm them. His robe hung open behind him and Blake was fascinated to see dozens of pockets zigzagging across its lining. Scrolls of paper stuck out from some of them like phials, while books bulged squarely in others. He was carrying a portable library inside his coat. Blake longed to know what sort of books they were, but the man said nothing and waited patiently for him to speak first.

The boy wondered where to begin and then, clearing his throat, asked the question that was uppermost in his mind:

'Who are you?'

Fifteen

The man considered the question for a moment, but said nothing. Then, to fill the silence, Blake voiced the idea that had occurred to him earlier: 'Are you Johann Gutenberg?'

Duck was the first to react. 'Are you serious?' she cackled. 'Of course he's not Gutenberg! Gutenberg died more than five hundred years ago, you idiot!'

Blake blushed. Curiously, however, the man's mouth softened into a smile. Blake was surprised by the transformation: It was as though someone had taken a crumpled sheet of paper and smoothed it out, revealing a hidden greeting inside. The stranger's eyes no longer seemed so distant or far away, but showed renewed signs of life – unlike the fire, which he prodded again with his staff.

The man opened his mouth to speak, but no sound emerged. Blake listened carefully, but the man's voice seemed to have dried up and only a distant sound of breathing could be heard. He closed his mouth again without uttering a word.

Blake frowned. 'I'm sorry?' He thought he might have misheard, but the stranger merely shook his head and pressed a fingertip to his lips. His eyes, however, were smiling.

Blake turned to his sister. 'Is he hungry, do you think?'

'Don't be silly,' she said. 'He probably hasn't spoken to anyone in ages. Perhaps he's lost his voice.'

Blake pondered this for a moment. Could someone actually forget how to speak? That must be horrible. He chewed on his lip. The man obviously expected him to know where to begin, how to lead the discussion, but too many questions were bombarding his mind and he didn't know which one to ask first – let alone how to express any of them.

'Thanks for the dragon,' he said at last.

The man doffed his hat and scratched at the thatch of scraggly hair beneath.

'What dragon?' said Duck.

He'd forgotten she didn't know. 'A dragon he dropped off at the house yesterday morning,' answered Blake.

'What?' she blurted out. 'That's preposterous! What do you mean by a dragon? There are no such things as dragons! How could he drop off a –'

'I mean an origami dragon he made with special paper,' said Blake. 'Like the paper in the book I found.'

'Why didn't you tell me?' cried Duck, offended. 'I could have helped you!'

'I didn't need your help. Besides, I figured out what it meant on my own.'

'Oh yeah? So, what does the dragon mean, Einstein?'

'It means we're – I mean, *I'm* – supposed to ask him about the blank book.'

The man nodded, but neither Blake nor Duck noticed. They were glaring at each other and had started to argue.

'And what exactly are you going to ask?'

'I don't know,' he responded lamely. 'Something will occur to me as soon as you stop interrupting.'

'Yeah, right. You wouldn't know what to say if he wrote down the question for you. Nice going, idiot.'

'Look, you didn't find the blank book and you didn't receive the paper dragon, so mind your own business. This doesn't concern you.'

He reached into the pocket of his jeans and pulled out the dog's bandanna, which he started threading round his fingers like a boxer taping his knuckles. 'You're just jealous,' he muttered, giving his sister a sideways glance.

'Oh yeah? Jealous of what?'

'Of the book I found.'

'You mean the one you lost,' she reminded him. 'Or have you forgotten that too?'

'Of course I haven't.'

She knew she had the upper hand. 'The book probably realized its mistake,' she taunted him, 'and went back into hiding until someone else could find it.'

'What's that supposed to mean?'

'It means you're too dumb to solve this mystery on your own,' she said.

'That's what you think.'

'Yep, and I'm smarter than you.'

'Well, you're not as clever as you think you are,' he said angrily, rising from his log. 'You're just a silly girl in a silly raincoat, who thinks Mum and Dad will stick together so long as you go on wearing it. But they won't, you'll see! They'll get divorced and then we'll have to live on different sides of the ocean. Then you'll be happy, won't you, because you'll never have to see me again! Anyway, Endymion Spring chose me, and not you, so get over it.'

He knew he was hitting her everywhere it hurt, but he was not prepared for her reaction. Duck looked about to sneeze, but her face crumpled instead into tears. Immediately, he reached out to hold her, but she shook off his clumsy attempt at an apology and covered her face with her hands. She rocked back and forth, sobbing.

He hadn't seen her cry like this – at least, not since the Big Argument. His words had opened a deep and dangerous wound.

The man had been watching them with a subdued look of tenderness on his face, as though he knew the pain and suffering the book could cause. Yet at the mention of Endymion Spring he stood up and approached them. The name seemed to fit like a key in a lock and released him from his inactivity.

He still did not speak, but sat down between them and reached into one of his voluminous pockets. He brought out an old battered book – the volume he had been reading outside the bookshop. It wasn't blank, as Duck had led Blake to believe, but full of densely printed words: old-fashioned words with barbed black letters and small illustrations of angels and skeletons and devils – not to mention men working on presses like the one Jolyon had shown them yesterday. Some of the pages were torn and others were covered in nasty brown blotches. The book was falling apart.

Duck stopped crying and looked up.

At last the homeless man turned to a series of blank white pages he had inserted near the back of the volume. They were as fresh as fallen snow compared to the slushy brown paper that preceded them: the finest tissue paper, veined with silver lines.

Blake gasped. 'How did you get this?' he asked, realizing at once that he was looking at part of Endymion Spring.

In answer, the man pointed to one of the blank pages, where Blake could see something forming. It was as if someone had breathed on a mirror and drawn a message on the foggy glass. Lines appeared – at first very faint, but then darker as more and more of the image was revealed. They were like pin scratches on skin before they well with blood. The boy's eyes widened in astonishment.

'What does it say?' squeaked Duck. 'Tell me!'

'Can't you see it?' he said, surprised.

'No. I could see the printed bits, but not this,' she said, sitting on the edge of her log. 'It's like it's the blank book I told you about.'

She sounded upset and more than a little bit jealous still, but her curiosity was getting the better of her.

Blake wasn't sure how to describe the apparition. It was an ancient tree with an odd beast dwelling in its leaves. He could see it quite clearly and reached forward to touch it. The creature seemed to sense his presence and flicked its head nervously from side to side before darting away from his enquiring finger.

And then, perhaps at his touch, the animal shivered and disappeared. The tree was no more than a memory on the page, a wintry outline, becoming fainter and fainter, until it had faded completely.

Blake held his breath. 'What was that?' he asked eventually, thinking it had looked like the dragon he had seen in the tree last night.

'What was what?' cried Duck.

'A dragon, I think,' he said less certainly, 'in a tree. Something happened. I don't understand. It didn't answer my question at all.'

Duck didn't know what the image meant either, but promised to find out something later in the library. Blake might be able to read from enchanted books, she remarked, but at least she could learn things from real ones.

Blake, however, wasn't listening. He had looked up at the homeless man. 'How did you – how did the book – do that?' he asked, but the man was miles away, staring at the book, as if he could see something else.

Blake glanced at the page. It was blank.

'Who are you?' he asked again. 'What is your name?'

The man seemed to emerge from a daydream. He shrugged off a memory and flipped to the front of the book, where he underlined a partially obscured word with a grimy fingernail.

Blake frowned. The syllables lodged like fish bones at the back of his throat. How was he supposed to pronounce it?

'It says his name is –' he started.

'I can read this, dummy,' said Duck irritably, cutting him off.

She pushed his head out of the way and studied the man's name for a moment. Then she looked up and smiled.

'I'm pleased to meet you, Psalmanazar.'

Blake's face wrinkled in consternation. *Psalmanazar?* What kind of a name was that? It reminded him of an angel or a djinn. 'Are you a wizard or something?' he asked finally.

Psalmanazar smiled, but shook his head.

'Then how did you know to contact me?' asked Blake, before Duck could interrupt.

Psalmanazar flipped to the end of the book, where several words were waiting for Blake, in ink as faint as ash. Even this message didn't make much sense. He mouthed the words to himself, unable to fathom their meaning.

'Come on,' Duck badgered him. 'What does it say?'

He read the lines aloud:

'The Silence will end – the Sun approaches.
Mark my Word – the Shadow encroaches.

'That's weird,' he added. 'The sun appeared in the other riddle, too. It's like an instruction or a warning of some kind.'

'And the shadow,' said Duck, ominously. 'Don't forget that.'

With a shiver Blake remembered Jolyon's stark warning about a Person in Shadow – someone who would stop at nothing to find the Last Book.

He was about to say something, when he noticed the following page had been neatly excised from Psalmanazar's book, possibly so that the man could construct the paper dragon.

On a whim, he asked, 'Did this message appear the other day, when we saw you outside the bookshop?'

The man looked pleased and nodded.

So that was it! Somehow, the paper – Endymion Spring's paper – must have told him to look up from the book. But why?

Blake reread the riddle. The suggestion that the Person in Shadow – perhaps the person Jolyon had warned them about – had been lurking outside the bookshop unnerved him and he looked around suspiciously. Only a few leaves shook on the branches of the surrounding trees.

'Ask what we should do next,' said Duck impatiently, sensing his hesitation. She reached out to pet the dog, which nudged her hand with its nose, urging her to continue. Its ears felt like warm silky gloves and she caressed them lovingly.

'OK, but this has to be quick,' he said, glancing at his watch.

Psalmanazar held the page open as Blake repeated Duck's question: 'What should we do next?'

He stared at the page for what seemed like ages, but no new message or instruction appeared. The page remained blank.

'Nothing,' he said at last, giving up hope. 'There's nothing there. I'm not very good at this.'

'Maybe the book can't predict the future,' said Duck. 'Maybe we have to figure it out for ourselves . . .'

But that wasn't true. The book had already made plenty of predictions. If nothing else, Jolyon had told them Endymion Spring's paper contained an answer to everything. It just didn't want to help them right now.

Blake felt let down by this realization. There were so many questions that needed answering, so many things he needed to know, and yet the book remained frustratingly silent.

'That's it,' he said suddenly, snapping his fingers. 'Sometimes it's harder to know the question than to find an answer.'

'Huh?' said Duck, puzzled.

'It's something Professor Jolyon told me,' he said. 'I can't ask vague questions like "what will happen in the future?" That's too general. I need to be more specific. Maybe then the book can help us.'

He took a moment to phrase the question in his mind and asked in a clearer, more confident tone, 'Where is the blank book I found in the library on Tuesday afternoon?'

Duck looked up, curious. Psalmanazar, however, had tightened his grip on the book. His knuckles gleamed, bone-white between the layers of grime. What had caused the change? Blake gave him a sideways look, but the man's face was locked on the book, inscrutable.

The boy followed his eyes down to the page.

'I can see something coming,' he whispered, 'but it's really faint. I can't make it out.'

He peered closer. His mouth felt dry. 'Great, it's another riddle,' he despaired when at last he could distinguish the words.

'Quick, read it to me,' said Duck. 'I'm good at these things. I can help you.'

Blake paused for a moment and then, unable to figure out the meaning on his own, recited the lines aloud. They seemed so simple, yet complex:

'The Present has passed – The Past has gone
The Future will come – once Two become One.'

He groaned. 'The poem's even more baffling than the first one I saw,' he said.

Duck, however, was repeating the words to herself over and over again, memorizing them. Her lips moved and her nose twitched – like a rabbit nibbling the air. Blake stared at her and then at the book, willing himself to see through the words, but he couldn't.

'I don't get it,' he said at last, a fringe of dark hair flopping over his eyes.

She held up a hand to silence him. 'I think I do.'

The words were so soft, Blake almost didn't hear them. 'What?'

'Well, I don't understand all of it,' she corrected herself, as he turned to her in disbelief, 'but I get the gist of it. At least, I think I know how we're supposed to locate the Last Book.'

'Huh?' said Blake, astounded. 'How?'

'Just read the poem again,' she said, 'but this time spell the words as you say them.'

Blake shook his head. 'What difference does that make?'

'It all depends on how you spell the past,' she said,

sphinx-like. 'It makes all the difference in the world.'

She started to pet the dog again. 'Just do it,' she commanded.

Blake did as he was told. Even with Duck's advice the words didn't make much sense. The present, past and future were hopelessly entangled, like a knot. Try as he might, he couldn't tease them apart.

'I still don't get it,' he said.

'Well, the book we're looking at now is falling apart,' she pointed out, as yet more bits of paper fluttered out from between Psalmanazar's fingers and fell to the ground like tattered moths. 'So its usefulness has passed or is passing as we speak. That explains the first bit: the present has passed.'

Blake regarded her with suspicion.

'And you don't have the volume you found in the library, so that's the second,' she continued. 'The past has gone. It can't tell you anything more specific than that. This leaves the Last Book, the one Professor Jolyon told us about, the most powerful book of all. That's the one still waiting for us – once we bring the other two books together!'

She looked up, expecting to be congratulated, but Blake frowned.

'But how are we going to do that?' he whined. 'We don't even know where the first book is. It's pointless!'

He kicked at the ground, sending a twig flying. It snapped like a bone.

'I know,' answered his sister vaguely, 'but I'm sure we'll find it soon.'

Unconvinced, Blake looked at his watch. 'Come on, we'd better go. Mum will be furious.'

'Ask who the Person in Shadow is, first,' she said.

Blake went pale. His heart leaped into his mouth. This was one question he didn't want answered. He turned to her, aghast.

'Go on,' she said. 'It's the obvious thing to do.' She continued combing her fingers through the dog's hair, pretending not to be afraid.

Blake nodded, but didn't say anything. The trees around him seemed to inch closer, clutching each other with their thin branches. The remaining leaves shivered.

Blake bit his lip, but found himself creeping closer to the blank paper, which Psalmanazar pinned open with his fingers. The corner of a page flickered.

Taking a deep breath, Blake then said the words that frightened him most: 'Show me the face of the Person in Shadow.'

Immediately he closed his eyes, afraid of what he would see once he opened them. It was like blowing out the candles on a birthday cake and wishing for something not to come true. He waited for a few seconds and then, slowly, prised his eyes open.

He could feel his courage trickling down his spine like a melting icicle.

He watched, appalled, as a mass of dark ink swirled over the page like dye unravelling in a glass of water, at war with the white paper. The battle seemed to last forever, a tug-of-war between light and shade, but eventually the page was coated completely in shadow – like an eclipse. Then, from the darkness, a figure began to emerge, a shape that grew larger, but no more distinct. It was like a mask or silhouette, concealing more than it revealed.

Despite his fear, Blake peered closer.

He sensed that he was looking into the face of evil, but could not tell who – or what – it was. The shadow seemed to reach out and engulf him. His heart and lungs filled with cold. His pupils dilated like holes in thin ice. He could not lift his eyes from the paper.

All of a sudden, the dog growled and Psalmanazar let the book drop . . . just at the moment Blake thought he could recognize the face. The volume fell to the ground, where it collapsed in a heap of paper. The spell was broken.

'What happened?' asked Blake in a petrified whisper.

The low rumble in the dog's throat revved into a snarl

as, hackles raised, it crept stealthily in front of Duck, shielding her with its body, its thin armour of ribs.

From behind him, Blake heard sounds of activity and turned to see joggers and dog-walkers crossing the bridge towards the towpath. Life was going on as usual.

'I don't understand,' he said, fearfully. 'What's wrong?'

'It's you,' said Duck at last, her voice trembling. 'Something came over you. You turned really pale all of a sudden. There was a gleam in your eye. What did the book show you?'

Helplessly, Blake turned to Psalmanazar, who refused to meet his gaze. He was staring into the distance as if impatient to be off.

'There was a face,' he said faintly. 'In the shadow. Only I don't know who it was. It could have been anyone.'

He couldn't bring himself to say more. He shivered, as though a cloud had blotted out the sun and coated the land in shadow. A touch of winter gripped the air.

The group stood motionlessly for a while, but finally Duck broke the silence. 'I want to go home.'

Blake nodded. He couldn't wait to get as far away from the clearing as possible. Still numb with fear, he reached down to pick up the remnants of Psalmanazar's book, which had been damaged even more in its fall. The spine had cracked and several pages lay scattered and torn on the ground. The boards felt curiously lifeless and empty in his hands, as though he was holding the memory – or ghost – of a book.

'Oh, Psalmanazar, what have I done?' he despaired when he realized the magical paper had slipped out, too. He twirled round in a panic.

Then he saw it. There, in the trees, was a large sheet of blank paper, caught like a kite in a clutch of branches. He ran over to untangle it.

A flutter of hope passed through him as he once again touched Endymion Spring's paper. Despite its unwieldy size, it folded naturally into a series of much smaller pages, like a miniature book that fitted neatly into the palm of his hand.

He hurried over to Psalmanazar. The man, however, refused to take it. Instead, he gently folded Blake's fingers over the edges of the booklet. The gesture was clear: Blake was meant to keep it.

Confused, Blake slipped the paper into his pocket. 'Um, thanks,' he murmured, unsure what else to say. He felt as though he had inherited a great responsibility. Even so, his heart was beating rapidly, an unmistakable buzz running through his veins. In exchange, he handed the man the dog's bandanna, which Psalmanazar promptly tied round the animal's grizzled neck.

As they were about to depart, Duck gripped her brother's arm. 'There's something we forgot to ask the book,' she said. 'What's the name of Psalmanazar's dog?'

Blake was tempted to laugh, but a weak, tremulous voice piped behind them: 'It's Alice.'

Both children spun round, startled.

Psalmanazar was smiling at them sheepishly, obviously ill at ease with his newly discovered voice. 'She was burrowing down a rabbit hole,' he continued, his throat rusty and sore. 'It seemed right somehow.'

Duck and Blake stared at him doubtfully for a moment, disbelieving what they'd heard; then, when no further sound was forthcoming, they turned and started the long trek back to the city.

They walked the rest of the way in silence, thinking exactly the same thing: there was something oddly familiar about Psalmanazar's voice, something that made it sound like an echo of a voice they had heard before. But they didn't mention their suspicions to each other. His silence had been contagious.

Sixteen

Blake expected to see a crush of police cars when he rounded the bend into Millstone Lane. He expected to find television cameras pointed at their front door and neighbours telling reporters how the foreign children had disappeared without a trace. Yet there was nothing. No megaphones, no television crews and no emergency tape cordoning off the front garden. The street was empty. Most of the people had left for work, their cars gone, the milk bottles taken in. It was as if nothing out of the ordinary had happened.

Blake checked his watch. They had been gone nearly two hours . . . two hours too long. He was worried how their mother would react. Each step brought them a little bit closer to the inevitable argument. Blake braced himself. He was no longer a hero in pursuit of a magical book, but a boy in trouble for sneaking out.

'Remember what I told you,' said Duck, sensing his anxiety. 'You caught me sneaking out of the house. Whatever you do, don't mention Psalmanazar or the blank book. She'll never understand.'

She'd been rehearsing the same excuse since they were within sight of the main road. She liked to take control whenever they were near home; it must be a female trait in his family. Well, she could shoulder all the blame if she wanted, he thought; he didn't mind.

He followed her up the garden path and inserted the key in the lock. He opened the door very slowly. It was like peeling back a plaster to see if the wound beneath had healed or was still inflamed and sore.

He got a nasty shock. His mother was slumped on the bottom step of the staircase facing the door. A rag doll. For one fearful moment, he thought she had collapsed, but then she looked up at him with tired, swollen eyes and his heart caved in inside him. They were in more than ordinary trouble.

'Um,' he said, not knowing where to begin.

His mother raised an eyebrow, waiting for more.

'Um,' he faltered again, feeling his pulse quicken.

'It's all my fault,' interjected Duck suddenly. 'I tried to run away, but Blake came after me and convinced me to come back. I didn't want to!'

She spoke in a great rush of words, as though she were

afraid the truth might recoil inside her if she paused or hesitated.

Blake listened to her, astonished, and then caught his mother looking at him for corroboration, testing him with one of her quizzical eyebrows. He glanced at Duck, who was staring straight ahead, like a wall. There was a slight flicker in the corner of her eye, but it could have been a wink, a tear, or even an angry twitch. He nodded unconvincingly.

His mother swore.

There was an uncomfortable silence; then Juliet Winters let out a long sigh. 'What am I to do with you?' she despaired at last.

Duck ground the edges of her boots together, while Blake studied the steps behind his mother's back. In his mind, he wanted to flee upstairs and, like the book, disappear.

'Do you realize how worried I was?' his mother said, her voice little more than a growl. 'What on earth made you go out without telling me? Where were you anyway?' She picked at him with her eyes – his muddy jeans and tousled hair – and Blake turned away, his cheeks reddening. 'You smell like smoke. What were you doing?'

'I'm sorry,' he said weakly.

'You're sorry?' she scoffed. 'Is that all?' She stared up at the ceiling and swore.

Blake closed his eyes, blood hammering in his head, and tried to block out the next assault of words.

'I thought that you, Blake, would have been more responsible than this,' she said in a chilling tone. 'A different country, a fabulous city, a new chance. You could have learned so much. Yet all I get from you is trouble – from both of you!' She glared at them each in turn, her eyes livid and sore. 'First, disappearing at night and now this morning. What are you up to? What game are you playing at?'

Neither child said anything. A tangle of emotions tore at Blake's throat. He was tempted to confess everything – to tell her about Endymion Spring, the Last Book and even the Person in Shadow – but he was silenced by her next comment.

'Do you want me to send you home?'

'Yes,' said Blake before he could stop himself.

Duck turned to him instantly in alarm, and he placed a protective hand over his pocket, which contained the sheet of Psalmanazar's paper.

'No,' he said, confused.

His mother eyed him savagely. 'Well, which is it?' she snapped. 'Your father or me?'

Blake felt the ground open beneath him and tried desperately to prevent himself from tumbling. The clock on the hall table ticked down the seconds, waiting for his response. He didn't know what to say. It was almost as if his mother wanted him to choose his father.

'I don't know,' he choked at last. 'I mean yes . . . I mean no . . . I mean . . . I mean . . . I don't know what I mean! I just want you and Dad to be together again, the way you were before you started working all the time and he gave up his job to be with us!'

His mother remained silent for a long, dreadful moment. Blake's hands were trembling and, to hide his feelings, he tightened them into fists.

'Is that what you assumed?' she said at last. Her voice was different. Beaten, unemotional. 'Well, perhaps we should have told you.'

Blake's knees went weak.

It was then that he learned the truth. His father had lost his job several months ago and she was working extra hard to keep them all together. Blake pressed his fingernails deep into his skin until they formed bruised purple moons in the palms of his hands. He was shivering.

His mother noticed his reaction and said, 'Honestly, Blake, you shouldn't go running off like that. You scared me. Anything could have happened to you. I'd be lost without you – without both of you.'

He barely heard the words she uttered next. She sounded just like a child. 'Please, I don't want to lose you too.'

Instinctively he moved closer and put his arms round her.

'I'm sorry,' he whispered, and this time he really meant it.

Seventeen

Everything after that happened in a blur. His mother told them to get ready; she needed to spend the rest of the day in the Bodleian Library. 'I really must get some work done.'

Obediently, Duck and Blake trudged upstairs.

In the bathroom, Blake studied his reflection in the mirror and frowned. What could Endymion Spring have seen in him? He wasn't the heroic type. He was just a scrawny kid with ribs like xylophones and irregular eyes that never looked anyone in the face. They had the unnerving ability to change colour according to his mood: pale blue when he was worried or upset, but darkening when he was angry. His dad likened them to wet pebbles. He wished his dad were here now to describe them; they were an enigmatic shade.

He scrubbed his face and patted his hair into place, trying to erase his feelings of doubt and failure, and then returned to his room to change into cleaner clothes.

He was examining the paper dragon, turning it over and over in his hands, comparing it with the section of Psalmanazar's book (they were a perfect match), when he heard his mother approaching. Hastily, he concealed the dragon behind his pillow and grabbed his knapsack, pretending to look busy.

'OK, let's go,' she said. 'I'm going to take you to the college library, where Mrs Richards can keep an eye on you. You're not to go off exploring without my permission. Have I made myself clear?'

Dutifully, Blake nodded and got up. He barely had time to stuff the wad of Psalmanazar's folded paper in his pocket before she marched him out of the room. He almost collided with Duck in the hall. She gave him a fleeting glance, but Blake ignored her and hurried down the stairs, still feeling bruised from the morning's proceedings.

He rushed out of the door without waiting for either his mother or sister to catch up.

His mother led them directly to the library, where she chose their seats for them: right next to the office. Paula Richards, however, was darting back and forth along the corridor, preparing for an invasion of the Ex Libris

Society, whose members had requested a chance to peruse the college's collections.

She glanced at the children each time she passed by, but didn't pause to speak or smile; she clearly had other things on her mind. Blake wondered privately if she suspected him of snooping around the library the other night and damaging the books on the floor. Her expression had little warmth in it.

He opened his knapsack and pulled out the worksheets his teacher had given him to complete during his absence. So far he had done his best to ignore them, but now his mother had warned him that she would check his assignments each night – to make sure he didn't fall even further behind. Duck, of course, had finished all of her homework ages ago.

He propped his elbows on the table and tried to concentrate. It was difficult. Duck was reading over his shoulder, tapping her fingers lightly on the back of his chair. He could feel the vibrations crawling all over him like a spider.

'Go away,' he said, brushing away her hand.

'I can help you.'

'I don't need your help.' He stared at the words without seeing them. 'Don't you think you've caused enough trouble already?'

Duck hovered for a moment and then said condescendingly, 'Well, if you don't need me, I'll see what else I can find out about Endymion Spring.'

Her words stung and it took every ounce of his willpower for Blake not to retaliate. He buried his head in his hands and stared fiercely at the words in front of him. *Identify the grammatical mistakes in the following paragraphs* . . . He groaned, then began to circle all the errors he could find.

Five minutes later, he looked up. Who cared about split infinitives and dangling modifiers when you had a whole library full of books around you, each tempting you with its secret knowledge? He scanned the rows of shelves. Who knew what sorts of information these books contained? He couldn't resist: he got up to take a closer look.

His mother had dumped them deep in the middle of the history section and each step carried him back a decade or two in time. There were fat volumes and thin, old books and new. The past, it seemed, was an unsolvable mystery, constantly being rewritten.

One of the books grabbed his attention. Unlike the others, it was a cream-coloured volume with a red silk ribbon tied round its body like a belt. It didn't have a title on its cover, but when he opened it, he saw the word *Bestiary* printed on the front page in fancy letters that reminded him of seahorses. He took it back to his desk.

Inside were lots of illustrations. Bizarre beasts with blue and silver scales, golden fur and elaborate tongues streaming from their mouths like banners stared out at him like exhibits in a medieval freak show. Some were familiar – hyenas, lions, pelicans and elephants – but many more were strange hybrids with horse-like bodies, colossal wings and razor-sharp talons. He'd never encountered anything like them before. With any luck, they'd be extinct by now.

He turned the pages slowly. Surrounding the creatures were short descriptions of their characteristics and attributes. These were written in the same spiky lettering, which he found hard to decipher, but gradually he came to realize that some of the animals were dangerous, while others, like the unicorn, had beneficial qualities: restorative powers and magical properties.

He flicked to a separate section – on dragons – and stopped.

On the page in front of him were four trees, and in each tree a well-camouflaged dragon. They were painted bright green, glossy gold, deep red and silver to coincide with the passing seasons. The fourth was almost invisible, barely discernible against its wintry background. He couldn't believe his eyes: they were just like the creature he'd imagined the night before, the dragon in the tree . . . the animal Psalmanazar's book had revealed to him only that morning. His heart thudded inside him.

He studied the inscription more carefully:

A Leafdragon ys that syngle creature whose skynne ys believed to contayne the twofoulde propyrties of immortalitee and wisdom, unknowne to manne since Eve dede eat of that moste sacryd forboden Tree. It atchievyth a cloke of invisibilitie, out of sighte of manne, by chaungyng colour accordyng to the sesons of the yeer; yet should manne or his kynde spotte such a beaste, shall he be granted powyrs like unto God and knowlydge bothe Good and Evill . . .

A shiver of excitement ran through him. The Leafdragon sounded almost exactly like the Last Book Jolyon had told them about – the power Fust had sold his soul to possess. Could the two be related? Did this dragon have something to do with the magical book he had found?

He glanced up and down the corridor, wondering if Duck would know, but he couldn't see her anywhere. She had disappeared.

Grabbing his knapsack, he went to look for her.

He filed past the philosophy section and entered the Mandeville Room, full of old maps and ancient atlases,

 Leaf dragon ys that syngle creature whose skynne ys believed to contayne the twofoulde propyrties of immortalitee and wisdom, unknowne to manne since Eve dede eat of that moste sacryd forboden Tree. It atchievyth a cloke of invisibilitie, out of sighte of manne, by chaungyng colour accordyng to the sesons of the yeer; yet should manne or his kynde spotte such a beaste, shall he be granted powyrs like unto God and knowlydge bothe Good and Evill . . .

He was about to creep upstairs, to see if she had gone up to the gallery, when a hand clasped him on the shoulder. He turned round. It was Paula Richards.

'Where do you think you're going?' she said firmly.

He pointed towards the gallery.

'No, I don't think so, Blake,' she said. 'Not today. It's off-limits. You're not to go causing trouble while the members of the Ex Libris Society are consulting the St Jerome Codex.' She indicated the glass cabinet on the landing halfway up the staircase and wagged her finger.

Blake blushed guiltily and turned away. Then, quite by chance, he spotted Duck dashing furtively across the lawn outside, heading towards the cloisters. What was she doing?

Luckily, they were interrupted by Mephistopheles, who had managed to sneak inside the library again and now tried to dodge past the librarian's legs. 'Oh no, you don't!' she roared, promptly giving chase. 'You're not supposed to be in here either!'

The cat made a game of her ferocity and scrambled up the stairs, followed by Mrs Richards.

Suddenly unsupervised, Blake rushed to the door. A frizzy-haired assistant was busily filing slips behind the main desk, her fingers flipping through a card catalogue like caterpillars on a treadmill. She was too preoccupied to take any notice. As silently as he could, Blake opened the door and slipped out.

Duck was easy to find. She was sitting cross-legged in the middle of the enclosed garden next to the Old Library, dwarfed by the enormous Jabberwock tree, which spread its coppery boughs high above her like large wings. She looked so small and vulnerable in her bright yellow raincoat that he felt an impulse to protect her. He stepped through an archway and walked across the cloistered lawn towards her.

He stopped. A small book lay open before her – a large white butterfly sunning itself on the grass. She was staring at it intently, lost in thought. His heart knocked against his ribs. Duck had found the blank book!

'What? How?' He stood above her, unable to speak properly. An unexpected surge of anger and jealousy rose in his throat.

'I was going to tell you,' she said, 'but I didn't know how.'

His cheeks exploded, red with rage.

'I meant to tell you,' she began again, wiping her nose on her sleeve, 'but the longer I had it the more I wanted to solve the mystery by myself.'

She lifted her face and he saw himself reflected in her large eyes – a silhouette blocking out the sun.

He didn't know what to say. He was fizzing with surprise and annoyance, but also with relief. More than anything, he wanted to hold the blank book again and feel the pages coursing through his fingers. He tried to make himself calm.

'How long have you had it?' he said finally, sitting down beside her.

'I went to fetch it after you found it,' she sniffed. 'You went to the Porter's Lodge, remember? It only took a minute. It was right where you'd left it. I wanted to know why you wouldn't let me see it.'

She flipped through the pages, all of which, Blake could see, were blank.

'I can't find any riddles,' she said. 'I've been through it hundreds of times. I've held it up to the light; I've considered using lemon juice to reveal any secret messages; I've even tried spilling ink on it; but nothing works. Ink doesn't stick to the paper. The words are invisible. How *do* you read it?'

She looked up at him and, for the first time in his life, he realized that she actually needed to learn something from him.

The trouble was, he didn't know how to explain it.

'I don't know,' he admitted truthfully. 'The words just find you. That's the only way I can describe it.'

He wondered whether she would laugh at him, but she didn't. She smiled sadly and held out the book to him. 'It's yours,' she said.

He felt the blood surge through his fingers as soon as he touched it. All of the anger and jealousy faded inside him. An instant connection to Endymion Spring, the printer's devil who had handled it so long ago, entered him. His skin tingled.

The volume realigned itself in his hand, just as it had done before, and the pages started to flicker, as if preparing to tell him its story.

His heart leaped with excitement.

Duck looked from her brother to the book expectantly. 'It didn't do that for me,' she said enviously.

Blake wasn't listening. A page had opened right in front of him, in the centre of the volume. He held his breath, convinced the first riddle he had seen would reappear. But nothing was there. The paper was blank.

'Can't you see anything?' asked Duck, sensing his disappointment.

He shook his head, unable to respond.

'Are you sure it's the right page? Perhaps if you –'

'Of course it's the right page!' he shouted irritably. 'It's no good! We're too late! I should never have let it out of my sight!' His voice reverberated around the cloistered passageways.

Annoyed, he slammed the book shut, but it immediately reopened, like a reflex. Once again, it showed him the blank page.

'Look!' said Duck suddenly.

At the heart of the book, where the sheets of paper had been bound together, a pale loop of thread, like a dragonfly wing, was coming loose.

'No! Don't pull it,' he cried, seeing her fingers veering towards it. Very gently, he tugged at the thread – more like a sinew or a fine loop of catgut than string – and watched, amazed, as it came undone at his touch.

'What's happening?' gasped Duck. Her breath tunnelled in his ear.

'I don't know.'

'Do you think the book is falling apart?'

'No, I don't think so. This is different.'

They stared in silence as a second and then a third knot pushed their way up from the spine of the book, like blossoming flowers.

Suddenly Duck had an idea.

'Quick. Do you have the page Psalmanazar gave you?'

'Why?'

'Because the riddle said that two books have to come together to find the third. Maybe that's what's happening now . . . Maybe you're supposed to bring the pieces of the puzzle together.'

'Maybe,' replied Blake, unconvinced. His heart, however, was beating very fast and his hand shook as he reached into his pocket and pulled out the neatly folded sheet of paper. It nestled in his palm like a small booklet, then began to quiver as he brought it closer to the book. He laid it carefully inside. It fitted perfectly.

Immediately, the loose threads began to worm their way through the new folds of paper, stitching Psalmanazar's page into the leather-bound volume. Like magic, they disappeared into the central gutter and the book clamped shut with a vicious, spring-like motion, its restoration complete.

Like an oyster guarding its pearl, the book remained closed.

'So that's that,' said Blake apprehensively.

'I bet it's going to show us the Last Book next,' said Duck excitedly. She wriggled beside him.

Blake was more cautious. 'I don't know. I expected the Last Book to look different somehow. Larger or more impressive.'

He eyed the battered brown book dubiously and then, just when he was about to give up hope, it sprung to life and the pages inside spun round like a whirligig. A light breeze fanned his cheek.

Eventually the blur of paper subsided and a suddenly still, silent page lay open in front of him. Blake looked down expectantly, wondering what he would see.

His blood turned to ice.

The page in front of him was deep black, almost

impenetrably so, as though a cloak of night had descended over the book and all it contained. Only a cusp of brightness like a gibbous moon shone through the upper right-hand corner of the paper.

Blake inhaled deeply.

Written in the darkness beneath were three words, etched in white:

I am watching

Eighteen

'What does it mean?' gasped Duck, frightened.

'I don't know,' Blake said, glancing over his shoulder at the dark colonnaded passages all around them. 'Maybe the book senses something's wrong. I think it's a warning of some kind.'

The tree behind them shivered slightly and dappled the ground with restless shadows. To their right stood the bolted door of the Old Library, its lion's teeth set in a silent roar. A gallery of gargoyles peered at them from the chapel roof, pulling nasty faces.

A noise like a hundred birds taking flight all at once rose from a nearby window, as applause greeted the end of a conference paper being delivered somewhere in the college.

Suddenly, Blake turned back to his sister. 'Hold on. Are you telling me you can see this?'

'Yeah, but that's not Endymion Spring, is it?' she said uncertainly, her eyes wide with fear.

'No, I don't think so.' Blake returned his gaze to the black page, where the ghostly message sent another chill through him. 'Maybe the Person in Shadow is communicating with us somehow. Maybe he can see us right now.'

'But that's impossible,' said Duck. 'Nobody knew I had the book. I didn't tell anyone, I swear!'

'Well, the Person in Shadow certainly knows we've got it now,' he said seriously. 'And I bet he or she'll be coming after us soon to get it.'

'What are we going to do?' squealed Duck, beginning to panic.

Blake went very quiet. 'I don't know.'

'We could tell Professor Jolyon,' she suggested. 'Maybe he can help us.'

Blake looked doubtful. 'I don't think that's such a great idea.'

'Why?'

'Because his office is up there,' he said, pointing at the tower of the Old Library, which rose above them. Its upper windows were a mirror of sunlit glass, reflecting the dark silver storm clouds slowly approaching. 'He could be watching us right now.'

Duck swallowed deeply.

'I don't know,' he said again, shudders crawling all over him. 'I don't know who we can trust.'

The page in front of him flickered.

'Hey, wait a minute,' said Duck. She ran a pearly pink finger over the surface of the paper and turned over one of the corners.

Blake, fearing she was going to try to rip out the infected sheet, raised a hand to stop her.

'No, look at the corner,' she said eagerly. 'There's still a piece of the book missing.' She lifted the edge of the paper with her fingernail and he saw what she meant: the round moon shape was where someone had torn off a corner of the page. It was a small scar revealing the perfect, intact sheet beneath.

'How did that happen?' he asked, dismayed. 'Did you do it?'

Duck was offended. 'Of course not! It's the page Psalmanazar gave you. Maybe he put a curse on it – or kept part of it for himself.'

Her imagination took off. 'Maybe he's using it to spy on us!'

He scrunched up his face. 'But that's impossible,' he said. 'Books don't work that way.'

'Come on!' she remarked. 'This book is hardly normal, is it? Perhaps the paper has other properties, ones we don't know about yet.'

She thought about it for a while. Her eyes widened.

'Maybe the Person in Shadow can see what we're doing whenever we open the book,' she said hurriedly. 'Maybe someone tore the section from the black page a long time ago and kept it as an eye into the book, just waiting for you to find it. Maybe you accidentally communicated something when you discovered Endymion Spring the other day – and that's why you were followed to the library . . .'

Duck was about to enlarge on the idea when a shadow stole across the lawn, creeping over them. Blake just managed to conceal the book in his knapsack before looking up.

Paula Richards was glaring down at them angrily.

'There you are,' she hollered. 'I've been searching for you everywhere. You're worse than the cat!'

She clapped her hands impatiently and they both rose to their feet, wiping the grass stains from their knees. 'I really don't have time for this. I promised your mother I'd keep my eye on you.'

Like criminals, they followed her back to the library.

A tall, familiar figure stood beside the table at which Blake had been working earlier. Jolyon.

Blake froze.

He eyed the professor warily: from the top of his heavily lined face to the tips of his long, inky fingers, which gripped the cream-coloured book he had left open on the table. And then Blake's heart skipped a beat. It was as though all of the blood pumping through his body had suddenly reversed direction; the ground lurched beneath his feet.

The professor had a bruised black thumbnail, almost exactly the same shape as the missing corner of the book.

The old man looked up, catching Blake's open-mouthed expression. A frown forked across his brow like a stroke of lightning and Blake tightened his grip on his knapsack, protecting the book inside, unwilling to let it near the man. He glanced away, unable to hold the professor's gaze.

Jolyon, however, had seen enough. He slipped a piece of paper between the pages of the bestiary, closed the volume, and pushed it gently towards Blake. Then he gestured Mrs Richards aside.

Blake watched as they walked out of earshot. He knew they were discussing him. Jolyon pointed at the section of the library where the books had been ripped off the shelves and murmured something in her ear. The librarian shook her head and turned to look at him.

'Get to work,' she admonished him quickly.

Blake glanced at the pile of worksheets awaiting his

attention. For once, his homework seemed like the safest option. He was still reeling from the shock of the shadowy message in Endymion Spring's book.

Rearranging the sheets in front of him, he started circling all of the mistakes he could find, taking special pleasure in lassoing other people's errors. He didn't want to acknowledge the suspicions creeping into his mind. The black page was invading his thoughts. He'd been wrong about his father, his mother, even Duck . . . so perhaps he was wrong about Jolyon, too. Perhaps there really was no one he could trust.

He kept his head down and didn't look up once – not when Paula Richards, carrying a heavy stack of books, took up a post close beside him, nor when Jolyon, leaving the library, brushed against him like a shadow.

Blake felt like one of the animals trapped in the bestiary. He and Duck were seated at opposite ends of the dark polished table, unable to talk, let alone pass notes. Occasionally, Mrs Richards scratched something in her notepad and he shuffled uneasily. Her pen made a dis-approving sound as it scraped against the paper, and he imagined her ticking a box next to some new fault or crime he had committed.

The black page was tugging at his imagination,

worrying him. The need to know whether the words had changed or whether a new message was waiting for him was irresistible. But there was no escaping Paula Richards' gaze. Magnified by her glasses, her usually sympathetic green eyes resembled Venus flytraps – and he was the fly slowly being devoured in the cage of her lashes.

Drumming his pencil on his worksheets, he looked around. A small pile of books was growing near him as Paula Richards scanned various reference works to do with Christina Rossetti, the poet Diana Bentley had mentioned at the college dinner. One of the volumes had devilish goblins and demons clawing up and down its gold spine, while another had a plain plum-coloured wrapper with ink blots on the leather. Paula Richards had left this propped open and he could just make out tiny scribbles in the margin – tight, minuscule words that looked like old-fashioned embroidery.

Not far from his elbow was the bestiary Jolyon had marked with his slip of paper. Slowly, so that Paula Richards could not see, he inched his fingers towards it and dragged the smooth white volume towards him.

Duck was watching him intently. Fortunately, the librarian was so engrossed in her research, she didn't notice.

Blake opened the book as casually as he could.

Jolyon hadn't been reading the entry on Leafdragons, but a different section altogether. A shudder of recognition passed through him: *Psalmanazar*. He blinked. No, it was a different word, but strangely similar: *Salamander*. Next to it was a picture of yet another tree – this time, full of snake-like branches. Each branch ended in a fanged head that was attempting to devour an apple.

Blake read the description carefully:

The Salamander, chefe among creatures, ys prooff against fyre, for it quenchyth flaumes wyth its bodie, while its skynne remaynes unscaythed. Yet beware: for thys beaste contaynes a secrete vennom, whych roted in trees will soure its fruit or releessed in a sprynge will polute its water and so cause an indyvyduall to die . . .

Blake scowled, puzzled. Why had Jolyon tried to alert him to this? The salamander sounded like a devious, untrustworthy beast, but it looked nothing like the dragon he had seen. Then he noticed the bookmark dividing the *Salamander* from its nearest alphabetical cousins, the *Raven* and *Sawfish*.

He turned it over and was even more surprised by what he saw. He read it twice before he understood it.

The Salamander, chefe among creatures, ys prooff fyre, for it quenchyth flaumes wyth its bodie, while its skynne remains unscaythed. Yet beware: for thys bearte contaynes a secrete vennom, whych roted in trees will soure its fruit or releessed in a sprynge will polute its water and so cause an indqvyduall to die . . .

JOLYON FALL

You are cordially invited to a plenary lecture
commemorating the 40th anniversary
of the foundation of the
Ex Libris Society

Whose Mortal Taste?
First Editions & Forbidden Fruit[*]

Sir Giles Bentley
Erstwhile Keeper of Books, Bodleian Library

All Souls College
Friday, 1 October, 8.15 p.m.

[*] Wine will be served.

Blake started breathing faster. Jolyon must have left this here for him to find. He wanted Blake to be at a lecture tomorrow night, but why? Blake couldn't work out what the professor was after.

His mind raced. Going to the talk would give him a chance to learn more about the origins of the society and perhaps find out who had found the blank book all those years ago. Not only that; it might tell him who had lusted after it, whose heart was already black. His mouth felt dry, as he considered the possibilities.

Duck was struggling to see the piece of paper in his hands, and he flashed it in her direction, careful not to let Paula Richards notice. She read the message quickly and a broad grin spread across her face.

He knew exactly what that expression meant: it meant they had to sneak into All Souls College, whether or not they had their mother's permission. It was an opportunity to uncover the past and perhaps solve the mystery for themselves.

Getting permission was not as difficult as they anticipated.

Juliet Winters returned from the Bodleian Library in a foul mood. This time she was annoyed with the librarians and not with them. Another scholar had requested the set of Faust books she needed to consult and she'd spent most of the afternoon trying to track them down.

'Who'd have thought so many people would be interested in Faust all of a sudden?' she said wearily, as they waited for the bus. 'It not only means that I'm behind schedule, but there's also a chance someone else is researching the same topic. I'm going to have to push even harder to publish my findings first.' She closed her eyes and kneaded her brow with tired fingertips.

The bus wheezed to a halt beside them and Juliet Winters piled into a seat near the middle. Duck and Blake positioned themselves behind her – like good and bad angels, one on either shoulder.

'If you need some extra time, we don't mind,' said Duck obligingly at the first set of traffic lights. 'We've been invited to a lecture. We could go to that while you work in the library tomorrow night.'

She was using her most soothing voice, like a hypnotist, to lull their mother into a false sense of security. Blake could not tell whether or not it was working. Her eyes were closed.

'We promise to be good.'

That did it. Their mother was instantly awake.

'What lecture is it?' she asked, her suspicions aroused.

'Sir Giles Bentley's. On collecting books.'

'You mentioned it the other day,' Blake added quickly. 'You told us we could go.'

'I did nothing of the sort.'

Blake held out the invitation for her inspection.

Juliet Winters frowned. 'Why are you interested in that all of a sudden?'

'Professor Jolyon thought we might be curious,' said Blake. 'Besides, Duck wants to ask some questions.'

'Sir Giles?' repeated his mother warily, scowling at the thick piece of paper. 'I'm not sure. All Souls is no place for kids. Plus, it's late at night.'

'But we've been invited!' protested Duck. 'We can't let Professor Jolyon down. He's relying on us.'

'Hmm, I wonder,' said their mother, still not convinced.

The bus swerved sharply to avoid an old man teetering on an even older bicycle, and she lost the thread of her argument.

'I promise to look after Duck,' said Blake, noticing they were approaching Millstone Lane. He reached out to press the button for the next stop. 'We could meet you outside the Bodleian Library afterwards. It's not too late. Besides, Professor Jolyon will be there. He'll be our babysitter for the night.'

He gave her a cheesy grin, but Duck tapped him on the elbow, warning him not to overdo it.

'Well, I don't know,' murmured their mother sleepily,

as the bus ground to a halt and the doors opened. 'I could certainly do with some more time to work, plus the Bodleian is advertising late hours this week, but . . .'

Blake knew he was almost there. One more push ought to do it. 'Just think of how much you'll accomplish,' he reminded her.

'OK, I suppose so,' said Juliet Winters, still with misgivings. 'Especially if Jolyon has invited you.'

'Thanks. You're the greatest!'

They both ran towards the house, smiling; but she was frowning. 'Are you sure you'll be all right?' she called out, perhaps remembering the trouble they'd put her to that morning. 'I don't like the idea of leaving you alone.'

'Don't worry,' the children chimed together. 'Nothing can possibly go wrong.'

That night, while their mother worked, Duck and Blake met in Blake's bedroom.

Blake knew what he had to do, but he was reluctant to go through with the procedure. It was a rite he didn't want to perform. The paper dragon was too beautiful, too intricate, to destroy; and yet, he needed to follow the instructions in Psalmanazar's book precisely and bring all the parts of the blank book together. The dragon was just one more piece of the puzzle.

With a heavy heart, he took the beast from behind the pillow, where he had left it, and started to unfold its many scales. The creases quickly disappeared, as if ironed by his touch, and soon the dragon was transformed into an enormous sheet of blank white paper, made from innumerable fine membranes of smooth skin. They flapped in the air, a gentle sail. Alive.

Feeling more confident, Blake folded the paper until it formed a small quire that fitted neatly in the palm of his hand. He then slipped it inside the leather volume and closed the covers, waiting for Endymion Spring to perform its magic. He could feel the book vibrating slightly between his fingers as the invisible threads began once more to weave the pages together . . .

And then it was over. The book lay still.

'This is it,' he whispered as he opened the cover. With trembling fingers, he turned the pages, impatient to know what the book would show him.

Nothing. The pages were blank – apart from the patch of darkness in the middle of the book, where the Person in Shadow's warning still haunted him with its three terrifying words.

'I am watching,' read Duck disappointedly. She sat back on her heels and sighed. 'Nothing's changed. What are we going to do now?'

Blake shook his head, but remained silent. Something

else had appeared on the page in front of him, something his sister couldn't see. He nearly dropped the book.

> The Sun must look the Shadow in the Eye
> Then forfeit the Book lest one Half die.
> The Lesion of Darkness cannot be healed
> Until, with Child's Blood, the Whole is sealed.
> These are the Words of Endymion Spring.
> Bring only the Insight the Inside brings.

Two words, in particular, grabbed his attention and refused to let go. They clutched at his throat and echoed in his mind like a horrible refrain: *child's blood*, *child's blood*, *child's blood* . . . Either he or Duck was going to die; he knew it instinctively, as though Endymion Spring had entered the room and whispered it in his ear.

'What's wrong?' asked Duck. 'You're sweating.'

'It's nothing,' he lied and shook his head again to dismiss the terrible thought. 'We'd better go to bed.'

Some things, he felt, were better left unsaid.

MAINZ

Spring 1453

ithout warning, a devil sprinted past the window and performed a grotesque, gyrating dance in the middle of the street. Peter and I ran to the front of the house to watch. The fiend made lewd gestures with its tail and mocked all those who came near.

Before long a gang of children had encircled it and started heckling. In a bid to escape, the devil dashed beneath their outstretched arms and raced towards the cathedral, pursued by a chorus of catcalls and whistles.

Almost immediately after, a procession of unsightly skeletons – faces powdered, eyes blackened and ribs painted across their chests – started walking along the straw-strewn streets, knocking on the walls of the surrounding houses, summoning the living to join the dead.

'Come one, come all!' they sang, beating their sticks

together and prancing from door to door. 'The time has come! All will be judged!'

Like obedient sheep, the citizens of Mainz emerged from their timbered houses to join the parade, all heading in the same direction: the graveyard beyond the city walls. Some were dressed in the false finery of kings and queens, which they had sewn specifically for the occasion, while others donned masks to disguise their faces and wore their normal clothes back to front. The more outlandish tied cowbells to their breeches and lowed like cattle, while younger children banged pots and pans together and cheered – or cried. Half-naked tumblers somersaulted up and down the length of the street, waving flags of multi-coloured cloth and adding their laughter to the general chaos and confusion.

Meanwhile, the players struck up their instruments. Bladder pipes, viols, lutes and lyres all belched and thrummed as madrigals began to weave in and out of the crowd, singing at the top of their voices:

'King or Queen, Pope or Knight,
Each lies equal in God's Sight;
Judge, Lawyer, Doctor, Fool,
None escapes Death's final Rule;
Merchant, Pauper, Friar, Thief,
Rich and Poor both come to Grief;

The Time has come to make Amends
Judgement Day for all ye Men.'

Hundreds of footsteps thundered in reply, as the congregation shuffled slowly towards the grave, forming its own relentless march through the city.

The Last Judgement had begun.

Herr Gutenberg sneaked up behind me.

'Aren't you going to join in the festivities?' he asked, laying a hand on my shoulder. 'It's considered bad luck, you know, not to participate in the Dance of Death.'

I turned round. Ordinarily, I would have laughed at his mismatched clothes – he was covered from head to toe in red and yellow squares, like a harlequin – but my heart was heavy. I shrugged. I knew that my time in Mainz was swiftly coming to an end and there would be no turning back. The day of my reckoning had indeed come.

Outside in the street a butcher with a pig's snout strapped to his brow jostled with a maid, as the Dance of Death continued.

'Do not dawdle, do not labour,' sang the madrigals. 'Join hands – now – with your nearest neighbour . . .'

The people in the street linked hands and began to

wind like a serpent through the crowded city. It was one of the spring's most festive occasions. The windows and doors were festooned with bright garlands of flowers, mixing their hopeful scent with the richer smells of meat roasting in the distance. Herr Gutenberg was stepping back and forth in a little jig of his own invention, completely out of time with the music, preparing to join in; but I held out a hand to detain him.

He glanced at me. 'You look as though the end is near,' he said, his worried voice full of compassion. 'What's wrong?'

Crouching down beside me, he gestured towards the cheerful faces of the crowd. 'This is a celebration, Endymion. You ought to be happy. The Dance of Death is merely a reminder of all we have to be thankful for. There is nothing to fear.'

He patted me affectionately on the head. Almost immediately, my lips started to tremble, as if they would speak.

'Don't mind him,' said Peter suddenly, grabbing me by the elbow and dragging me back into the house. 'His costume isn't finished yet, that's all. There are a few minor adjustments we need to make. I'll take care of them.' His hand gripped me like a vice.

Herr Gutenberg looked up. 'Well, hurry,' he said. 'You especially, Peter, must not be late.'

Peter nodded, a certain satisfaction in his face. He and

Christina had been given pride of place in this year's festivities: the most important roles of Adam and Eve, whose job it was to lead the dead into the graveyard and then sing to them about their mortality. Once the bodies of all the citizens in Mainz were lined up in a symbolic death, God would descend and resurrect the crowd. Then the real merriment would begin: dancing and feasting to continue long into the night.

And I wouldn't be there to enjoy it . . .

'Don't worry about us,' said Peter. 'We'll meet you at the city gates.'

I watched helplessly as Herr Gutenberg nodded and left. Almost immediately, his long bearded face was lost in a surge of bobbing, dancing heads. He had no idea that I would not be returning from the grave. I had to harden my eyes to prevent the tears from falling.

'Here,' said Peter, shoving a shallow wooden bowl into my hands. 'This will complete the look – and allow you to beg for money along the way. You'll need all the help you can get.'

He winked at me in an effort to cheer me up and then stepped back to assess his handiwork.

I glanced shyly at the mirrors on the wall. An old man stared back. Peter had taken care to dress me as the poorest beggar this side of Christendom. A rough hessian cloak had been pulled over my small, hunched frame and a long pointed hood, like a jester's cap, hung loose behind me. My eyes were unnaturally round and large, my back misshapen.

The change in my appearance only heightened my sense of foreboding. I was headed for Oxford. An unknown landscape unrolled before me: frigid territories to the north; mysterious cities to the east and west; marauding Turks somewhere to the south; and a limitless expanse of water surrounding the island I needed to find. My legs shook beneath me. I was already at sea.

I had hoped that Peter would accompany me – he had travelled far and wide and could protect me from cut-throats and thieves – but I had underestimated his love for Christina. She had proved the greatest temptation of all. Peter was indebted to her father . . . at least until he achieved his independence and claimed her hand in marriage. He promised to take care of Herr Gutenberg and defend him, should the need arise.

I grabbed my short wooden staff – half walking stick, half weapon – and followed Peter towards the hearth.

We had rehearsed this moment several times since returning from Frankfurt four days ago, but that didn't make it any easier now that the time had finally come.

We approached the open chest with a shared sense of misgiving.

As if aware of the monumental journey ahead, the loose sheets of dragon skin had undergone a magnificent transformation – withdrawing from the snakes' fangs and binding themselves into a wondrous book that looked impossibly heavy to carry, yet weighed surprisingly little. It was guarded by new talon clasps and armoured with jagged silver-green scales. Fust was fascinated by the alteration, but unable to account for its sudden metamorphosis. He had no idea of my immi-nent departure. Nor could he read yet from its pages: stories began, but ended in mid-sentence; potions appeared, but lacked the one or two vital ingredients to achieve their full potency; and all doorways to the future remained sealed . . . at least until he discovered I held the missing sheets in my toolkit. And that was only a matter of time.

Peter stared into the chest, while noises from the crowd outside lapped beneath the open windows.

'I wish there were another way,' he sighed, as he took the fabulous book made of dragon skin and fitted it into a makeshift harness, which he had secured to my back, making me look even more hunched over than ever. The toolkit, which even Peter did not know about, was safely concealed beneath my girdle.

He refused to meet my gaze, but worked steadily and methodically, tightening the straps of cloth around my body and then covering the whole again with my rough yellow cloak. He kept his thoughts to himself, as though words would be a sign of weakness.

I tried to imagine Fust's face when he next peered inside the chest and found the dragon skin missing. Surely his wrath would be insurmountable! I quivered at the thought. Would he pursue me to the ends of the earth, searching for it? Would I ever be able to return to Mainz?

My knees buckled beneath me, but Peter put out a hand to support me.

'Are you ready?' he asked, giving me a sad smile – his most brotherly gesture yet. Before I could react, he raised the hood of my cloak, so that I could not see to either side: only straight ahead. That way, he thought, I could not detect the tears in his eyes.

But I could.

Christina surprised us by bounding down the street to meet us. Her flyaway hair showed her distress.

'My father knows!' she called out over the din of jubilant voices. 'I tried to hide it from him, but he knows! He's coming for you now!'

She shoved and battled her way through the throng of

dancers. Peter had entrusted her with the job of keeping Fust preoccupied while we prepared for my departure; but the man, ever wary, had wrested the truth from her. There was no end to his jealousy or suspicion. Even now, he was visible at the far end of the street, fighting through the crowd. By sheer force of will, Christina had beaten him to us.

My heart bolted inside me. I looked frantically to right and left, desperately seeking a means of escape, but my legs had turned to water. Bodies boxed us in. Cries of 'Thief! Thief!' rose in the distance, Fust's voice unmistakable above the roar of the crowd.

'Hurry! There's no time!' shrieked Christina. 'You've got to go!' Like a frantic hen, she started shooing people away from her with lifted skirts – which only made them rowdier.

Luckily, Peter had a plan. He grabbed me by the arm and propelled me through a knot of merrymakers.

'Quick! Act as if you're dancing!' he shouted to me, as kings, queens, knights and jesters whirled round us in a blur of masks. I did a poor imitation of a leap and caper behind him, unable to match the fervour of his steps, and pretended to smile – but inwardly, I was stiff with terror. I grinned like a death's-head.

Fust was rapidly closing in, his jewelled hands pulling people aside.

Our diversion finally started to take effect. Recognizing the principal characters, Adam and Eve, dancing towards them, most of the revellers stopped to point and stare.

'Why are you waiting here?' cried Peter, giving the nearest onlookers the order to start the formal procession towards the grave. 'Let's go!'

The words seemed to release the citizens of Mainz from a spell. With a mighty cheer, the crowd surged after us, dancing in our wake, all heading in the same direction: the graveyard at the edge of the city. Ahead of us, strangers jumped aside to let us pass and then clapped their hands and leaped in our trail, joining the carnival atmosphere. The street was sheer pandemonium.

'Stop!' I heard Fust cry as more and more people blocked his way. 'Let me pass, you fools! They've stolen my book!'

I glanced behind me. Fust, in his vanity, had dressed as the Pope, one of the foremost members of the procession. While some taunted him with jibes and jests, others bowed before him and allowed his Holiness to advance unimpeded. If anything, the stream of bodies was pulling him closer.

Feeling me waver, Christina tightened her grip on my other hand and together we charged through the streets and alleys, picking up more stragglers. Breathless and dizzy, I clung to my rescuers as they pulled me under the shadow of the large rose-coloured cathedral and up the cobbled lane towards the North Gate.

Suddenly, like an assault of brass angels, a triumphal fanfare greeted us from the heights of the city wall. Musicians scurried along the parapets, dancing and playing their instruments. The flames of the apocalypse were upon us! Horns and trumpets sparked in the sunlight and red and gold pennants, fixed to the gate, rippled like silken fire. Already, a great crowd had assembled by the tall, turreted tower, close to the graveyard. Voices burst into song the moment we appeared.

Fust pursued us, showing no sign of letting up. His cries hounded us like a baying dog.

Desperately, I searched for a sign of Herr Gutenberg, but couldn't see him anywhere in the confusion of faces. We tore through the crowd.

Ahead of us loomed the large wooden gate and, beyond that, the entrance to the graveyard. If we were not careful we would soon be sucked into its embrace and trapped for good. Fust would surely have us then.

Peter and Christina seemed to have reached the same conclusion. Without warning, they flung me ruthlessly aside, into a multitude of awaiting arms. I bobbed and bounced from person to person, until I landed, winded and bruised, near the giant stone ramparts, on the city-side of the wall. Bent double with exhaustion, I struggled to regain my breath. The book felt suddenly too heavy for my back; my body ached. By the time I looked up, Peter and Christina had gone, swallowed by the graveyard.

For a moment, I stood where I was. People yelled and applauded and danced all around me, but I neither heard their songs nor felt their joy. I was numb with shock. I had not expected Peter to fling me aside so roughly, so impersonally, without even a word of farewell. I knew why he had done so – to give me time to escape – but still I felt betrayed. I didn't want it to end this way. Slowly, shouldering my burden, I began to pick my way through the crowd. Tears blinded my path.

As if sensing my mood, the revellers suddenly fell quiet. A hush shifted through the crowd like a snake. The musicians' frantic playing faded.

Fust had arrived.

He stood barely a stone's throw away, prowling through a mass of spectators, hunting me down. I crouched by the wall, trying to make myself invisible. He had not been fooled by Peter's ploy. He must have seen me escape. He was coming for the book . . .

I held my breath.

The crowd opened before him in a quivering circle, surprised by the vehemence of his actions, which were no longer those of an innocent bystander. His eyes had narrowed to dark slits and his nostrils flared, like a wild animal sniffing me out.

Fortunately, a brave horn-player broke the silence with an untimely belch and a nervous ripple of laughter passed through the crowd. Fust paused to glare at the ring of offending faces.

'Fools,' he spat. 'You laugh now, but you have no idea what will come!'

The few titters stopped. Peter, dressed as Adam, strode into the arena. Bare-chested and brave, he faced his Master. To a chorus of approval, Christina then walked up behind him and, like Eve, coiled her arm seductively around his waist.

Fust, as the Pope, pointed at them accusingly.

'You!' he hissed, barely able to contain his fury. 'You two are to blame for all this! It's your fault!'

A couple of spectators, thinking this was part of the performance, chuckled.

Fust, livid with rage, turned on them with his heavy ring-clad fingers. 'Fools!' he cursed again, his jewels catching fire in the light. 'You're all damned fools!'

This only served to increase the general sense of hilarity. People broke into a chorus of laughter and insults, taunting the Pope.

Immediately, Peter and Christina raised their hands to

silence the commotion. Gently, with voices tinged with sorrow, they began to sing:

> *'King or Queen, Pope or Knight,*
> *Each lies equal in God's Sight;*
> *Earth to Earth and Dust to Dust,*
> *We claim your Soul: Johann Fust . . .'*

Fust looked at them in disgust and then, as the full comprehension of his situation dawned on him, his mouth curled into a sneer.

'No! I won't go! You can't make me!'

Peter and Christina – as Adam and Eve – repeated the verse, emphasizing Fust's role as Pope, a pre-eminent member of the procession and the first to be led to the grave. While they sang, a host of skeletons emerged from hiding and moved stealthily towards him, about to claim their first victim. Once summoned to the grave, Fust would have to wait in quiet compliance – death – until all the citizens of Mainz lay beside him, from the noblest knight to the poorest beggar. Finally, at the end of the symbolic dance, God would descend and raise them all from their slumber . . . by which time I would be gone.

One by one the skeletons approached Fust and bowed before him, inviting him to participate in the Dance of Death.

Fust became hysterical. 'No! I won't go! Never! You can't take me!'

He ran from one side of the crowd to the other, appealing to people to let him pass, scrabbling at them, but the spectators, now a wall of bodies, blocked his way.

Peter and Christina walked steadily closer.

Fust attempted once more to run away, but a mischievous devil, sensing trouble, rushed up behind him and kicked him in the backside, causing him to fall down. On his hands and knees, he scrambled away from his daughter and chosen son-in-law, crawling like an infant.

Even now, the skeletons barred his way.

Impassive, Peter and Christina looked on as Fust, reduced to no more than a child, was dragged away by his arms and legs, struggling furiously against the ignominy of death. The crowd gave an enormous roar of approval – like the earth opening up – and the musicians on top of the wall struck up their instruments. The last I saw he was pinned to the ground by an army of devils and demons in the realm of the dead and forced to remain still by an open grave. He was writhing desperately beneath their hoofs and claws, trying to pursue me and regain the book.

Peter and Christina shook their heads and scanned the faces of the crowd for the next person to join the Dance of Death. I longed for them to pick me out of the mass of heads, but I forced my steps away.

Blindly, I stumbled through the excited throng of people – an unnoticed beggar, hampered by a burden on his back – working my way towards the protective shadow of the great cathedral. I glanced back just once, when I heard Peter's voice soaring above the crowd like an angel's chorus:

> 'Naked we're born, Naked we'll go.
> See how the Vain are soon brought low.
> Godspeed the poor Boy on his Way.
> Fear not, we'll meet some other Day . . .'

I turned and made my solitary way through the suddenly cheerless city, walking towards my future.

OXFORD

Nineteen

B lake felt uneasy. A wind had picked up and leaves were blowing against the sides of the locked-up colleges, which towered above him like massive shadows. Gargoyles gripped the ledges of the buildings with chiselled claws and angels peered down at him from the roofs. He was making his way through the dark city streets towards All Souls College.

Duck trotted behind him. 'Did you bring Endymion Spring?' she asked excitedly.

'Of course I did,' he answered, 'but you're not to mention it, OK? We can't let anyone know we've got it until we figure out who's the Person in Shadow.'

'And then what?'

It was such a simple question, but it made him stop in his tracks. He wasn't sure.

'I don't know,' he said uncertainly.

Beside them an enormous drum-shaped building with

blackened windows and a silver dome – the Radcliffe Camera – grew out of an islanded garden in the middle of a cobbled square. Just behind them was the Bodleian Library, a vast stone crown with windows lit up like jewels. Somewhere in the Upper Reading Room, beneath the rows of glowing lamps, their mother was working into the evening.

Until now, Blake had expected someone – either Jolyon or Psalmanazar or even Duck – to tell him what to do, but he no longer felt he could trust anyone. It was up to him to solve the mystery on his own.

Even Endymion Spring, it seemed, had abandoned him. All day long the book had taunted him with its silence. The black page was still there, warning him of the Person in Shadow, but there was no sign of the original riddle he had seen, nor any clues about the future.

To his left he could see the imposing walls of All Souls College, its thistle-like minaret and distinctive towers steeped in shadow. Inside its gates was yet another library, a chapel-like building with row upon row of leather books, reached by curving wooden staircases. The entire city, it seemed, was built of books. Stacked on top of each other, slotted side by side, they fitted together like bricks to form a tremendous fortification of reading, a labyrinth of words. There were even miles of books beneath him now, in tunnels below the ground. The university was an immense walk-in library. The Last Book could be hidden anywhere.

Endymion Spring squirmed suddenly in Blake's knapsack, thumping him in the small of the back.

'Hold on,' he said. 'I need to take a look.' He grabbed Duck's elbow and steered her towards a large, old-fashioned lantern hanging from a sconce on the wall, opposite the Church of St Mary the Virgin.

The wind was gathering strength and the pages of the blank book whipped back and forth like a thing possessed, flickering past his eyes so quickly he couldn't tell whether they contained any new information. Once or twice, he thought he glimpsed streaks of words, but they could have been smudges, shadows, anything. The lamp threw restless shapes against the stone buildings like autumn leaves.

Suddenly, a gust of wind tunnelled through a nearby alley and seized the book from his hands. It almost flew away from him, rising towards the church, but he managed to cage it against his chest like a frightened bird before it broke free. Heart racing, he stuffed the volume back inside his bag. It wasn't safe to take any chances – not here, not now, not with the members of the Ex Libris Society so close.

'What's happening?' cried Duck, her voice grabbed by a fist of wind and hurled down the street.

'I don't know! The book seems to be afraid for some reason.'

'Blake, I don't like it,' she whimpered. 'I'm scared.'

'I know. I am too.'

'Maybe this is all a mistake,' she said. 'Maybe we shouldn't have brought the book with us.'

'But we had to,' he insisted. 'It's not safe to leave it behind either. I'm not letting it out of my sight ever again.'

He tried to give her a reassuring smile, but was rapidly losing his nerve. The quivering book alarmed him. The Person in Shadow might be waiting for them just around the corner. Endymion Spring might be telling them to turn the other way.

'Don't worry,' he said again. 'It'll be all right, you'll see. Everything will work out fine in the end.' The wind forced the words back down his throat.

He noticed the long golden hands of the clock on the church tower overhead passing eight o'clock. The meeting would soon begin. They had to hurry.

Taking Duck's hand, he guided her towards the High Street, where the main entrance was located. Buses pounded past, sending tremors through the pavement. He glanced up at the sky once more for reassurance, but the night seemed to glower back – like the black page in his book. A few ragged clouds scudded across the moon.

The college was guarded by a slender door set into a fancy wooden gate. The arched door was slightly ajar, but an iron chain barred their way in. All Souls College was clearly closed to visitors.

Blake looked around for a bell to ring, but all he could see were three dim statues glaring down at him from above. One wielded an orb and a sceptre, another a crosier, while the third seemed to be perched above the others like God, sitting in judgement over everyone who passed by.

A voice suddenly growled at them from the other side of the door. 'What do you want?' A face like a gargoyle peered at them through a crevice between the door and the frame.

'We're here to attend a meeting,' said Blake nervously, swallowing a lump of fear in his throat. 'The Ex Libris Society.'

'You are, are you?'

'We're members,' lied Duck.

'You're members,' repeated the man mirthlessly. 'You expect me to believe that? You're a bit young.'

Duck was about to give him a piece of her mind, but Blake nudged her to keep quiet. A bus rattled by. As soon as the vibrations subsided, he added more reasonably, 'We've been invited.'

The porter took off his bowler hat and poked a stubby finger in his ear, as if he had misheard. Wild hedgerows of curly grey hair sprouted around the sides of his bald head. 'I'm not going to open the gate to any kids,' he said at last. 'Especially foreign kids who waste my time.'

He moved as if to slam the door in their faces.

'But we have an invitation!' cried Duck in alarm. 'Show him, Blake.'

Reluctantly, Blake took the invitation from his jacket pocket and, carefully concealing the professor's name with his thumb, showed it to the man. The porter peered at it closely.

'The Ex Libris Society, huh? Come on, show me the real name on the invitation.'

Unwillingly, Blake peeled his thumb from the top of the card.

'Professor Jolyon Fall, eh? Well, I'm honoured to meet you, sir.' The porter made a poor attempt at a bow. 'You're a bit young, aren't you?'

'That's enough!' a sharp voice rang out behind them suddenly. The children spun round in surprise. Diana Bentley, dressed entirely in white, stood out like a marble statue in the dark, the wind whipping a few strands of silver hair around her face like electricity.

She glared at the porter with contempt. 'They're with

me and here's my invitation.' She handed him her card. 'Now open the door.'

The porter nodded and obediently unchained the door. The children followed Diana inside.

Diana regarded them with interest as they passed under a stone archway towards the front quadrangle.

'Well, this is a surprise,' she said mildly. 'It's nice to see you, Blake, and this must be your sister –'

'Duck,' said Blake, introducing her.

She smiled. 'How . . . cute.' She chose the word rather like a candy, which she bit.

'I preferred the porter,' Duck muttered gloomily under her breath, but Blake hissed at her to be quiet.

'Just be grateful we're in, OK?' he said. 'Behave yourself.'

Thick walls of stone surrounded them on all sides, shutting out the sounds of the city. It was as quiet as a tomb. To their right rose two tall, silhouetted towers, which speared the clouds with their spires. A small rectangular lawn, brilliant green by day, but black by night, lay in front of them: a pool of darkness moated by a silver path. On the far side of the quadrangle was a chapel with what looked like ghostly saints floating barefoot in the faintly illuminated windows.

Diana clearly knew the way. She led them round the lawn and down a small stairwell into a dusky crypt beneath the chapel. Echoes shuffled around them in the dark and the air smelled dusty and stale. In the twilit shadows Blake could see rows of short pillars bearing the weight of a low vaulted ceiling, under which several sarcophagi had been stashed.

'What are those?' he asked timidly, reaching out to take Duck's hand. Diana, however, laughed softly and glided in between them, steering them towards a hidden court-yard at the back of the college. Stopping outside a heavy wooden door, half-obscured by vines, she swiftly seized a round iron handle and twisted it open.

They entered a long room with a trussed roof made from blackened beams. A tapestry dominated the far wall. In it, a white stag leaped nimbly through a needlepoint forest, filled with pale trees and tiny embroidered flowers, endlessly pursued by baying hounds – their slavering jaws agape for centuries.

Numerous people were seated before a podium at the front of the room and Blake shied away from their glance as they turned around.

Diana, however, pushed him forwards. 'We've got some new recruits,' she ventured happily. 'Dr Juliet Somers' children, Duck and Blake.'

There were murmurs of surprise, more than approval,

but only Prosper Marchand, seated lazily in the front row, seemed unfazed by the intrusion. He was disputing the advantages of digital paper and electronic ink with a group of grey-haired scholars beside him.

'All the books in the world available at your fingertips,' he was explaining. 'No more crumbling paper or fading print. It's a universal library.'

Blake caught sight of Sir Giles Bentley standing nearby, listening to the conversation. His hands were clenched round the neck of a wine bottle, as if he wanted to choke it.

'Codswallop!' he roared suddenly. 'Nothing can replace the feel of a nicely bound book. The printed word is sacred.'

Involuntarily, Blake stiffened, but the leather-jacketed professor merely took the interruption in his stride. 'Don't be such a Luddite, Giles,' he responded calmly, with a smile. 'It's an invention worthy of Gutenberg himself.'

Sir Giles eyed him coolly as finally the cork squeaked open and he poured the red liquid into a row of glasses.

Diana had gone over to investigate an assortment of old books on a large polished table next to the podium. Blake followed her, grateful for the diversion. She was wearing elbow-length gloves, which made her hands look like long-stemmed lilies. He guessed you had to wear these if you wanted to handle Sir Giles's books. They must be extremely valuable. Just a tinge of dust, like pollen, smirched her fingertips.

He itched to pick up the books – some were bound with clasps, others studded with jewels – but he could feel Sir Giles watching him as he distributed glasses of wine among the assembled members. He decided to wait for permission first.

'Keep your eyes peeled,' he whispered to Duck, who had sidled up to him. 'We need to figure out who found the blank book originally – and, more importantly, who's after it now.'

There were so many faces. Blake recognized some of them from the dining hall, but many more had crept out of the Oxford woodwork just for the occasion. Mostly, they were academics like his mother, speaking a multitude of languages and clutching thick notebooks, ready to take notes. They spoke in low voices, as though in a library – or a church for worshipping books.

The reverential air was soon broken by Sir Giles, who rang a brass bell on the podium and encouraged everyone to take their seats. The room buzzed with expectation.

Diana Bentley summoned Blake and Duck to her side in the front row and they sat down next to her, feeling excited and yet nervous at the same time.

The meeting of the Ex Libris Society was about to begin.

Twenty

Wearing an elaborate black robe with spidery gold embroidery on its sleeves, Sir Giles positioned himself behind the lectern and with fierce blue eyes surveyed the room.

'First, may I extend a warm welcome to you all on this memorable occasion,' he addressed the members formally, 'the fortieth anniversary of the foundation of the original Libris Society.' There was a polite ripple of applause. 'Indeed, it was on a night like this, close to the start of Michaelmas, that a few of us gathered in a college library to track down the world's most elusive books . . .'

Blake shivered with anticipation, feeling as though he had travelled back in time and was embarking on the same treasure hunt. Fortunately, Endymion Spring had settled down in his knapsack and was no longer drawing attention to itself.

'. . . a quest that continues to this very day. I see we have attracted some new members,' he continued, eyeing the children sternly, 'but I regret that not all of our founding members are able to attend.'

A hint of a smile curled his lips and Blake felt there was a deeper, more malicious meaning to his words.

At this moment, Jolyon burst into the room. 'I'm sorry I'm late,' he announced, 'but I was unexpectedly detained. I bumped into an old member who incidentally, Giles, *says* hello.'

Sir Giles responded with a cold, forbidding look. His eyebrows darkened his face.

The professor, however, took no notice. He caught Blake's eye and nodded. The boy coloured automatically and turned away. He pressed his legs against the bag beside his chair, feeling particularly conspicuous and vulnerable among so many authorities on rare books.

Sir Giles waited for Jolyon to take a seat.

'As I was saying,' he resumed haughtily, once the lumbering professor had found a chair next to Paula Richards a few rows back, 'a warm welcome to everyone. And may I take this opportunity to remind all present to sign the register, which Mr Fox-Smith is now placing by the door. Many of you will know that we have been signing this book since the original meeting forty years ago, and so we would be honoured to continue marking the success and expansion of the society, devoted as it is to the preservation of the printed word, by including your names here tonight.'

Blake squirmed in his chair, straining to see what he meant. A young man in a pinstripe suit was holding aloft a thick book full of ribbon-like signatures. He placed it on a stand near the door.

Blake nudged Duck with his elbow. 'We've got to see inside that book,' he whispered. 'It'll . . .'

'Ssh!' hissed a woman behind him.

Sir Giles was beginning his lecture. 'And so, without further ado,' he said, tapping a sheaf of notes on the lectern, 'the reason you are here. My lecture, *Whose Mortal Taste? First Editions & Forbidden Fruit . . .*'

While Sir Giles droned on at length about the history of collecting books, mentioning people who had lusted after rare volumes or broken into libraries to seek lost or forgotten tomes, Blake shuffled impatiently in his seat. The other members of the society bowed their heads and listened respectfully, coughing discreetly at intervals, but he was desperate to see the ledger by the door. Here, at last, he might learn the identity of the person who had first found Endymion Spring . . . and the person who had lurked in the shadow, desiring it.

He glanced over his shoulder and caught Jolyon

watching him with a knowing expression. He blushed and turned away.

Finally, Sir Giles clapped his hands together and announced, 'And now some of my personal treasures.'

There was an audible exclamation round the room as books started exchanging hands, the scholars delving into the printed worlds they knew so well. Quiet murmurs of approval became raptures of delight. Blake was surprised to see that Prosper Marchand made the greatest show of all of examining the books: he stroked the covers, caressed the pages and even held the paper up to the light like a connoisseur of fine wine. Only then did he read the words on the page.

Blake was beginning to despair that the books would ever reach him, when Sir Giles slapped a pair of gloves in his lap. 'Put these on if you're tempted to touch anything,' he growled, his dark eyebrows knitting together. 'Children and books don't mix.'

Blake was about to complain, but Diana murmured in his ear that gloves were merely to protect the books from the acid on his skin.

'See, I need them myself,' she said with a smile. That made him feel better and he pulled them on obligingly, sliding his hands into the long, snake-like gullets. He wasn't sure that he liked the sensation: it was like wearing a blindfold at the end of each finger.

Yet when the books finally reached him Blake was pleased to have them on. Despite their treasure-like status, many of the volumes exhaled tiny clouds of dust that made him want to sneeze. Copies of *The Tragical History of Doctor Faustus*, *Paradise Lost* and *The Rape of the Lock* passed before his eyes – a blur of words and menacing black and white illustrations. Duck peered over his shoulder, breathing enviously. Sir Giles had refused to let her touch anything.

Diana then handed him a slender green volume decorated with gold swirls. 'It's a copy of *Goblin Market*,' she murmured in his ear. 'The goblins look sweet and harmless, except they're not. They have real claws and sharp teeth . . .'

Breathlessly, Blake opened the covers and saw a multitude of cat-faced, bird-beaked, weasel-furred creatures wearing large hats and long coats. They were smiling and snarling and grovelling in an attempt to seduce two young girls to sample their bushels of fruit. 'Come buy, come buy,' they sang in a chorus that repeated throughout the book like a trail of breadcrumbs, leading him further into the story.

'It's quite safe,' she purred. 'If you feel a little frightened, all you have to do is close the covers and the danger will disappear. That's the wonderful thing about books.'

He wasn't sure that he agreed with her – some books

stayed with you long after you read them; they lingered in the unswept corners of your mind – but he wanted to impress her. He sensed that she believed in the power of books just as much as he did. She read them with a child's eye. A child's magic.

Sir Giles, however, broke into his reverie. 'What's this?' he barked. 'Another book? This isn't one of mine.' He lifted a red-coloured volume with inky blotches on the cover into the air.

A chair scraped back and Paula Richards stood up. Blake looked behind him.

'I'm afraid I've taken the liberty of bringing in one of the more tempting books from the collection at St Jerome's,' she addressed the room. 'It's a coincidence really. It's another copy of *Goblin Market*.'

'Yes, and a fair example of nineteenth-century publishing, too,' started Sir Giles, turning over a couple of pages and expertly assessing its value.

'I'd forgotten we owned it actually,' continued Paula Richards, raising her voice slightly and interrupting the domineering man in mid-flow, 'until a chance remark from you reminded me of it the other day. I'm impressed. You seem to know a lot about our library's collection.'

There was nothing malicious in her tone, but it suddenly occurred to Blake that she was privately accusing Sir Giles of something. Was he the person, perhaps, who had broken into the library the other night and disturbed the books on the shelves? Was he the book-breaker?

The man glared at her coldly, but said nothing.

'Our collections must have a special significance for you, Sir Giles, to make you familiarize yourself with them so well.'

'Naturally. I take an interest in all the Oxford libraries,' the man explained himself.

Paula Richards sharpened her smile somewhat. 'Yes, but this is an extremely rare book. Christina Rossetti's own copy of *Goblin Market*, one she expressly asked her publishers to bind in red leather – puce, as you called it – when all the others were blue. I must congratulate you. This book is one of a kind. Not many people know it exists . . . but you did.'

Blake sat very still. She might be describing Endymion Spring for all he knew, but he was relieved to hear that she was merely referring to a child's book. Nevertheless, he was surprised to see Paula Richards flash a private smile in Jolyon's direction, as if he had prior knowledge of her accusation and supported her. Clearly there was something he didn't understand going on between them. He couldn't help wondering if this was really about Christina Rossetti. Was it possible that Sir Giles, like Jolyon, knew about Endymion Spring?

'Well, thank you for the compliment,' said Sir Giles, graciously inclining his head. His eyes, however, were livid and his brow had turned a brighter shade of scarlet.

He glanced at his watch – a gesture repeated by many people in the room. 'I believe I have spoken for long enough, but I am happy to answer any other questions, or assess any other books, in private. I hereby adjourn the meeting.'

There was a short applause before people scurried to the back of the room to consume the remaining glasses of wine.

It was already after nine and Duck and Blake had only a few precious minutes to consult the register by the door before meeting their mother by the library. They were off like a shot, battling their way through the crowd of grown-up arms and legs.

They waited impatiently for a few more senior members of the society to sign the book, and then grabbed the ledger. Blake flipped back through the pages, cartwheeling through time, watching row upon row of signatures concertina past his eyes.

Suddenly a hand clasped him on the shoulder. 'You're supposed to sign the page with today's date, not go nosing about in the past,' said a familiar voice.

Blake turned to find Prosper Marchand smiling at him. The professor calmly took the register from him and turned back to the page that was clearly indicated with a silk ribbon. An expensive fountain pen, as fat as a cigar, lay on the table beside him and he picked it up to sign his name. After a Zorro-like finish, he handed the pen to Blake and watched as both he and Duck signed their names painstakingly under his.

'There, now your names are recorded for all posterity,' he said, bringing his face just close enough for Blake to smell a spicy cravat of aftershave around his throat. 'Just like these unfortunate rascals at the dawn of time.'

To Blake's astonishment, the professor flicked back to the very first page of the ledger, where a black and white photograph had been pasted above a line of faded signatures. He had only a few seconds to gaze at the grainy image, but like a camera he captured the faces and names. Part of the mystery was solved.

'Mum's the word,' whispered Prosper Marchand like a naughty schoolboy and then, with a playful smile, headed back towards the other members of the Ex Libris Society.

Blake turned to Duck in surprise. She, too, looked amazed by the discovery. The photograph had shown a group of young students in old-fashioned clothes, standing in front of a bookcase. It could have been any Oxford library. Most of them were staring woodenly at the camera, their faces washed out by time, their hair-styles preposterously dated; but four figures had grabbed his attention immediately.

Jolyon towered above the other students, a giant of a man with a storm of wavy curls and an already thread-bare suit. Attached to his arm, caught in a flirtatious laugh, was an attractive girl with sleek, dark hair, while standing stiffly behind them, dressed in an expensive dinner jacket, was a bullish man who resembled Sir Giles, with just the hint of a moustache crowning his upper lip. And in the far right-hand corner of the picture, almost out of the frame, was another figure, a shy blur, whose nest of wild hair and shabby cloak were instantly recognizable.

Psalmanazar. The lost member of the Libris Society.

Twenty-one

Blake was still shaking his head as they hurried through the dark streets towards the Bodleian Library. 'Who would have guessed Psalmanazar was one of the founding members of the society?' he said. 'He must have discovered Endymion Spring all those years ago. I wonder what happened.'

Duck remained silent and thoughtful for a while. 'But we still don't know who the Person in Shadow is,' she remarked gloomily, her breath shining like tinsel in the air. 'It could be any one of them.'

Or someone else entirely, Blake thought to himself. He and Duck were surrounded by adults, all consumed by their own bookish passions.

It had rained heavily and the street lamps smeared patches of electric blood on the pavement. They rounded the corner into Broad Street and rushed to the entrance of the Sheldonian Theatre, a dark domed building next to the library, where they had arranged to meet their mother. Above them a tall curved railing jutted into the darkness, crowned by a series of crudely carved stone heads: large bearded men who guarded the ceremonial hall beyond. Blake wasn't sure whether they were meant to represent emperors or philosophers. They stared blindly into the night, frowning at the noise spilling out from a beer-lit pub on the opposite side of the street.

Duck and Blake sat quietly on the short flight of steps for a while, thinking over the events of the meeting. It was cold and they pressed together, trying to steal each other's warmth. Stars trembled in the now cloudless sky. There was no sign of their mother.

Blake shifted uncomfortably. The book had stirred again, thumping him in the small of the back, grabbing his attention.

He checked behind him. Nothing – apart from the now-darkened buildings.

'That's weird,' he said.

'What's weird?' said Duck, glancing up. She pulled back her hood to see him more clearly.

'The book's behaving strangely again. It was acting like this before the meeting, but why now? It ought to feel safe.'

Cautiously, Blake took the bag from his shoulder and

opened the main compartment – just an inch. He peeked inside.

The book crouched like a trapped animal in the depths of the bag, an agitated shadow that seemed to sink towards the ground, as if drawn by a magnetic force.

'What's wrong with it?' said Duck, peering over his shoulder.

'I'm not sure. It feels like a paperweight or something. A brick. Really heavy.' He frowned. 'It's almost as if it's pulling me down there.'

He indicated the kerb.

'Into the sewer?'

Blake paused, trying to figure it out. 'No. I mean, into the ground,' he said.

Suddenly his heart started to pound and the blood rushed into his head. He felt giddy with excitement. He stood up, unable to sit still. 'I mean,' he said, growing ever more confident, 'Endymion Spring wants us to go where all the books are kept – beneath the library, into the stacks Mum told us about. That's where the book is leading us. The Last Book must be hidden somewhere in the depths of the Bodleian Library!'

Just then their mother appeared, looking pleased with herself.

'So, did you learn anything new?' she asked.

Duck and Blake glanced at each other covertly.

'Oh yeah,' they said.

Later that night, while they slept, the telephone rang. The sound crept up the stairs and tapped on each of their doors, but they were fast asleep. Duck burrowed her head beneath her pillow, dreaming of Alice; Blake twitched uneasily, tormented by another nightmare that pursued him like a shadow through the stacks of the Bodleian Library; and Juliet Winters rolled over on to the empty side of the bed, holding out a hand to answer a phone that went on ringing, unanswered.

Thousands of miles away, Christopher Winters put down the receiver and then, after a moment's thought, picked it up again and dialled a different number.

'City cabs,' responded a voice on the other end.

'Yes, I'd like a ride to the airport.'

Twenty-two

Blake could hardly wait. He'd been awake for several hours, riffling through Endymion Spring, trying to uncover its secrets; but nothing new had appeared. Both he and Duck were up and dressed long before their mother joined them for breakfast, and they nearly ran to the Bodleian Library, pulling her behind them.

'What's got into you?' she asked, struggling to keep up.

Blake and Duck said nothing, but smiled at each other. Despite the fear creeping into his body, Blake tingled with anticipation, egged on by the book, which flickered and jumped in his bag. He passed through the gates of the four-hundred-year-old library into a paved courtyard surrounded by ancient iron-studded doors and tall, fortress-like ramparts. Pushing past a swarm of tourists who had already gathered to take photos of the Earl of Pembroke, a statue standing proudly on its marble plinth, he came to the main entrance. He heaved open the heavy glass doors and walked inside.

He stopped in amazement.

Facing him was a magnificent chamber flooded with an ethereal, unearthly light. Slender columns supported an ornate roof covered with finely chiselled leaves, crests and angels, all carved from the same honey-coloured stone that filled Oxford with gleams of gold. Delicate stone bosses descended from the ceiling like marvellous stalactites.

In the far corner was a large wooden chest, decorated with painted flowers and birds, fortified by an intricate system of locks. Blake guessed that this had once housed the university's treasures, when the library was expanding its collection of books.

He gazed around him in wonder, feeling as though he had been swept back hundreds of years to medieval Oxford. A deep, damp smell of learning seeped into his bones.

To his right, he could see a small gift shop full of bookish knick-knacks and cat-themed souvenirs for the present-day tourists, while to his left was a depository for coats and bags, guarded by the first of two porters. Blake had been careful to press his mother for more informa-tion about the layout of the library. There were two stairwells, he learned, each leading up to the box-shaped reading rooms where the scholars worked. Both were guarded by porters who checked readers' cards on the way in and ensured that none of the university's precious collections went missing on the way out. It wasn't going to be as easy as he thought to sneak in, undetected.

'I'll meet you here in about two hours,' said their mother. 'Then we can do something special. It's early closing today.'

'Take your time,' they replied. 'We won't go far.'

She eyed them warily, her suspicions aroused. 'Well, be careful,' she said, moving towards the south stairwell. She showed the porter her reader's card and ascended the stairs.

While she wound her way up to the Upper Reading Room at the top of the library, Duck and Blake wandered over to the gift shop and pretended to interest themselves in the items for sale. There were book-themed tea towels, book-themed scarves, book-themed ties and even more book-themed books.

Another porter sat behind a small desk in an over-looked corner of the room, close to a second stairwell that disappeared into dimness. The children chose this as their best target. Thankfully, there were plenty of tourists to provide them with cover. Like spies, they leafed through the postcards and posters, all the while watching the porter carefully, trying to figure out the best route to the stacks.

Blake's mother had told him that there was a special lift transporting books up and down from the stacks, all day long, located in the north stairwell. Each time you requested a title from the reading rooms, a mole-like librarian scuttled underground and scurried through the miles of shelves to find it. Out of the corner of his eye, he now glimpsed a rectangular shaft, encased in wire mesh, in the centre of the staircase. This must be the conveyor she had mentioned. His heart galloped with excitement. They were on the right track.

The porter, a surly-looking man with stubbly jowls and hair the colour of cigarette ash, was frowning at his watch, counting down the minutes until his coffee break. A partially filled-in crossword lay on the desk before him.

Occasionally, students and scholars brushed past, unclipping their trousers from their socks and removing hard, beetle-like bicycle helmets from their heads. They showed the porter their library cards and quickly ascended the stairs. Those leaving had to have their bags inspected, just in case they were smuggling out rare books.

After fifteen minutes of waiting, Duck sidled up to Blake. She looked worried.

'How are we going to get inside?' she said. 'He looks ferocious.'

Blake was pretending to study a paperweight with dark medieval letters trapped beneath the glass like insects in amber. He glanced at the porter, who had rolled up his newspaper into a baton and was tapping it against the side of the table. A thermos stood on the desk beside him.

'Maybe there'll be a change in shift soon and we can sneak down then,' he said.

Duck looked unimpressed. 'Is that it?' she sneered. 'Is that your plan?'

'Have you got a better one?'

'How about I ask if I can use the bathroom?' she suggested. 'There must be one somewhere inside.'

She slid her hands between her legs and bobbed up and down.

'Do you need to go?'

'Well, I have to make it look realistic, don't I?' she growled.

'OK,' said Blake, doubtfully. 'It's worth a shot.'

Together, they walked up to the porter, who frowned at them. 'Only readers beyond this point,' he said automatically. He unrolled his newspaper and tried to look busy.

'Is it OK if she uses the bathroom?' asked Blake, pointing at Duck. 'She really has to go.'

The porter pretended not to hear. He read a clue to

his crossword, counted the number of squares and then tried to think of a word that would fit.

'Please,' said Blake. 'She's desperate.'

Duck squeezed her legs together and grimaced.

'The nearest public toilets are located in the bookshop on the opposite side of the street or just around the corner in the Covered Market,' said the porter, without looking up.

A student passed by, flashed him her card and rushed upstairs. Enviously, the children watched her disappear.

'Only readers beyond this point,' said the porter again.

'Come on, mister,' pleaded Duck this time. 'I really need to pee.' A pained expression crossed her face. Even Blake was beginning to believe her.

'Across the street or –'

'– right here if you're not careful!' exploded Duck, raising her voice.

The porter dropped his pen and stared at the children, astonished.

'Look,' said Blake, trying to defuse the situation. 'We're not allowed to leave the library, OK? Our mother's working upstairs and told us to stay put while she consults something. She'll be really annoyed if we're not here when she comes back. Please, it'll only take a minute.'

Duck squeezed her eyes shut, ready to burst. The man squirmed uncomfortably.

'Please!' implored Duck. 'I'll be quick.'

The porter checked his watch and then grumbled, 'Oh, go on, then.' He glanced at his steel thermos. 'Just hurry. My shift ends in a few minutes.'

'I can go with her, if you like,' volunteered Blake.

'Fine. Just be off with you, the pair of you,' snapped the porter. He hurried them towards the stairwell and pointed them in the right direction. 'The women's facilities are upstairs on the left and the gents', if you need them too, young man, are downstairs. Just don't mention this to anyone. And, whatever you do, *don't* go anywhere you're not supposed to. This is more than my job is worth.'

'Thanks, mister,' they chimed together and branched off in separate directions.

One look inside the damp, clammy toilet was enough to persuade Blake to wait for Duck outside.

He paced up and down the dim corridor, just out of sight of the porter, behind the old wire elevator shaft. Occasionally a dark, box-like shadow drifted past, trailing a noose-like cord behind it. Spectral shapes moved up the walls.

Midway across the corridor was a heavy wooden door with several iron bands slatted across its front. It looked ancient and forbidding. A discoloured plaque, adorned with black letters, suggested that something important was hidden on the other side: 'NO EXIT THIS WAY'.

A faint tug in Blake's knapsack, which he had concealed beneath his jacket, just in case the porter decided to search it, convinced him. Like a steady, insistent hand, it pushed him towards the doorway. There was no mistaking it: Endymion Spring was guiding him.

He decided to take a look.

Furtively, he grabbed the large iron handle and twisted it in his hand. He wondered faintly if it would activate an alarm system, but nothing happened. The door swung open quite effortlessly, as though it had been waiting for him all along. A whitewashed passage sloped away from him like an industrial rabbit hole. His heart knocked against his ribs and his legs trembled.

Hearing voices, he hastily shut the door.

Outside, in the gift shop, a young man with auburn hair had replaced the porter on duty and was chatting amiably to a pair of tourists in matching windcheaters, who poked their heads into the stairwell and enquired about the size of the collections.

'Millions upon millions of books,' the porter was saying, 'all shelved beneath the ground . . .'

Blake ducked behind the wire shaft and crossed his

fingers that the other porter had forgotten to mention the two kids in the toilets.

He glanced at his watch. His sister had been gone a long time. What was keeping her?

Just then, he caught the sound of soft, skipping footsteps descending from above.

'What took you so long?' he hissed, when Duck finally appeared. She looked pleased with herself. He pulled her by the elbow, away from the porter.

'You should see upstairs,' she said, unapologetically. 'There's this amazing blue and gold door, and a room behind it full of hundreds of old books. I mean, really, really old books. It's like another world in there. That must be the Duke Humfrey . . . I love it!' She fingered the wire cage and peered up into the gloom.

'Well, come on,' he urged her. 'I've found the way.'

Checking to make sure the coast was clear, he inched open the door and stepped inside.

'Where are we going?'

'Down there.' He pointed down the long white tunnel and felt his nerves tingle again with excitement. Duck followed him into the passageway and he quickly shut the door. It closed with a final, unexpected click.

He gulped. This time they had really done it. They weren't just creeping around the college late at night, but trespassing on private property, breaking who knows how many rules. They would be in serious trouble – if they got caught.

Yet the book was clearly leading him this way. He could feel it flapping and shuffling in his knapsack, wanting to be released.

Endymion Spring was coming home.

Twenty-three

Duck led the way.

'What are you waiting for?' she asked, her voice booming around the claustrophobic corridor.

Blake looked around him, vaguely disappointed. He had expected a dank dungeon full of mouldering books and mummified spiders. This was more like a hospital corridor. Safe and sanitary. Even the floor was coated in a special non-slip substance. Beside them, running along the wall, was an iron cage full of writhing, twisting cables. He wondered what they were for.

At the end of the tunnel was a small steel door and Duck cupped her ear to it like a safe-cracker, listening for any signs of movement on the other side. Hearing none, she inched the door open and peered inside.

Shelves, shelves and more shelves. Shelves led away from them in all directions – like a maze.

Together, they crept into the adjoining room and crouched by a tall metal cabinet. There was hardly a book to be seen. Instead, hundreds of identical grey cardboard folders, each tied with string, stretched into the distance.

Blake gazed around him.

Below them was an iron grille, allowing them to see through on to another floor – and another below that. He let his eyes slip through the cracks. Red and gold volumes glinted dimly on the densely packed shelves like coals in an oven. There was no end to the labyrinth. They were suspended on just one catwalk in a great iron spiderweb. He was already lost.

The dim, dusty air thrummed with machinery. All around him he could hear the regulated clicks of temperature controls, fire detectors and security systems monitoring the collections. And beneath it all was an indistinguishable rumble, a mechanical thunder. An image of a Minotaur, half-bull and half-man, dragging piles of books through the heart of the library, flashed through his mind.

Overhead copper pipes zigzagged across the ceiling like complex plumbing. Occasionally, he thought he heard a papery rustle inside the pipes, as though they were crawling with insects, but he shook off the suspicion. It was probably his imagination. Libraries fought an ongoing war with pests. Surely the Bodleian wouldn't allow any in its stacks.

One doubt, however, remained with him. Was there a CCTV camera somewhere monitoring their actions? He half-expected the porter to clamp hands on his shoulders and pull him out of hiding . . . but nothing happened. No one came. They'd been down here too long. The stacks, it seemed, were unsupervised.

Even so, he remained quite still for a moment, getting his bearings, trying to devise a plan. Duck was running her fingers along the cardboard folders, tempted to open them to see what treasures they contained.

'What do we do now?' she said finally, sidling up to him.

'I don't know.' He watched as a network of tiny red and green lights blinked on a circuitry board above her head. Stop, go, stop, go . . . 'Start looking for the Last Book, I guess.'

'Are you crazy?' She motioned towards the surrounding shelves. 'We don't even know what it looks like. It's impossible!'

'No, it's not,' he raised his voice, unwilling to give up. 'The blank book has led us this far. Now it's going to take us the rest of the way.'

'How?'

He didn't answer. Instead, he shrugged off his jacket

and knapsack, took out the blank book, and caged it in his hands.

Duck was shaking her head. 'What's it going to do? Fly off and show us where to go?'

'Maybe.' Nothing would surprise him at this point. 'Let's just see what happens.'

Gingerly, he lifted one of his hands from the cover. Like a butterfly, the blank book stretched its papery wings and tested the air. Ever so slightly, the pages flickered. A tremulous sound filled the air.

Blake held his breath and listened.

From somewhere on the surrounding shelves came a responding flutter – the scuttling noise he had heard before. This was followed almost immediately by a murmur from high above and then one from the depths below. Pretty soon, the sound was taken up and repeated by hundreds of thousands of books in the library. Blake looked around him, amazed. The air was alive with books! Each volume was passing on its secret: Endymion Spring had returned!

Duck, who had pulled down one of the boxes from a nearby shelf, paused in the process of untying its wrappers to stare at Blake. Then she delved hungrily into the contents of the folder.

A sorry-looking volume with a bruised leather cover was whirring like a frantic insect inside the cardboard container. It made a dry scuttling sound – like a cock-roach – feverishly spinning its pages.

Startled by the noise, she slammed the box shut and immediately retied the string, gagging the book, but not before the blank book in Blake's hands had responded by fanning its pages even more urgently.

Blake could not believe his eyes. The books were communicating with each other.

Suddenly Duck hissed in his ear, 'Ssh! Someone's coming!'

He clutched the book against his chest, muffling it.

'Where?' he asked anxiously, straining to catch any sound over the drum-like march of blood in his ears. 'I don't hear anything.'

Duck held up a finger.

Blake heard it too. A series of short, scuffling footsteps, accompanied by a tuneless whistling.

They crouched even lower and waited.

Eventually a woman with wild, troll-like hair appeared. She was wheeling a trolley loaded with books down an adjacent corridor, stopping occasionally to shelve them. Fortunately for Duck and Blake, she was wearing head-phones that buzzed in her ears like angry bluebottles. No wonder she hadn't heard the commotion.

The children eyed each other nervously as she approached and then breathed a sigh of relief as she passed. Abandoning her still-loaded trolley, she opened the door to the underground passage and disappeared.

As soon as she had gone, Blake released the blank book and, pinning down its pages with his fingers, whispered, 'Please show us where to go, but be quiet, OK? There might be more people in the stacks.'

This time, the paper flickered more slowly and an extra large sheet unfolded in front of him. The vein-like lines he had seen before were visible, but illuminated from within, as though the book were lighting up a path for him to follow.

So this was it! The marks in the paper were a sort of map.

He watched as the lines bent and intersected with each other, branching off in unexpected directions, before finally stopping . . . roughly, he figured, where they were now hiding.

'So?' Duck breathed in his ear, unable to see the route it was revealing.

He said nothing, but waited for the paper to disclose the next part of the path. A glimmer of light grew on the page in front of him and unveiled a new section of the library: a narrow line surrounded by a network of shelves. He began to creep in that direction.

'Hey, where are you going?'

'Just follow me,' he murmured, without turning round. 'I think it's this way.'

The book guided them through a series of intersecting shelves and a long, poorly lit corridor and then down an iron staircase, which clanged underfoot. Warning his sister to keep quiet, Blake passed through a scuffed wooden door at the bottom and entered yet another iron-grilled chamber full of books.

This far underground, the air smelled chalky and stale. Some of the books were coated in a fine layer of dust, as though no one had touched or opened them in ages, while others showed evidence of too much activity: bound with string like mummies to prevent their insides from spilling out. The shelves were made from thick black iron and extended into the distance. Scabs of leather littered the floor like the husks of dead insects.

Duck trailed her fingers along the spines of the books, mapping their path through the ever-deepening library. Inchworms of dust scurried away from her fingertips.

Blake was beginning to lose all sense of direction. For some time, he had been perturbed by a rusty, creaking noise pursuing them through the stacks. The noise grew louder the further they progressed – like a mechanical snake slithering along the ground. He could feel the hairs on his arms standing up like antennae, sending ripples of anxiety all over him.

And then he saw it. A huge motorized beast lurked only a few feet away, in an open area in the depths of the library.

Large, bronze wheels whirled round and round like the tireless cogs of a clock, every now and then propelling thick plastic containers, some loaded with books, along a conveyor belt beside it. The apparatus creaked and moaned, an ancient relic, but was still serviceable: books appeared and disappeared, transported from the stacks up to the reading rooms high above and then back down again.

'Quick!' said Blake, grabbing Duck's wrist and rushing towards a dark channel between two walls of shelves. 'Someone's been here recently.'

A series of footprints, like a dance pattern, lay in the papery dust surrounding the machine.

Heart pounding, Blake ducked between the rows of book-lined shelves. Cords dangled from the strip lights overhead, tapping him on the shoulder, but he opted to proceed in darkness – unobserved. Keeping his head down, he continued along the narrow passage, guided only by the blank book, which emitted a safe, soft glow.

Midway through the tunnel, he stopped. Books towered above him like an invincible army; shelves crushed against him. Yet for some reason the line in the map had reached a dead end.

Duck tugged on his sleeve. 'What's wrong?'

Blake crouched on his heels, looking in both directions. 'I don't know. Maybe the book has lost the way.'

Peering into the gloom, he could see a faint pool of light spilling on to the floor. A bare light bulb blazed above a small wooden desk a short distance ahead. A battered chair with worn wooden arms had been positioned nearby.

Blake caught his breath. There was a black shape – a shadow – hovering close beside it, pressed against the side of a metal cabinet loaded with books.

Duck had seen it too. 'Who's that?' she whispered, her eyes wide open.

Blake shook his head and reached out to hold her hand. Barely able to restrain the impulse to flee, he watched the figure closely.

The shadowy form showed no signs of life. It did not move.

Blake consulted the book. The map very faintly indicated that the path lay beyond this black figure. He could feel the sweat beginning to trickle down his neck. His mouth was dry. He had no choice. He had to edge closer.

Duck clung to the hem of his jacket. 'No, don't,' she whined.

'We have to,' he hissed.

With trembling limbs, he crawled nearer.

The shape materialized into a black coat – a hooded gown dangling from a hook that had been secured to the side of a metal shelving unit.

Blake let out a sigh of relief, but his senses were on heightened alert. Someone had been sitting here recently. The leather seat was dimpled. He ran a finger over it. It was warm!

Wasting no time, he tugged on Duck's sleeve and they raced to the end of the corridor, trying to put as much distance as possible between themselves and whatever spectre had been sitting in that chair.

The book seemed to have regained its focus and pulled them down yet another dark corridor, past a mound of broken furniture and through a series of ever-narrowing shelves, into the heart of the maze. They came face to face with a wall of solid steel. A dead end.

Blake scratched his head, confused.

'I don't get it,' he said. 'The map's pointing straight ahead, but that's impossible.' He re-examined the twists and turns on his map, but they all seemed to be leading to this spot.

'So, what's the problem?' said Duck, moving past him. 'Let's just go through it.'

He turned to her in disbelief. 'How?'

She rolled her eyes. 'Haven't you seen one of these before?' She tapped the steel, which let out a hollow din.

Small circular handles, like steering wheels, had been set into the metal barrier at intervals, making the wall resemble a series of bank vaults.

'It's a collapsible bookcase,' she said. 'To save space. How else do you think libraries cope with the increasing number of books?'

She made a great show of rotating the first handle, which released a catch. A sharp metal sound exploded in the air like a gunshot and he jumped back. Automatically, the other wheels started spinning in a clockwise direction, reminding Blake of a race of scurrying spiders.

Like someone letting out a deep breath, the units eased open, rolling apart on metal tracks. Numerous parallel shelves, each lined with hidden books, opened in front of them – a hall of mirrors, all identical.

'See?' she said, wiping her hands on her yellow coat. 'No problem.'

'OK, so which corridor now?' he asked, irritated.

'I don't know. You're the one with the book.'

He checked the map. Endymion Spring indicated a passageway next to the wall, in the very corner of the library. It was a tight squeeze, but they could just pass through in single file. They joined hands like paper dolls.

Sure enough, at the end of the corridor, obscured by a curtain of cobwebs, was an old, unmarked door. A very old one – barely visible against the stone foundation of the library.

Blake's heart was beating fast; the whole library seemed to shake around him. The book had become agitated, flapping in his hand, almost catapulting itself towards the opening.

Brushing aside the webs, which clung to his skin like candyfloss, Blake cleared the way.

A stone portal with eroded teeth, just like the one guarding the entrance to the Old Library at St Jerome's, faced him. He stared at it in stunned silence. It was the ghost of a door, half-sunken into the floor.

Duck gripped him by the sleeve.

'I don't like this,' she said, her voice a pale whisper. 'I don't think we should go any further.'

Blake's hand was already on the door, propelled there more by the book than his own courage. 'Don't worry. Endymion Spring is with us,' he said, trying to sound brave.

With trembling fingers, he turned the skeletal handle. It twisted in his hand with a brittle, bone-dry click. Very slowly the door opened.

A breath of fetid air rushed out to greet him and a million goose bumps erupted over his skin at once. The passage oozed a damp, cold, earthy scent that clogged his nostrils.

Nervously, he peered into the void.

A spiral staircase descended steeply away from him, curling into darkness. A few moss-mottled stone steps, that was all. He could see no further.

He wanted to run away, but the book was drawing him closer, pulling him irresistibly into the shadow, its silver pallor extinguished by the suffocating dark. He needed more light.

Then he remembered.

Patting the front of his jacket, he soon found what he was looking for: a cylindrical object tucked into one of his pockets. His torch. He'd forgotten to remove it after his incident in the college library.

He grinned and pulled it out, struggling to hold both the book and the light at the same time. Duck's face was a moon of fear beside him.

He turned back to the hole and watched as the thin beam of light tumbled down the ancient steps. Even now, he could not see the bottom.

'Great, another spiral staircase,' he muttered, feeling Duck clinging to his elbow. Her eyes were wet.

With a shiver, he stepped into the shadow. It was like wading into a moonlit pond; the dark came up to his waist, like very cold water.

'Don't!' squeaked Duck, her voice small and fragile. 'I don't want to go down there. It's not funny any more.'

She hung on to him tightly, pinching his skin.

'Come on,' he grumbled. 'We have to!'

The book was dragging him down, pulling at him like a weight. He was sinking into darkness.

'It'll be OK,' he tried to reassure her. 'I'll protect you.'

His voice cracked and he fought hard to keep back the fear scratching at his throat. He reached out to support her, but her sweaty hand eluded his.

'No, I don't want to,' she said again, backing away. Tears slid down her cheeks.

'Look,' he said. 'I don't like this any more than you do, but we have no choice. The Last Book is nearby; I can feel it. It *wants* us to find it.'

'I'm scared.'

'I know, I am too,' he confessed; 'but I swear I won't let anything happen to you.' The darkness was seeping up his legs, chilling him. His teeth were rattling. They had to keep moving. 'We'll be OK so long as we stick together.'

Duck's bottom lip quivered, but eventually she nodded. She edged closer to the stairwell like a little kid dipping her foot in a pool. She clung to the hood of Blake's jacket, nearly choking him.

Together they stepped into darkness.

Twenty-four

The staircase spiralled steeply down before it gave way to an uneven, earthen floor. A damp mossy smell filled the air. For a moment it seemed to Blake that they had stumbled into a graveyard, a reliquary for dead or forgotten books. Endymion Spring's bones might be hidden nearby, he thought with a shiver.

Apart from a frail shaft of light falling like a veil from the pages of the open book in his hand, the chamber was thick with shadow. He swept the beam of his torch around the room, chasing away layers of darkness. Ancient pillars supported a low, rounded ceiling from which cobwebs dangled like sticky chandeliers. All around him were open chests, like plundered tombs. Rudimentary shelves lined the walls, but these had cracked and splintered centuries ago. Most of their contents had spilled to the ground.

Everywhere Blake looked there were books: ghostly

355

white volumes in plain wrappers that gradually began to emit a faint silver glow – like the pages in Endymion Spring. Quires of paper filled the chests, while heavy reams, too large to pick up, lay on worn plinths, shrouded in dust. It was more like a crypt than a library.

Black doorways gaped at intervals, ready to receive them. Blake peered into the deeper, darker rooms, his breath coming in ragged gasps. They were surrounded by a honeycomb of cell-like chambers.

Duck had lifted one of the large folios. 'It's blank,' she muttered as she let it fall. Instantly, a dusty detonation filled the neighbouring rooms and a lisp of paper passed through the air. *Endymion Spring*, the sheets seemed to whisper in an unearthly refrain.

Blake whirled round, startled. His eyes were dark, his pupils dilated.

Shakily, he held out the blank book in front of him and used its lantern-like light to guide him. It was more effective than his torch; it picked up a trail of scintillating paper on the floor.

Duck followed, unconsciously leaving fingerprints like bird tracks on the books and shelves she touched.

The rooms were all alike: lined with blank books that seemed to be waiting for someone to fill them with words. The whole library appeared to be watching, waiting for Blake to find the Last Book. He felt incredibly small and insignificant in comparison. He shrank against the walls.

As if responding to his growing sense of uneasiness, the book jittered in his hand and fell to the ground. Its comforting light went out. The room was plunged into sudden darkness.

Duck's fingers clawed at him. 'Blake!' she screamed, her voice reverberating against the shelves in a shrill shriek.

Frantically, Blake swung his torch around the chamber, trying to locate the blank book.

There it was. A small square of leather lying against the endless reams of fine white paper. He reached down to pick it up.

His heart leaped into his throat. The book opened not to the map he had been following earlier, but to the black partition in the centre of the volume.

The ghostly message was still there, but it had changed – ever so slightly. His blood ran cold.

His torchlight trembled over the awful words:

I am waiting

Suddenly, the shadows seemed more menacing, more terrifying, and he began to run.

Blindly, he dashed through the surrounding rooms, no longer following the map in the book, but a path of his own devising. 'Come on,' he yelled, grabbing Duck's hand.

'What did the book say?' she squealed, struggling to keep up.

He didn't answer, but pulled her after him, rushing headlong into the darkness. He made desperate detours, turning first one way and then another, past rows of silent, watchful waiting, books. His torchlight scrabbled over the walls.

The riddle he had seen a couple of days ago flashed through his mind:

The Sun must look the Shadow in the Eye
Then forfeit the Book lest one Half die . . .

Its meaning seemed even more sinister down here in the dark depths of the library.

Gradually, there was a change in their surroundings. A luminous chamber shone just ahead of them – a beacon in the distance. Or a trap. Blake didn't have time to think. The blood screeched through his body. He raced towards the light.

A faint tittering noise, like rustling leaves, started up again around him, urging him on, and his pulse quickened. This must be the way. The books were communicating with each other.

He burst into the light-filled room and came to an abrupt halt. There was no other exit. A circle of book-lined walls surrounded him. Only a deep hole in the ground opened at the centre of chamber: the source of all the light.

Shielding his eyes, he tiptoed closer and peered down . . .

Another library, a whole universe of reading, stretched elastically beneath the floor. Books filled the shimmering space: identical volumes in plain white wrappers fitted on to concentric shelves that spiralled down the edges of the shaft like a helix, connected by long, thin ladders. There appeared to be no end to the number of volumes contained in this bottomless well.

He recoiled from the sight. His head spun. How could he possibly find the Last Book among so many?

Endymion Spring was quiet in his hand, as though it had reached its destination. What was he to do?

The books flickered around him expectantly.

And then he noticed something. A long way down the narrow chute was a slight shadow, a barely visible seed of darkness in the gleaming wall of light.

'There's something down there,' he told Duck. 'A black space. I think there's a book missing. I'm going to take a look.'

Duck panicked. 'No! Don't go!' She gripped him tightly by the back of his knapsack. 'I can't go with you. I'm scared.'

'Come on, I have no choice!'

'Yes, you do! You don't have to do this! We could pretend you never found it. We could turn back.'

Blake hesitated, then Endymion Spring moved in his hand and urged him that little bit closer to the lip of the well. It wanted him to go down into the stack of books. It was guiding him.

Blake glanced again at the small, unassuming volume in his hand. Its faithful glimmer of light gave him renewed confidence. Endymion Spring had brought him here for a reason. Jolyon had told him that many people had searched for the Last Book, but failed. This was *his* chance. He felt sure the Last Book was nearby – almost within reach. He had never been so close to achieving something amazing in his life before.

'I've got to try,' he said aloud, his mind made up.

Pushing Duck aside, he quietly took off his knapsack and jacket and placed them on the paper-strewn ground beside the hole. Then he slipped the blank book between his T-shirt and the waistband of his jeans and slid his torch into his pocket. He could feel the restless flutter of Endymion Spring's paper against his skin – an additional heartbeat.

'I'm going to find the Last Book,' he said. 'You can watch me from up here, OK?'

Duck danced uneasily on the spot.

'Just don't go anywhere. Wait until I get back.'

She fixed him with her large, fearful eyes, but said nothing.

'Promise!' he barked.

She nodded obediently and backed away from the hole.

Blake took a deep breath. His mind focused on the sliver of shadow far below – and what it might contain – he stepped towards the threshold of the well and reached with his toe for the first rung of the ladder. His shoe caught a firm foothold and he swung himself over.

Duck started to moan.

'It's all right,' he told her one last time. 'I'll be back soon.'

Gripping the sides of the ladder, he descended slowly, taking tiny steps, refusing to look down. The rungs were placed close together, nearly tripping him. It was as though they had been constructed in a far-off century: the wood was uneven, knotted with whorls of bark – more like branches than proper footholds. He continued carefully, grasping the vine-bound slats in his tight fists. His entire body was shaking.

Every now and then, he paused to make sure that Duck was all right at the top of the well. Her head was just visible: a small yellow sun, eclipsed by the growing wall of books.

He climbed still lower, ignoring the fear rattling at his nerves. His fingers ached; his muscles were tense; and his teeth set in a determined grimace. Endymion Spring juddered against his belt, encouraging him downwards. He glanced at the dark space below. It was getting nearer.

All around him the waiting books whispered like leaves in a breeze. Curious, he picked one from the surrounding shelves and, monkeying his arm around the ladder to improve his leverage, flipped through its pages. They were not blank, as he had suspected, but contained a vast number of words, all written in a transparent silver light, as if frozen or suspended in ice. There appeared to be no end to the number of books: made from the same soft, enchanted paper as Endymion Spring, all waiting for some reader's imagination to unleash the writing inside. A trapdoor swung open in his mind. He suddenly comprehended the concept of infinity.

He looked down. A few feet away was the shadowy crevice he had glimpsed from above, the space that divided the limitless wall of books. At first, he thought it might be a black leather-bound notebook, a book different from the others, but now he realized that it was a small opening – a gap in the heart of the library. The blank book seemed to be guiding him towards it.

He slipped down the next few rungs, almost falling, until he was on a level with the black hollow on the shelf. He could feel Endymion Spring urging him closer, its irresistible desire to be reunited with the other books drawing him nearer. He removed the blank book from its position in his belt. Part of him didn't want to let go, but as he inched his hand towards the available space no force on earth could have stopped it. Endymion Spring propelled itself between the other volumes, a perfect fit.

The other books, which had been lisping quietly, suddenly became silent. The air trembled with expectation. The whole library appeared to be waiting for just this moment, as if the stability of the well and its tower of books hung in the balance.

All of a sudden he became aware of a shiver in the air, a slight quiver of paper. Then, suddenly, in a blinding blizzard of books, the volumes on the shelves started to whirl round him, sucked into a maelstrom of paper. They whipped past his head, brushed against his shoulders and nipped his arms and his legs, slashing him with paper cuts, jettisoning themselves towards the small space on the shelf where moments before he had placed Endymion Spring.

He screamed in terror and pressed his head against the rung of the ladder to protect himself, fearing something had gone disastrously wrong, closing his eyes against the snowstorm of spinning, spiralling pages. He thought he heard a high-pitched shriek from above, but the din in his ears was near-deafening and all he could do was hang on as the books flew past his face, flapped round his body and got caught in the whirlwind of paper.

And then, like the aftermath of a violent rain shower, the air was suddenly quiet, refreshed. Only a few loose scraps of paper dripped into the surrounding silence. The ladder wobbled beneath him.

Tentatively, he opened his eyes. The darkness was overpowering. With fumbling fingers, he reached into his pocket, took out his torch, and shone the light around him.

The brown battered book – Endymion Spring – was still on its shelf, as though nothing had happened. Except, Blake noticed, sliding his light up and down the sheer sides of the well, the other books had gone. The shaft was as barren as a mountain after a landslide.

Carefully, he reached out to touch the remaining volume. Was this it? Was this the legendary Last Book?

The name 'Endymion Spring' was still visible on the scabbed leather cover.

He edged his fingers round the spine and gently pulled it towards him. Recognizing his touch, the book immediately eased into his hands. The broken clasp coiled tightly round his little finger and the same nervous buzz of excitement rushed into his blood. Ignoring the pain in the crook of his arm, he opened it.

The pages were no longer blank, but covered in minute panels of words that opened like invisible doors the moment his eyes fell on them, leading him into different stories, different languages . . . each stairwell of paper taking him on a new adventure. Every now and then they froze, stopping in mid-sentence, on the verge of revealing an amazing truth, and he leaped to a new entry. The amount of information was overwhelming. Each page was divided into an infinite number of thin, indestructible membranes.

And then his heart stopped. Turning over one last luminous page, Blake found what he most dreaded: the black page. It was still there, an ominous bookmark at the heart of the volume. Compared to the wonderful whiteness of the surrounding paper, the purity of its words, this shadow was a chilling, inescapable void – a black hole sucking all the goodness of the book into its absent soul. And at the top of the page was the torn corner.

There was still one piece of the book missing.

All of a sudden, Blake remembered Duck. He looked up. There was no sign of her at the top of the well.

Breaking into a cold sweat, he clutched the volume in his hand and scrambled up the ladder as quickly as he could, climbing past the empty shelves, desperately trying to retain his hold on the uneven wooden struts. He slid, exhausted, over the edge of the pit, panting hard.

'Duck,' he whispered. 'I've found it! I've found the Last Book! But it's not what we thought . . .'

He stopped. There was no response.

'Duck,' he said again, poking his torchlight into the shadows. 'You can come out now.'

The room, illuminated only by the faint glow of the Last Book, was empty. He scoured the remaining corners with his torch. Nothing. The books on the shelves and the paper on the floor had vanished. Only a disturbed trail of dust lay on the ground.

He picked up his knapsack and jacket, which had been flung to the far side of the room, and put them on. He started to hunt for his sister.

'Duck! Where are you?' he called, his voice a fragile whisper in the dark immensity of the library. Frantically, he checked the other chambers. He found the trail of fingerprints Duck had left on some of the empty shelves and followed them, but there was no sign of her bright yellow raincoat anywhere.

She was gone.

A few minutes later came a muffled explosion from above: a door slamming far away. The noise echoed through the underground chambers like a popped paper bag.

Duck!

Blake raced through the surrounding rooms until he came to the tight, twisting staircase up to the next level of the library. He forced his legs up the sunken stone steps, scraping at the walls with his fingers. He ended up face-to-face with the collapsible bookcase, which someone had hastily, but ineffectually, closed. A pile of books blocked his way.

'Duck!' he yelled.

No response.

He scrambled over the heap of fallen volumes and battled his way through the narrow partition of shelves, scratching his elbows against the sharp metal edges. Pushing the cabinets aside with all his strength, he emerged on the other side.

The wreckage of furniture was visible nearby and beyond it the battered chair with the light bulb blazing over the desk. Blake sprinted towards them, then slowed to a crawl as he caught sight of the shadow against the wall.

The black cloak was gone. In its place hung Duck's yellow raincoat, dangling like a lifeless body from the hook.

His heart lurched.

The raincoat looked so small and alien without Duck's cheerful form to fill it and he picked it up uneasily. It felt so light.

Then he looked down. A coiled notebook lay open on the desk in front of him. A scribbled message waited just for him. The words wobbled before his eyes:

13:00, Duke Humfrey's Library.
Bring the book.

There was no mistaking the author of the message. It was the Person in Shadow.

Twenty-five

There was no time to ask the Last Book for help. A bell shrilled above him, ripping through the stacks, and Blake checked his watch. He had less than fifteen minutes. The library must be closing.

Duke Humfrey . . . Duke Humfrey . . .

He was sure he'd heard the name before, but where? *Where?*

The large machine responsible for sending books up to the reading rooms had grown silent. Unsupervised, its cogs and gears had creaked to a standstill, somehow eerier now they had been suspended than when they were alive. A deathly hush filled the air. Somewhere far above, it suddenly occurred to him, his mother would be packing up her work, completely unaware of the danger her children were in below.

Duke Humfrey . . .

Blake started to run.

Rows of leather volumes gave way to modern textbooks, which turned into books with bright dust jackets, as he streaked through the stacks. Ahead he could see an endless line of grey cardboard folders. He was on the right track.

Spying a wrought-iron staircase in the corner, he sprinted towards it and clambered up the tight corkscrew of steps, his feet ringing out on the cold metal.

And then he remembered: *Duke Humfrey* . . . Duck had mentioned it after visiting the bathroom. It was somewhere up the main stairwell. He knew where to go!

Bursting through the brightly lit tunnel, which connected the entrance of the Bodleian to the stacks, he emerged into the dim corridor just outside the gift shop. The main entrance had been sealed off, closed for another day, and the walls echoed with the lonely sound of his footsteps. No one was around to help him.

He worked his way up the deserted staircase, climbing the wide wooden stairs. Each step filled him with a chilly sense of foreboding. Would Duck be all right?

The sight of two regal blue and gold doors, partially open, brought him to a standstill near the top of the stairwell. *The Duke Humfrey Library* . . . A fusty smell of learning seeped from the darkness within.

The chamber was almost exactly as Duck had described it. Thousands of ancient volumes sat on the wooden shelves, set behind thick balustrades. Sturdy ladders climbed to a further tier of books, all crammed beneath a decorated ceiling, covered with scrolls of painted flowers and majestic crests. It looked like a chapel devoted exclusively to reading.

A porter in a navy-blue suit was clearing a desk in the middle of the room, preparing to lock up. Blake paused on the threshold of the library and then, as soon as the man's back was turned, slid into position behind a banister directly opposite. He squeezed himself between the railing and a bench, which he hoped would shield him from view.

On the underside of the shelves above him gleamed a constellation of stars, gilded on to a chequered background of red and green squares. Otherwise, the room was thick with shadow. He checked his watch. Only three minutes left. His pulse throbbed wildly as the seconds ticked away.

Very carefully, he unzipped his bag and put both the Last Book and Duck's jacket, which he had rescued from downstairs, inside. He then sealed the bag and threaded his arms through the straps and gripped them tightly to his back. He would not surrender anything until he knew she was safe.

Whistling to himself, the porter fetched his keys from the desk, locked the far doors and then started towards Blake's hiding place. Blake shrank even lower and held his breath. He was shaking all over.

The porter took a last look around the closed-up library, then pulled the doors shut and locked them behind him with a prison-like finality.

Silence fell.

The room was eclipsed in darkness.

All Blake could do was wait.

Minutes dragged by, agonizing in their slowness.

Then, when Blake could stand the suspense no longer, he heard a metallic quiver thrum the air as an invisible clock chimed the hour. This was followed almost immediately by a tiny, scratching noise at the opposite end of the room.

He raised his head, alert. A key whispered in the lock.

The door opened – just a little – and a shadowy form slid into the room. The hooded figure was dressed entirely in black.

Blake barely breathed.

The person glanced round the murky room and then drifted on soundless feet towards his hiding place.

Blake closed his eyes, not daring to look. He hoped that by remaining perfectly still, by shutting out the outside world, he, too, might disappear.

The shadow drifted nearer.

One thing was clear. Duck was not with the Person in

Shadow. They were alone in the ancient library. He had been tricked.

Crouched like a sprinter, he considered making a mad dash for freedom, hoping to summon help from outside; but then he felt the floorboards beside him stiffen slightly and a black shape fell over him.

A gloved hand slid silently over the railing near his shoulder and grabbed him by the wrist.

'Hello, Blake.'

The chilly female voice sent shivers up and down his spine. He knew instantly who it was. He looked up.

'Isn't this a surprise?'

Diana Bentley greeted him with a cold smile.

Blake couldn't bring himself to respond. The sound of her voice, the touch of her glove, both seemed icy now, despite the special butterfly clasp she always wore as decoration and the dark woollen cloak she had draped over her shoulders.

Blake blinked, confused.

The butterfly had singed wings, like burnt paper.

'You should mind your knees,' she said, pulling him to his feet. 'They'll get dirty.'

He looked down at the hard wooden floor and dumbly rubbed his jeans, which were patched with dust. His clothes were torn and filthy.

'You poor boy,' she murmured. 'You really are in

trouble. Sneaking into the Bodleian like this. What will your mother think?'

'She doesn't know,' he said miserably, then bit his tongue.

Diana observed him with mock sympathy. 'Ah, I see. You're on your own.'

Blake grimaced, realizing his mistake. 'Where's Duck?' he barked.

'All in good time,' she said. 'First, where is the book?'

'I don't know what you mean.'

She locked his arm in a tight, vicious grip and wrenched it behind his back. He yelped, surprised by her strength.

'Be careful,' she warned. 'You don't want to make things worse than they already are.'

Her words brought the gravity of his situation home. He stopped struggling.

'The book,' she said again. 'Where is it?'

She levered his arm slowly upwards and he gasped as hot spears of pain shot across his shoulder.

'My mother,' he managed at last, between clenched teeth. 'She'll be furious if we don't turn up soon. She'll go to the police . . . and . . . aah! . . . tell them we're missing.'

He risked a look at Diana, but she seemed unfazed by the remark. She eyed him with steely composure. 'What's in your bag, Blake?'

He squirmed and she jacked up his arm one notch. He winced.

Blake could feel her fingers spidering along his back and wriggled to prevent her from discovering the book inside his knapsack. Once again, she tightened her grip on his arm and he fought back tears. It was as if her desire to obtain the book had given her superhuman strength – and ruthlessness.

'Of course,' she said, breathing softly into his ear, 'there would be no reason to go on inconveniencing your mother – or Duck – if we came to a mutual agreement.'

The image of Duck's lifeless yellow coat, stuffed hastily into his knapsack, filled Blake with guilt. All of this was his fault. He'd got obsessed with the book – to the point of abandoning her. Still, he couldn't help it: the book was *his*. Endymion Spring had chosen him. For hundreds of years scholars had searched for what he, Blake Winters, had found. And the Person in Shadow – Diana – wanted it for all the wrong reasons.

Slowly, she tilted his chin towards her, so that he could see into her cold, grey eyes. They were as hard and unflinching as stone. 'Where is the Last Book, Blake?'

His heart cowered inside him. He had no choice but to hand over the book to save his sister. The sinister riddle from two nights ago had warned him as much:

The Sun must look the Shadow in the Eye
Then forfeit the Book lest one Half die . . .

He started to shiver uncontrollably.

'I'll help you on one condition,' he said finally, gritting his teeth. The words tasted like ash in his mouth.

'You have a condition?' She almost laughed. 'And what might that condition be?' She considered him like a cat toying with a bird.

'I've hidden the book,' he lied. 'I'll take you to it, but only once I know my sister is OK. I need to see her first.'

Diana sounded bored. 'Do you really expect me to believe that?'

Blake was thinking fast. 'You need me to read from it,' he said quickly.

His response seemed to trigger a reaction, for she regarded him less certainly for a moment.

'I want to see Duck,' he said again.

'Enough!' cried Diana, losing her patience. 'I'll take you to see your odious little sister, but then you'll hand over the book. No funny games!'

Still gripping his arm tightly behind his back, she marched him towards the far door. He fought desperately to come up with a plan, a way of escape, but the pain shooting across his shoulder blocked out any coherent pattern of thought. He was terrified. All he could do for now was obey.

'One careless move and I assure you your sister will suffer the consequences,' lisped Diana behind him, almost biting off his ear.

Diana ushered Blake through the blue and gold doors and sharply to the right, up a final flight of steps to the Upper Reading Room, nestled beneath the roof of the library. The thin double doors were open a fraction and she guided him into a large room full of study carrels and hard wooden chairs.

The air was stuffy and dim, like a museum. Frescoed faces watched them from a frieze above the book-lined shelves; yet the ancient scholars who had helped to shape the university's illustrious history now turned a blind eye to his predicament. There was no one to help him.

The blinds on the windows had been pulled down, shutting out the outside world, and the cork linoleum deadened their footsteps. There was no sign of Duck anywhere – neither here in the vast reading room, nor around the corner, where Blake encountered yet more tables, followed by a series of computer terminals and a central desk, where library staff presumably distributed books.

Hidden in the corner was a thin cream door that led up to the tall square tower that formed the principal peak on the library's prickly skyline. Diana motioned him towards it.

Another spiral staircase corkscrewed away from him – this time rising to what must be the very top of the library. What was she going to do? Throw him off the roof?

She forced him inside.

'Where are we going?' he asked nervously as she locked the door behind them and followed him up the stairs. The steps were tight and treacherous; his legs trembled. The bottom was a long way down.

Diana responded by prodding him sharply in the back with the tip of her key. He kept going, marching upwards – past two thin lancet windows and a tiny wooden door.

Blake's eyes narrowed with suspicion. 'Where's Duck?' he asked.

His question was answered by a frantic hammering on the other side of the door.

'Duck!' he cried, leaping towards it. He grasped the handle and pulled. 'I'm here! I've come to get you out!'

The door was locked and would not budge. His sister was thrashing even more urgently now she could hear him. He knew she must be terrified. Duck hated confined spaces.

He turned to Diana, enraged. She was dangling a

precious silver key from her fingertip. He lunged to grab it, but she deftly closed her hand in a fist.

'What's wrong with her?' he hollered. 'Why can't she speak?'

'I took the liberty of gagging your sister's mouth,' replied Diana curtly. 'She was driving me to distraction.'

Blake could not contain his anger. 'Let her out!' he screamed. 'She can hardly breathe in there! If anything happens to her, I'll –'

'You'll what?' asked Diana savagely, shoving him forwards. His ankle twisted and he fell, his knee catching the edge of a sharp stone step. He cried out in pain. Remorseless, Diana pulled him to his feet and pushed him further up the twisting staircase.

'I'll come back . . .' he called out to Duck, his voice cracking.

They came to a tall door with 'UNIVERSITY ARCHIVES' engraved above it in the stone. A brass plaque on a central panel read: 'DR D. BENTLEY, ARCHIVIST'.

Blake looked behind him, surprised. 'You work here?' he asked.

Diana frowned. 'Naturally. Do you think Giles is the only person in a position of power?'

She unlocked the door and shoved him inside.

Blake stumbled against a desk in the middle of the

spacious room and fell to the floor, winded. Dazed, he took in his surroundings. Four enormous windows, partially obscured by large wooden cupboards, provided spectacular views of the surrounding domes and spires. A choir of angelic figures stood on top of one of the nearby buildings, playing their silent instruments, while a statue of blindfolded Justice turned her back to him on the other side of the glass.

He raced to one of the giant windows and tried to flag down help from the people in the street far below. Tiny figures, no more than matchstick men, marched back and forth. The window had no latch and all he could do was hammer on the glass with his fist. The muffled sound did not travel far.

'Had enough?' asked Diana, behind him. 'I have kept my part of the bargain. Now I suggest you keep yours.'

He turned to face her. She was calmly inspecting a row of books in one of the cupboards.

'These are my favourites,' she said, indicating several volumes, as large as Bibles, fastened with iron clasps. 'I keep them up here, so that no one – not even Giles – can touch them.' She stroked the dimpled black surfaces with her fingers. 'They're books that date back to the foundation of the library.'

Blake didn't respond. His eyes dashed to the door, which Diana nudged to with her foot.

'Don't even think about it,' she said. 'You can't go far. Besides, I have all the keys between you, your sister and freedom. The only way out of here is to give me what I want.'

'I told you I don't have the Last Book,' he said defiantly. 'I couldn't even find it.'

'Oh, I doubt that,' said Diana with a knowing smile. 'You were chosen.'

She slowly advanced towards him and he took two steps back.

'Give it to me,' she said.

Blake flushed. 'No,' he defied her again and involuntarily tightened his grip on the straps of his knapsack. He backed into a glass cabinet full of hand-written documents sealed with flattened dollops of red wax, like squashed bugs. Two more lines from Endymion Spring's riddle floated unbidden into his mind:

The Lesion of Darkness cannot be healed
Until, with Child's Blood, the Whole is sealed . . .

His eyes landed on a sleek, silver paperknife placed crosswise on a pile of unopened correspondence on the desk.

'If you want the book so badly,' he lashed out, 'why don't you come over here and take it?' His heart felt like a bomb ticking down inside him. At any moment, it might explode.

'Yes, I suppose I could,' said Diana, without enthusiasm. He noticed her long white gloves and panicked, realizing that she had been careful not to leave any fingerprints behind. He could imagine her sliding them around his neck and throttling him.

Sensing the direction of his gaze, she slowly removed one of the gloves. She peeled back the smooth white material and pulled it from her fingers. Blake gasped. All of the fingernails on her left hand were black.

'It's like Professor Jolyon,' he blurted out.

'Oh, this?' she said calmly, assessing her bruised nails. 'Yes, I was snubbed by the book, too. Just like Jolyon.'

'Do you mean you're in on this together?' he asked, his mind working furiously. A recollection of a dark-haired Diana flirting with the youthful Jolyon in the Libris Society photograph flashed in his memory.

Diana was appalled by the insinuation. 'Heavens, no. Jolyon and I haven't agreed on anything since the foundation of the Libris Society. However, we are *both* interested in the Last Book and would love to get our hands on it . . . for different reasons.'

She watched his face register surprise. 'Jolyon isn't such an angel either,' she said coldly. 'Disappointing, isn't it?'

'I don't understand,' he said.

She reached for a piece of powdered confectionery in a crystal bowl on her desk. Turkish delight. She bit into it with relish.

'I'm disappointed in you, Blake. Are you really so dim?'

He nodded; it was safer to keep her talking.

'Oh, very well,' she muttered, brushing a smattering of icing sugar from her lips. 'Jolyon broke the clasp on the blank book a long time ago, soon after the Libris Society was formed. He was convinced he could find the Last Book without any help from the rest of us. Of course, he was mistaken. He tried to steal the book from George Psalmanazar, who had found the book originally, but the clasp broke off and stabbed him in the thumb, branding him a traitor.'

Blake inhaled deeply. His mind was spinning. No wonder the professor had seemed so agitated when he'd first mentioned Endymion Spring at the college dinner. No wonder he'd been unwilling to confess his involvement in the past . . .

Diana glanced at her blackened fingernails. 'Of course, I rather fancied him more after that,' she said drily, clearly enjoying pulling off the scabs of Blake's delusion, 'but he became so incredibly penitent afterwards. It was tiresome. He vowed never to go near the book again.'

Her voice filled with scorn. 'He became boring.'

'And what did you do?' asked Blake, eyeing her fearfully. 'What turned your fingernails black?'

The smile died instantly on her face. 'After the book rejected Jolyon, I had to connive my way closer to that ugly wretch, George.' She spat out the name with distaste. 'I could tell he was going to hide the blank book and I needed to lay my hands on it before the key to the Last Book eluded my grasp forever. It was my only chance – or so I thought.'

Her eyes gleamed and her fingers clawed the air. 'It was almost in my hands,' she said, reliving the experience, 'but then that wretch saw what I was doing and slammed the book shut on my fingers. The clasp stung me! It was sheer agony! Yet I managed to hold on to one section of the book and ripped that from the volume.'

'The section Psalmanazar gave me,' Blake whispered to himself.

Diana was rubbing the tips of her charred fingers. 'I didn't know his strength,' she remarked. 'He wrestled even that away from me, unwilling to let a single part of the book escape, saying that even the tiniest scrap of paper held the strongest magical power, that the Last Book would never work without all the pieces.'

'But why go to so much trouble?' asked Blake. 'It's only a book. Surely, it can't be that powerful.'

All the while she talked, he was inching closer to the desk and the temptingly sharp paperknife.

Diana snarled at him. 'Foolish boy! You have no idea what the book contains! It is the key to everything you've ever desired. All the power and riches in the world!' Her face contorted, as if possessed by greed. 'The book demands an innocent to unleash its words, but only a person with true ambition can fully know their worth. Johann Fust knew as much . . . as did Horatio Middleton, Jeremiah Wood, Lucius St Boniface de la Croix and all the others who have searched for the book for years.'

As she said this, a ray of sunlight broke through the clouds and transformed the surrounding spires and domes to a shimmer of burnished gold; but its warmth stopped short at the window. Blake had turned ice-cold. He recognized those names. They had been staring at him from the walls of St Jerome's College ever since he arrived in Oxford. They were the ancient scholars in the portraits, all clutching their sacred, unidentified leather books, feeding on him with their eyes.

As if in answer, Diana withdrew a thin black book from her pocket and waved it in the air. He saw a shadowy *F* stamped into its unsightly cover and realized with a start that it was the *Faustbuch* he had found in the second-hand bookshop.

'That book . . .' he said, confused.

'Yes, you really were most considerate, finding this for me,' she said with a devious smile. 'The *Faustbuch* holds the key to the entire history of Endymion Spring. Not only how the Last Book came to Oxford, but also how to see inside it, to decipher its riddles and make use of its power. Of course, it's rather ruined now – it's been handed down for centuries, ever since the anonymous author first penned it – but it really has come in useful . . .'

Blake shivered. His eyes returned to the desk and the paperknife, which disappeared into Diana's fingers. She was regarding him steadily.

'Did you really think you could outsmart me?' she said. 'You're just a boy. Now hand over the book.'

Knees quivering, Blake crabbed sideways to the window.

Diana followed him, balancing the tip of the paperknife against her fingers. His skin prickled with fright, but she merely placed the knife and the *Faustbuch* on top of one of the cabinets, out of reach.

'Tell me,' she said. 'Have the pages come alive? Have the words emerged from hiding?'

He stiffened as she drew up beside him and prised his chin in her hands. Her fingers were long and cold, like icicles, except they didn't melt.

Snake-like, she peered into his eyes. Blake glanced away.

From far below came the sound of crowds milling in the street. A dog barked somewhere. The noise caught his ear and he checked the window. The glint of an iron fire escape leading up the side of the tower flashed in the corner of his eye. Perhaps, after all, there was a way out . . . He wanted to run, but felt trapped by the cold hands on his face, the fierce glare of her eyes.

'Show me the book!' roared Diana and flung him furiously towards the centre of the room. He collided heavily with the desk and slid to the floor. A throbbing pain cleaved his chest and a strange iron tang filled his mouth. Blood.

Defenceless, he watched as she stooped over him and casually plucked the bag from his shoulders, throwing it on the table.

Like a beast ripping into prey, she tore open the main compartment and cast Duck's coat aside. Then she found what she was looking for: the unspectacular brown leather book at the bottom of the bag. *Endymion Spring*. She dipped in her hands to retrieve it and whisked them away, as though stung.

'It bit me!' she howled with rage.

Blake gazed at her, his vision blurry, barely comprehending what was going on.

She drew on her long white glove and tried again to

withdraw the book. Succeeding this time, she laid it care-fully on the table.

She stared at the cover closely – Endymion Spring's name was still inscribed on the leather in rounded letters – and then began to turn the pages with the tips of her gloves, impatient to garner their knowledge.

'But that's not right!' she hollered, lifting her face from the book. 'Why, you deceptive little beast, what have you done?'

She grabbed him by the collar and pulled him sharply to his feet. Dazzling lights popped and fizzed before his eyes. She slammed her fist on the table.

Speechless with surprise, Blake forced himself to focus on the page in front of him. Apart from the black section in the middle of the book, the remaining pages had reverted to their natural, unsullied white. There were no words to be seen.

'I don't understand,' he began. 'They were –'

'Well, they've gone now!' screamed Diana.

He blinked again. As his eyes adjusted to the glowing whiteness of the paper, he realized that the words had not disappeared, but were recoiling into the book like snails into their shells. They were still there, but only for those with eyes to see them.

The deception, he feared, would not last long. Already, he could see a faint shadow of ink leaching through the paper, as though all of the books and the marvellous secrets they contained would soon reappear.

Thinking quickly, he said, 'It's not yet complete. I tried to tell you. Something's wrong.' He hoped the statement would deter her.

'Yes, but what?'

Presuming he had outwitted her, he added more confidently, 'There's still a section of the book missing. It won't work without that.'

He turned to the black page and showed her the torn corner. 'See?'

Diana hissed with fury, but then a smile slowly returned to her lips. 'Ah yes, how very foolish of me,' she said. Her mouth curled into a sneer. 'I can fix that.'

Unclasping the butterfly pin from her cloak, she carefully plucked the paper wings from its body and lined them up with the book. They were a perfect fit. The delicate black paper fluttered with life.

'But . . .' Blake stammered.

She smiled at him victoriously. 'I didn't say George was successful, did I? I managed to steal just one corner of one page, which I kept as a little reminder of what I most desired: the Last Book!'

Blake stared at her, appalled. Paying no attention, she pressed the blackened wing of paper on to the page in front of her and he watched helplessly as it began to reattach itself to the book with an invisible seam. Like a dark snowflake, the ash-like paper melted into the volume and the pages inside started to spin. The book shone with a fierce white light.

'Yes, imagine my surprise when this little slip of paper alerted me the other day to the fact that someone had rediscovered Endymion Spring,' she said. 'It seemed too good to be true. All I had to do was look for someone sufficiently . . . idealistic . . . to draw Endymion Spring out of hiding. I was quite pleased to make your acquaintance and then to see you slipping out, oh, so surreptitiously, you thought, from the college dinner.'

'So you were the person behind me?' gasped Blake, as the book continued to stir with jubilant, ecstatic, powerful life. He could see the ink beginning to grow darker, taking on a more permanent form, as the words were released from their hibernation. 'You followed me to the library that night?'

'Oh, I've had my eye on you – and the library – for a long time,' said Diana boastfully. 'I always suspected that Psalmanazar returned Endymion Spring to St Jerome's for safekeeping, but I was never entirely certain where. You, however, led me right to it. Except, of course, the book had already disappeared by then.'

'And is Sir Giles after the Last Book, too?' asked Blake stupidly, trying to catch up.

'Of course he is,' snapped Diana. 'Giles collects books on forbidden knowledge. What could be more spectacular than the most tempting book of all?'

Her expression hardened. 'Mind you, he almost ruined everything by mentioning that elusive copy of *Goblin Market* – a book he couldn't have known about without a prior knowledge of the library's collections. But I don't think your brave little librarian had any idea what we'd really been looking for all this time.'

'And you?' asked Blake. 'What do you want the Last Book for?'

She smiled at him icily and then whispered in his ear, 'I'm after the power it possesses: the ability to foresee the future, to know the past. The opportunity to make children's nightmares real. What is the power of witchcraft or wizardry compared to that?'

Blake shivered.

'And now,' she said triumphantly, holding the book aloft, 'to read the Last Book.'

Just at that moment, there was a loud, ferocious baying from the street outside, as if a pack of hounds had descended on the library all at once. Blake ran to the window to see what was happening.

There was just one dog: a scruffy mongrel leaping against the gates in an attempt to get in. Alice! Psalmanazar was barely able to restrain her. He tugged on her bright red bandanna, but Alice pulled free and charged against the library. The noise of her barking reverberated against the sides of the building with a harsh, percussive echo that caused a crowd of spectators to stop and stare.

'Get away from there!' screamed Diana, dropping the book and racing towards him. She slashed a long, black fingernail across his neck and he winced as the sharp edge seared his skin. In an instant, he doubled back to the desk and seized the book and the butterfly clasp – anything to defend himself – from the tabletop.

The dog's howl grew more insistent. New voices joined the din. Duck pounded on the door below.

'Give that back!' said Diana fiercely.

Blake was surprised to feel the clip in his fingers curling towards the palm of his hand like a claw, as if to prick him. It was just like the clasp on Endymion Spring's note-book – the one that had scratched his knuckle once before.

And then, with sudden clarity, he knew what he had to do.

In one quick motion, he stabbed the point of the clasp deep into his finger and extended the injured digit over the edge of the Last Book. It was what the volume had first tried to accomplish in the college library; it was what the riddle had been telling him all along. *Until, with Child's blood, the Whole is sealed . . .*

He watched as blood welled in the wound and spilled on to the exposed pages.

'You beast!' screeched Diana. 'What are you doing? Get away from the book!'

She rushed headlong towards the table; then froze, horrified. The blood from Blake's finger had formed an immediate seal, a rusty red clot, on the side of the Last Book. The pages were sealed. Blake's heart burst with relief and he sank to the floor.

Diana grabbed the book from his weak fingers and clawed at the covers like a wild animal, yet the Last Book – no more than a battered brown volume – remained closed. She could not dislodge the crusty seal of blood. The bond held fast.

'What have you done?' she roared. 'Why won't it open?'

She glared at him furiously, but there was no answer.

Blake had already scooped up Duck's yellow raincoat from the floor and bolted towards the door. He opened it and scrambled up the uneven spiral staircase before she could react.

There was no time to rescue Duck. His best chance was to summon help from the roof. He sprinted up the remaining stairs, stumbling on the old stone steps, scraping at the walls with his sore fingers, and continued all the way up to the top of the tower.

Diana was close behind.

'Come back, you monster! Open the book!' her voice boomed in the narrow passageway.

Blake spotted an emergency exit just beneath the enormous turret and propelled himself towards it. Without thinking, he rammed his body against the door, grunting as the stiff metal bar punched into his stomach. Pain pummelled through his body. He tried again.

Luckily, the door gave way and he broke through on to a hard, uneven surface. The copper tiles tripped him and he went sprawling.

An alarm system trilled deafeningly in his ears.

For a moment, he rolled along the top of the square rooftop. Spires and gargoyles wheeled past his eyes. He landed on his back, groaning with pain, and stared up into blue space. Then, rising to his feet, he looked frantically for the fire escape.

A stone trellis surmounted by tall, knobbly turrets ran along the edges of the tower – far too high to clamber over. Through one of the carved quatrefoils, he could make out crowds of people in the street below.

'Hey! Up here!' he called out, waving his arms up and down to grab their attention; but his voice was smothered by the alarm bells and nobody noticed the terrified boy on the roof of the tower.

Sirens roared into life in the distance, responding to the emergency call, but they were still so far away.

Hobbling, Blake tried to make his way to the iron ladder on the opposite side of the rooftop, but Diana suddenly blocked his way. Her face was ruthless and cold. Losing all hope, he waved Duck's coat in the air and cried again for help.

Below him, people were struggling to restrain Alice, who was leaping crazily at the gates. Others were pointing at the library's many windows, trying to locate the source of the disruption. Finally, someone spotted a yellow shape flapping in the wind and caught sight of Blake. A number of startled faces peered up.

There was an astonished silence – then shrieks filled the air. People yelled and jumped, pointing behind him.

Blake turned round . . . but was too slow. A blinding blow – the Last Book – thwacked against the side of his face and he reeled backwards against the guard rail, hitting his head hard against the stone. He let go of Duck's jacket, which fluttered uselessly to the pavement far below.

He rubbed the side of his face and was sickened as his fingers came away wet with blood. Suddenly the world swam before his eyes. Everything slowed down. Helplessly, he appealed to Diana, who was clutching the Last Book to her chest – a look of murderous rage in her eyes.

'You will do as I say and open the book,' she said. 'Or I will kill you.'

He shook his head, barely able to form the words to defy her.

'No,' he muttered weakly.

She studied him with silent hatred and then said: 'So be it.'

With sudden vehemence, she locked one of her elbows round his neck and pulled him off his feet. His face felt as tight as a red balloon. 'If I don't get the book,' she snarled into his ear, 'then neither do you.'

Blake was powerless to resist. His arms fell to his sides, too heavy and too tired to fight back. He was exhausted. The shadow had won.

Diana's glove chafed against his skin, tightening its grip on his neck. He could barely breathe. He raked in dry, desperate gulps and his knees went weak.

Faintly, he could hear people yelling in the street. Hundreds of faces were looking up in horror, some taking pictures, but the sights and sounds reached him only dimly, drifting in on waves. He was drowning in mid-air. There was nothing anyone could do to help.

'I will not lose the book,' spat Diana, and pinned him against the stone railing. He could feel the sharp edge of a quatrefoil biting into his side. 'What a pity it has to end this way.'

'No!' he roared one last time, twisting and turning and biting and fighting with all his might.

Taken by surprise, Diana opened her hand and accidentally dropped the book. They both watched, horrified, as it fell through the open quatrefoil and into empty space.

Diana immediately released him from her grasp and groped at the air with her gloved fingertips, desperate to recapture the book as it tumbled over the side of the tower and plummeted down . . . down . . . down . . . into the waiting arms of Duck's yellow raincoat, which lay like a dead body a hundred feet below.

And then Blake slunk, senseless, to the ground.

OXFORD
Summer–Winter
1453

felt like I was flying.

Crowds reeled drunkenly around me, spinning on their heads, while houses, taverns and spires turned somersaults. Booths with canvas awnings swung at weird angles.

I could not tell where I was. The ground was thatched with mud and straw, and the sky stretched far above me like an impossibly blue ocean. My arms flailed uselessly to either side, the limbs of a dead man.

A stranger, I realized dimly, was transporting me through a market in the back of his cart. My head jolted painfully each time the wheels struck a loose stone, and twice I vomited.

A round, worried face peered down at me from the side of the cart. 'Be not afraid,' it said in the softest of voices – first in English, which I could not understand, and then in Latin, which I could. 'You are safe with me, Endymion.'

My brow furrowed. How did he know my name?

Then, sensing my confusion, the man smiled and added, 'I am Theodoric. I am taking you to St Jerome's.'

A circle of unruly hair crowned his head like a halo and a long black robe cloaked his body. His hands were as smooth and white as vellum, but covered in inky scribbles – like my Master's.

For a moment I feared an angel had come to take me up to heaven and I struggled to be set free. I still had my task to complete. I could feel the book of dragon skin strapped to my back, cutting into my flesh. Yet try as I might, I could not move. I could not even sit up.

The world swayed sickeningly around me and my head lolled weakly in the straw.

'Faster, Methuselah,' Theodoric urged the grizzled mule, which pulled the cart behind it and brayed objectionably at the extra load it was carrying.

Then everything plunged into darkness.

I dreamed a lion swallowed me. Its teeth were set in a silent roar, a shoulder's width apart, but luckily they had no bite. I passed through its stone mouth into a chamber full of books. The walls were pierced with light and the room divided into alcoves by a number of sloping desks and large chests. The air was quiet with the sound of quills and whispering parchment.

Bleary-eyed, I looked around me. Black-robed figures hunched over the desks, hard at work. Some were writing in a beautiful script that flowed from their quills in streams of ink, while others pressed thin sheets of gold to the capital letters they were adorning. Still more dipped their brushes in oyster shells of crushed crimson powder, which they applied to the flowers they were painting in the margins of a wonderful manuscript.

All of a sudden I understood the marks on Theodoric's hands. He was a scribe, an illuminator. He had taken me to one of Oxford's monastic colleges.

The book of dragon skin stirred again on my back and I squirmed, trying to get down; but Theodoric refused to let go. He carried me in his arms to the front of the room, where a small, white-haired man was seated on a large, throne-like chair. The Abbot was deep in prayer: his eyes closed, his fingers fumbling with the beads of a rosary.

An ancient librarian with skin like melted wax sat close beside him, reading from a tiny book. His lips made a soft sound like a sputtering candle as he recited the words to himself and traced them in his psalter. Suddenly, he stopped. One of his eyes was milky blue and rolled alarmingly in his head; the other, as clear as day, drifted towards me and fixed on my face.

Unnerved, I glanced away. Through the window, I could see a sapling in an enclosed garden, its pale green leaves shuddering in a breeze.

Luckily, the Abbot took one look at me, crossed himself and rushed to my aid. Despite his wild thistledown hair, he showed no signs of a prickly disposition. He clamped his hand to my forehead and checked for symptoms of disease. Then, ignoring the protests of Ignatius, the librarian beside him, he indicated that Theodoric should escort me to the infirmary.

Words were unnecessary. They communicated by means of a system of simple hand gestures.

Theodoric, however, stood his ground and slowly drew the Abbot's attention to the leather toolkit I normally wore beneath my belt. It had transformed itself into a sealed notebook ages ago. Somehow it had worked itself free.

I reached out to grab it, but Ignatius was too quick. He snatched the book before either I or the Abbot could lay our fingers on it.

I watched helplessly as the old man turned the notebook over in his hands and tried unsuccessfully to prise the covers apart. He studied the clasps more intently. No matter what he tried, he could not get the book to open. His brow creased in consternation and he shot me a suspicious look, as though the Devil lurked somewhere behind my eyes.

Theodoric, amused by the older man's struggles, calmly took back the book and showed it to the Abbot. Shifting my weight on to his shoulder, he underlined the name on the cover and gestured towards me. *Endymion Spring.* No wonder he had known my name.

The Abbot nodded thoughtfully and then, after gazing at the notebook for a while, made a curious writing motion with his hands. The message was clear: he wanted to know if I could read or write.

Theodoric shrugged.

I didn't have the strength to enlighten them. Despite the sunlight streaming in through the windows, I was shivering uncontrollably. My face was clammy and hot, and my body felt as though I had rolled in splintered glass. Every little noise boomed in my ears like thunder.

Theodoric looked at me worriedly and then, returning the book to my possession, cradled me in his arms and hurried me through the cloisters to the infirmary. My hands curled weakly round the book like an additional clasp.

We passed under another archway engraved with lion's teeth and dashed across an open area full of herb gardens and neatly cultivated flowerbeds. Wicker hives, daubed with clay, hummed in the distance. The air was sweet and honey-scented; but I barely noticed. Already, I was sinking into a deathly cold delirium.

By the time we reached the infirmary, a long low building close to the latrines, a fever had gripped me – and would not let go.

Fust waited for me in the darkness.

No matter how far I ran, no matter how hard I tried to escape, he always caught up with me the moment I closed my eyes. He swept into my dreams like a shadow, filling my heart with dread. Endlessly, he pursued me; endlessly, he hunted for the book . . .

From Mainz, I had fled not to Frankfurt, nor to Paris, as he had imagined, but to Eltville, a pretty little village on the banks of the River Rhine, where Herr Gutenberg had a niece. For a few days I sheltered among the fragrant grape-green hills; then, when Peter sent word that Fust had stormed off towards the Library of St Victor, hoping to overtake me, I grudgingly began my route north to Oxford.

For weeks, I kept to the grassy banks of the river. Fust had placed a bounty on my head and I was no better than a wanted criminal. I avoided the inns, which were infested with lice, fleas and thieves, and bedded down with the cows in the fields at night. Nowhere was safe. No one could be trusted.

The book was my sole companion, but even this did not contain any news of Herr Gutenberg or Peter. For all its power, it could not bring them back to me. I was befriended only by the past, by the memories of those I had left behind.

As I neared Coster's homeland, the birthplace of the book, the place where Coster had slain the dragon, I began to fear that Fust had finally caught up with me. His name was never far from the lips of the people I passed in the woods or villages; but it was a name spoken of with loathing and distrust. His theft had not been forgotten. It rankled in the hearts of Coster's country-men. Yet, even here, the book was not safe. Haarlem was too close to Mainz and Fust could follow my tracks too easily. Only in the depths of the vast new library William had described in the Little Lamb could its pages be properly hidden. I kept going.

In Rotterdam, where the Rhine meets the sea, I found a vessel bound for England and two or three days later emerged from it, dazed and disorientated, in a city far larger than any I had known: London. Hungry and cold, I shivered through the densely packed streets, shunning strangers and disappearing into anonymous cracks. I could not wait to be free of the city. Yet there seemed to be no end to the wharves, houses and alleys that flanked the busy river, spewing their filth into the mighty waterway that cut through the land like a gash. Boroughs festered outside the city walls.

Nevertheless, as the drunkard William had promised, the river eventually narrowed into a more navigable stream and I followed its wriggling course through the more pleasant countryside, overtaken by boats loaded with luxury silks and linens. Half-starved, I stole from farms and hamlets, sheltered beneath the lychgates of old stone churches and watched miserably each night as the day's reflections sank in the turbid water.

Finally, Oxford lay, huddled in mist, on the other side of the river. The spires were not nearly so grand as I had imagined – they squatted closer to earth than aspired to heaven – but I was cheered by the thought of colleges and libraries, and the expectation of somewhere warm to rest my weary feet, which were rubbed raw with blisters.

I rushed forwards, joining a pilgrimage of labourers up to the South Gate, but my cheerfulness turned almost immediately to despair.

'Your kind is not welcome here,' snarled the shorter and smellier of the guards at the gate. I could barely comprehend his language. His face, however, said it all. His partner stared fixedly over my head at the restless line of people behind me.

My bright yellow cloak was no more than a soiled rag and my skin covered with sores and abrasions. I looked like a victim of the plague.

I began to unfold my notebook, hoping to prove that I could read and write – surely a valuable skill in a university town – but they were not impressed.

'Look, be off with you,' said the more officious guard. 'If you don't move on, I'll throw you in the boggards' prison myself.'

He shoved me roughly back and I tripped over the edge of a cartwheel that had been drawn up close behind. I collapsed in a pool of muck and thought I heard a mule snigger. Tears of humiliation pricked my eyes.

I got up and brushed the dirt from my already tattered clothes. I had faced too many obstacles to be turned away so easily. While the guards inspected the other travellers, checking their loads and wagons, I concealed myself in a cartload of squawking chickens and sneaked into town. Theodoric, however, must have noticed my notebook and kept a safe distance behind, biding his time . . . until my fever overcame me, my world went black and I collapsed in the filthy street.

I awoke to find Theodoric examining the little notebook by my side, wondering why the clasps would not open even for him. He noticed me eyeing him from the edge of sleep and welcomed me back to the world of the living with an immense grin.

We were in a long infirmary lined with straw-filled beds. I was the sole occupant.

Sheets of radiant light streamed in from the vine-trellised windows, offering glimpses of the garden outside. Chests and cabinets stood with their backs to the walls.

The afternoon hummed with heat. Flies circled the air in drowsy loops and bees droned near their hives. Bunches of dried flowers had been tied to the rafters to obliterate the smells of death and disease, the room's previous tenants.

Theodoric looked around him apprehensively. I could tell that a question was burning his lips, but he seemed uncertain how – or if – to ask it. Despite my aching bones, I sat up, grimacing with the effort.

'You can read?' he said at last, when he judged the room to be free.

I nodded.

'And write?' he asked, even more doubtful. He glanced at the window, through which we could see black-robed monks tending the garden, hopping from plant to plant like crows. Theodoric had phrased both questions in Latin, which it pleased him to know I understood.

Again I nodded.

'But this,' he said, pointing to the book and stroking the letters on the cover. 'This is a different kind of book. You are blessed with a secret knowledge, yes?'

Wearily, I smiled. I was too tired to explain. Besides, who would believe my story?

Theodoric did not appear to mind my silence. 'You must rest,' he said finally, and then got up as a solitary bell clanged outside, summoning him to prayers.

The bed they had placed me in was as soft as a cloud. I could have lain there forever. It had freshly laundered sheets, sprinkled with lavender and tansy to keep the fleas at bay, and the straw mattress smelled every bit as sweet as the day it was threshed. I did not care that this could be my deathbed. After the ditches and fields I had slept in, it felt like heaven.

For days, I drifted in and out of consciousness. Each time I surfaced, I found Theodoric doting over me like a faithful puppy. He treated the chilblains on my feet with a poultice made from marjoram and prepared bitter-sweet remedies for me to drink. At first, the feverfew and lemon balm made my skin erupt in prickles of sweat, but gradually I began to recover my appetite and regain my strength. Soon I was able to sit up and take note of my surroundings.

My clothes lay in a paltry heap on the floor at the foot of the bed – a dingy skin I had sloughed off like a past life. The bright yellow cloak, which Christina had so lovingly sewed for me, was now no more than a flimsy burial shroud. In its place I wore a garment of white cloth, its sleeves far too wide for my skinny arms. They spread out from my shoulders like wings.

To amuse me, Theodoric tried on the long yellow hood I had worn on my arrival. It sat on his head like a dirty sock, a tiny jester's cap, making me laugh. Whereas the other monks shuffled past as discreetly as possible, keeping a respectful distance, though vows of silence were not strictly observed, Theodoric seemed unable to remain quiet or still for long. He was too full of questions.

Where had I come from? Why had I chosen Oxford? What was so special about the books I carried?

I tried my best to satisfy his curiosity with a system of nods and smiles, but said nothing. He trusted that I would speak when the time was right.

The book strapped to my back had caused no end of speculation when the monks first undressed me. Theodoric told me there were rumours, perpetuated by Ignatius, that I carried the Devil on my shoulders: the sealed volume was surely a sign of my wicked heart. But if my strange cargo troubled Theodoric he gave no indication of it. Instead, he tried to assure me that both books were safe in a chest close to my bed. He had one key, and I the other. He would let no one near them.

Occasionally, the librarian visited the infirmary.

Cowled in black, he made a pretext of checking the properties of the herbs he was including in a book of medicine, but I could feel his eye on me whenever he was near. It was as though he could sense the nature of the dragon skin I was concealing. He was forever scribbling notes in a private journal, muttering to himself, his fingers scurrying like spiders.

Sadly, I began to realize that no hiding place – not even in Oxford – would be safe for the book. There would always be people like Fust, or Ignatius, desiring the knowledge it contained. It was a temptation too great to resist; it attracted evil like a magnet. The curse of Adam and Eve lived among all men.

Luckily, the Abbot was sympathetic to my plight. Books were valuable commodities in Oxford – scholars devoted their lives to them and the town teemed with bookbinders, papermakers and stationers, all busy copying manuscripts in the vicinity of the Church of St Mary the Virgin – and so he invited me to stay on at St Jerome's even after I began to recuperate. Impressed by my ability to read and write, he delighted in showing me the work of the college scribes.

For years, they had been copying a translation of the Bible, supposed to have been written by their patron saint, Jerome. It was a labour of love: a book full of beautiful calligraphy and devout illustrations.

413

Theodoric, in particular, was a gifted illuminator. When he was not busy lampooning the other monks as foxes and gargoyles in the margins of the manuscript, he was imagining a world full of saints and angels.

Slowly, in my own way, I began to teach him the principles of printing. I lacked my Master's skill and equipment, but relied on clumsier methods – whittling letters from strips of willow that we found near the river, instructing him with messages written on a wax tablet with a stylus. Theodoric, to his credit, caught on quickly and began to incorporate some of the innovations and techniques in his work.

On one occasion, he pressed a large O he had carved from wood on to the surface of the vellum he was illuminating and decorated it with a fancy picture of the two of us. I was seated on his lap like a tiny yellow puppet, speaking volumes. Ignatius objected to the monstrosity, proclaiming it an abomination, but the Abbot allowed it to pass, indicating that I was a welcome initiate of the Order.

If Ignatius viewed me with suspicion and hostility, then Theodoric was my saviour, my guardian and my friend. More than anything, it was his love of life that nursed me back to health.

Days lengthened into weeks, and weeks drew slowly into months. Trees thatching the hills in the distance gradually lost their colour and chill mists blistered the landscape. Winter closed in.

Memories of Mainz continued to fill me with wisps of longing, but I was gradually building a new life here in Oxford. I quickly learned the layout of the streets. Not surprisingly, a large proportion of the scholars – like William – spent their time in the taverns, their rooming houses much too squalid or dilapidated to live in. The Swyndelstock Tavern and the Bear Inn were the most popular, and I often dived into their boozy, warm interiors to escape Ignatius, who took it into his head to follow me on occasion. The rooms were rife with unwholesome discussion and I began to suspect that some of the scholars learned far more here than in their tutorials.

My excursions, however, did little to diminish Ignatius' suspicions. Word began to arrive from the continent of a Black Art, a mode of artificial writing that produced mirror copies of books. It was no more than a whisper, but Ignatius believed I held the key to such secrets. He thirsted to know more. He began to keep vigil by my bed at night, his blind eye rolling in its socket and his good one hunting for the truth – a truth he never learned. I took to carrying the book of dragon skin again on my back, and the toolkit concealed beneath my girdle, anything to keep its knowledge safe with me.

I had to find a more secure resting place for them – and fast.

The answer came on a frosty December morning.

Theodoric was summoned to the Congregation House in the centre of town to discuss the performance of three young novitiates who had embarked on a course of undergraduate study.

While he met with the university officials in a small stone chamber attached to the Church of St Mary the Virgin, I was free to roam through the Old Library above. A long rectangular room, it was full of gowned scholars, mainly standing at dark wooden lecterns, memorizing lengthy tracts from books. The moth-like flutter of lips drowned out the sound of my book of dragon skin, which, strapped to my back, responded to the setting with excited flickers of movement.

At the far end of the library, under an arched window overlooking the recent foundations of the College of All Souls of the Faithful Departed, was an immense chest. Longer than I was tall, it was fortified with thick metal slats, like an iron maiden, which the librarian calmly told me no living man could break. Five locks awaited five keys from five separate key-holders to unleash its secrets. Inside lay irreplaceable documents pertaining to the university's origins and a pile of books belonging to students who could no longer afford their tuition. They had to pay their debts in books – for books, in Oxford at least, were as precious as gold.

For a moment, I considered hiding the book of dragon skin inside. What better place could there be than a guarded chest in a spectacular library? But there was no way of picking the locks unaided and the bearded librarian was regarding me with suspicion. Besides, the magical paper was pulling me in a different direction.

A hundred or so paces from the Old Library was another structure, a half-built edifice girded by ladders and wooden scaffolds. For almost three decades, masons had been working on an exquisite chamber to house a collection of books bequeathed to the university by Humfrey, Duke of Gloucester. This was the room William had spoken of in the Little Lamb, the library to rival Alexandria!

Everything seemed to be leading towards this moment. I hurried towards the building, my heart full of joy. My journey was almost at an end.

And yet, when I looked around me, I could see that the chamber was hardly a hallowed depository for books: workmen clambered over the wooden platforms, industrious as ants, and tall fluted columns supported a ceiling of open sky. Reeds matted the ground, bundled against the walls to prevent the damp from seeping in. The time was not yet right. The book and I would have to wait.

Disheartened, I ventured outside and stood in the cold, desolate square. Clouds of powdered stone hovered in the air as masons chipped a forest of foliage from the massive slabs of rock that had been drawn up close to the library. Squinting away my disappointment, I peered up at the lonely spire of St Mary the Virgin. The church seemed no match for the magnificent cathedral I had left behind in Mainz. Once again, I felt empty, alone.

For a while, I paced back and forth between the two libraries, the old and the new, unable to settle, beginning to despair that my mission had been in vain. Around me the town heaved with activity. From the south came the competing calls of peddlers and street-sellers, while the anguished cries of cattle in the slaughterhouse close to the castle sluiced through the lanes from the west. Flies buzzed everywhere – around the heaps of salted fish on the market stalls, the carcasses of meat dangling from the butchers' shambles and the ropes of entrails slung across the streets. Scribes ducked into the nearby binderies, keen to replenish their supplies.

And then I glimpsed something. On the far side of the church, obscured by a stunted, twisted tree, a series of stone steps led down to a tiny door set into the wall of the chapel. My pulse quickened. Could there be a hidden chamber beneath the church? A vault, perhaps, silted up and forgotten?

Like a hand pressed to my back, the book of dragon skin propelled me towards it.

Careful to ensure I was not followed, I stepped over the knot of roots and tiptoed down the stairs, wrestling with the worm-eaten door at the bottom. With some difficulty, I managed to wrench it open and entered the darkness beyond. The air was as chill as a grave, but virtually dry.

My eyes took time to adjust. Archways led into even colder, dimmer rooms and I ventured into some of these, eventually encountering a dead end where I felt the brown breath of earth close in all around me. Shadows stood guard in the corners; webs grew like moss on the walls. Apart from a few scraps of leather and scrolls of parchment – pickings from the neighbouring binderies perhaps – the shelves that lined the walls were bare. Whatever its previous purpose, this barren catacomb was now derelict and abandoned.

In the middle of the chamber was a shallow depression, a font of darkness. On an impulse I took the book of dragon skin from its harness on my back and laid it carefully inside the pit, then covered it quickly with the surrounding dirt, planting it like a seed. It seemed like a perfect hiding place: halfway between the House of God and the new house of learning. In my mind at least, another tree of knowledge began to grow – an amazing tree like the one Coster's granddaughter had first espied, a tree containing all the knowledge in the world.

Hearing Theodoric's worried voice calling me from outside, I wiped the dirt from my hands and emerged into the bright, restless world, blinking away the sudden light. Life went on. Peddlers flogged their wares; masons tapped at stone; and flies bickered over the ever-growing mounds of dung. Nothing had changed. And yet everything had.

My trembling body felt lighter and freer than it had in ages, as though a great burden had been lifted from my shoulders; but there was also an unexpected emptiness there too, a hole deep inside me, as though I had mislaid part of my identity. The paper had absorbed my thoughts and feelings for so long, as though it could read my mind.

All of a sudden, I realized that I had not included my own little toolkit with the rest of the dragon skin. The final, completing section of the paper was still in my possession.

My hands delved beneath my cloak, where my fingers brushed against the familiar leather notebook. My name was still printed on its surface, as though it rightfully belonged to me. I did not have the heart to surrender this remaining piece of my story. Not yet. It was my connection to the past, my link to the future. More than anything, it was my voice.

A friendly hand tapped me on the shoulder and the beam of Theodoric's smile fell full on my face and removed any doubt. I patted the little notebook once more, its secret safe with me, and followed Theodoric towards the North Gate and the open doors of St Jerome's.

This, for now, was my home.

OXFORD

Twenty-six

A kiss woke him.

Blake had been dreaming once again of snow – it settled on top of him like a blanket – but at the touch of a solitary snowflake melting on his brow, he surfaced to find his father sitting beside him, watching over him with tired affection. How had he got there?

Blake blinked, confused.

His father's face was worn and haggard, and there were bags under his eyes. His clothes were creased; but somewhere beneath the stale, ashy scent was the familiar fragrance of home.

It made Blake feel warm and safe. He rolled over on to his side and dozed off again, smiling happily.

A few hours later, he awoke with a start.

Had it all been a dream?

He opened his eyes. At first he was aware of nothing more than a quiet white light, which settled all around him like a pillow. Then his mind started scrambling up a heap of discarded images and he clawed his way back to consciousness. His body ached just enough to remind him that the nightmare had in fact been real.

He took in his surroundings. The bed was thin and hard, like a stretcher, and the starched sheets almost surgically sharp. Blips and beeps filled the silence. There was also the regular sucking sound of a breathing apparatus – which luckily was not attached to him. Furtively, he brushed his fingers against his nose.

He must be in a hospital.

His parents were sitting near him, nursing him with anxious expressions, while Duck, wrapped in a shiny silver blanket, was watching a doctor administer something to a clear plastic bladder above his head. Liquid dripped into a tube attached to his wrist.

'He'll be all right,' the doctor was saying. 'We've bandaged his right index finger and stitched the other cuts, but he suffered a nasty blow to the head. We'll keep him in overnight to rule out concussion. He's been through an ordeal.'

Blake's head felt like it had been stuffed with cotton wool. He swallowed back a rising tide of nausea.

'Of course,' said Blake's father. 'We can't wait to get him home, that's all.'

Home . . . Somehow the word sounded different.

Blake lay where he was, catching glimpses of his family between the curtains of his closed lashes. His father placed a reassuring hand on Duck's shoulder and then gripped his mother – tightly – round the waist. To Blake's astonishment, she was crying.

Blake didn't have the strength to say or do anything; he just pretended to go on sleeping. He was unwilling to open his eyes fully in case the vision of his family, safe and reunited at last, disappeared.

It was like a dream he didn't want to end.

'Isn't he awake yet?' muttered Duck, sensing some animation behind his eyelids.

'I don't think so,' said her father.

'Don't wake him,' added her mother.

This didn't stop Duck, however, from approaching and tapping him on the forehead. 'Hello in there. Anyone home?'

A vicious pain tore down the side of his head. He moaned.

'Duck!' both parents admonished her and quickly pulled her away.

'See? I told you he was awake.'

Blake's body felt like it had been dismembered and then stitched back together again with barbed wire. Despite the snags of pain, he tried to sit up.

'Hunh?' he grunted groggily, as the pain welled again in his head and he sank back down, exhausted.

'Don't move your head, darling.'

'Diana Bentley's been arrested!'

'Duck!'

'We're just relieved you're safe, darling. There's plenty of time for you to tell us everything.'

Blake shook his head, struggling to make sense of the bombardment of voices. Sounds echoed in his ears.

'But how?' he asked vaguely, feeling sick.

'You rescued me!' cried Duck.

'Well, it was the dog actually,' stated her mother. 'It started barking hysterically and leaping at the library gates. I thought it was rabid at first. The owner was a peculiar man; he kept pointing at the roof, muttering something I couldn't comprehend . . .'

'It was Alice!' cheered Duck, but her mother took no notice.

'And then, of course, the alarm went off,' she continued. 'I saw you waving Duck's coat from the top of the tower and struggling with that wretched woman. It was like a scene in a movie. I couldn't believe my eyes.'

'Then the police arrived . . .' Duck fast-forwarded the narrative.

'Yes, they clambered up to the roof to save you,' said his mother, 'but for a moment I thought Diana Bentley was going to kill you.'

'She was,' Blake tried to say, but the words stuck in his throat.

To his surprise, his mother started weeping.

'And Dad?' he asked wearily. 'How did you –'

He reached out a hand that he couldn't quite control and ended up pointing at the floor.

'I was already on my way here,' said Christopher Winters, taking his son's hand and tucking it beneath the covers. 'I'd been trying to contact you for days. I missed you.'

His story was punctuated by a yawn.

'Besides, I heard from yours truly here –' he patted Duck on the head, who squirmed uncomfortably – 'that Prosper Marchand was back in the neighbourhood. I couldn't have him making advances on your mother, so I rushed to the airport, boarded a plane last night and arrived in Oxford early this afternoon . . . to a chorus of shrieks and sirens. I knew that you and your sister must be up to your usual tricks.'

Blake grinned, but was unable to take it all in. 'You know Professor Marchand?' he said at last.

His father stiffened slightly and nodded. 'He and your mother were once quite an item before I, um, complicated matters.'

Juliet Winters shook her head. 'What makes you think I would –' she started.

'I just wanted to make sure,' he said, meekly wrapping an arm around her shoulders. 'I missed you . . . all of you.'

'I missed you too,' said Blake, with a tired smile. 'I'm glad you're here.'

'Come now, the boy needs his rest,' said another voice from the edge of the room.

Blake craned his neck to see a familiar white-haired figure blocking the door with his giant frame. The movement set off an explosion of fireworks in his head and he winced.

Sensing they needed some privacy, Blake's parents got up. 'Excuse us,' they said. 'We'll step outside for a moment.'

'It's good to see you again, Jolyon,' added Blake's father privately.

'And you, my boy, and you,' murmured the professor. They dragged Duck after them.

'I know what you're going to say,' said Jolyon, as soon as the room was clear. Blake focused his intent blue eyes on the man's face. 'I was after the book . . . once. I was as desperate as Diana to get my hands on it.'

'She said you broke the clasp.'

Jolyon contemplated his thumb for a moment.

'Yes.'

Duck, who had managed to sneak back in, gasped.

'Go away!' shouted Blake, but his voice was no more than a husky croak.

Jolyon intervened. 'No, no, your sister has a right to hear this, too. I'm afraid I've not been entirely honest with either of you.'

Duck tiptoed closer. 'What happened?' she asked, curious.

'I was jealous of George Psalmanazar,' said the professor bleakly. 'He found the blank book. We were good friends, but I ruined everything by trying to see inside it for myself. I wanted to solve its riddles.'

'Like me,' said Duck softly.

The old man did not seem to hear. He had retreated into his own private world of memory. 'Yes, the book does that to you,' he said. 'It makes you greedy for knowledge, for power.'

His voice clouded. 'I tried to steal it from him,' he remembered, 'an action I regret to this day. The book must have sensed I was unworthy, for it rejected me and George disappeared shortly afterwards. He remained somewhere near Oxford, I believe, probably to keep an eye on the book, but he never uttered another word to anyone. That is, not until the night of Sir Giles's lecture, when he told me the shadow was getting closer.'

Jolyon paused. 'I thought he was referring to me,' he said, shuffling guiltily, 'but I was wrong.'

'Diana Bentley wanted it even more than you,' said Blake.

'Yes,' said the professor, examining the floor. 'She desired the Last Book more than anything – anyone – else. She seduced me, she used George and she finally took advantage of Sir Giles's money and influence to try to get her hands on it. The power it contained consumed her.'

'But she couldn't find it,' said Blake. 'At least, not until we came along.'

'I'm afraid the book awoke shadows in us all,' admitted Jolyon, broodingly. 'Except in you.'

Blake's confidence suddenly collapsed. 'But, Professor Jolyon, I don't know where the book is! I dropped it from the library roof and . . .'

'Relax,' said the professor mildly, resting a reassuring hand on his shoulder. 'The book is waiting for you, I promise. It will find you again – once you're ready.'

'But how?' asked Blake doubtfully.

'Trust me. You are its rightful guardian, Blake. Endymion Spring chose you for a reason.'

Blake shook his head. 'I still don't know why,' he

muttered to himself, as a nurse entered the room to tell them that visiting hours were over.

Jolyon heard the boy's last remark and smiled.

'Perhaps you should ask your father,' he said mysteriously, as he led Duck to the door.

Twenty-seven

B lake was once again in the college library, waiting
for his mother.

'What's keeping her?' said his father, letting out
a long, exasperated sigh. He glanced at his watch. 'It's
been an hour.'

'You have no idea,' said Blake, and together, they started
walking up and down the corridors, running their fingers
along the books. Christopher Winters peered at the shelves,
revisiting old memories, while Blake pondered more recent
ones. He couldn't help suspecting the portraits were still
watching him – hunting for the book, even in death.

They paused as they came to the central staircase
leading up to the gallery.

'Have you seen this?' asked Blake, eager for a diversion. He steered his father up the steps and showed him
the illustration of the hunched yellow figure on the
monk's knee in the illuminated manuscript.

Christopher Winters smiled. 'Oh yes, Theodoric and I go way back,' he said, gazing fondly down at the tonsured monk. 'There was a time when I spent most of my waking hours studying this book. I had quite a theory about it.'

'No kidding?' said Blake, feeling the blood rush through his veins.

'It's all a bit complicated . . .' His father shuffled uneasily from foot to foot. 'You probably wouldn't believe me.'

'Try me.'

Christopher Winters glanced down at his son. 'Well, this little yellow figure here almost perfectly resembles another on a coat of arms found in Germany at around the same time. The Gutenberg coat of arms, to be precise.'

Blake tried not to show the shiver of excitement that ran through him.

'Scholars have disputed the identity of the yellow figure for years, but how anyone, let alone a monk in Oxford, could know of this enigmatic character is a complete mystery,' remarked Christopher Winters. 'I've always suspected that there's a direct link between this manuscript and Gutenberg's first printing press in Mainz. I'm not sure exactly how, but if you look closely, you can see that the figure is actually . . .'

435

'. . . a young kid like me,' said Blake, with a grin.

His father gawped at him in amazement.

'Exactly,' he said, shaking his head slightly.

Blake had tried several times in recent days to explain the strange goings-on to his parents, but until now they both attributed much of his story to his fanciful imagination. They believed Diana had desired an important book he had inadvertently found in a secondhand bookshop. For his part, Blake had been careful to describe the *Faustbuch* to them, instead of Endymion Spring.

'Yes, he's a young boy like you,' said his father, 'but with a hunched back, as though he's carrying a heavy burden. There's something on his shoulders.'

'Oh no, not this again,' interrupted Juliet Winters, joining them from downstairs. In her hand she held a draft of her most recent article, 'The Faust Conspiracy', fresh from the printer in her office. Duck was with her and had bent down to stroke Mephistopheles, who arched and curved around her legs – his tail held high like an exclamation mark.

Christopher Winters looked hurt. 'You never know,' he said. 'I might have been right.'

Juliet Winters shook her head and led them out.

Duck was giggling.

'Don't listen to your mother,' said Christopher Winters privately, as Blake followed him down the library steps.

'There's a fascinating story that a devil once travelled to Oxford with a strange book of knowledge on his back. I think this could be . . .'

It was another unseasonably warm day and they decided to take the long way home.

That night, as he was preparing for bed, Blake heard a soft scratching sound outside the house on Millstone Lane. He rushed to the door and looked out.

A bright yellow package lay on the front step: Duck's raincoat. Its sleeves were neatly folded across its chest, but the body was filthy and smeared with dirt after her exertions in the library. Blake wondered if she would ever wear it again. He doubted it.

He scanned the dark, frosty street for a sign of Psalmanazar or his dog, but they were nowhere to be seen. He longed to speak to the man about everything that had happened. Quickly, he picked up the coat and closed the door.

Wrapped inside the sleeves was another object – a book. Blake unfolded them, his heart beginning to pound. Endymion Spring was there, still sealed with his crusty patch of blood. His injured finger, cocooned in gauze, throbbed with the memory.

Carefully, he stroked the leather cover. It didn't look

like much, but the book contained the secrets to the whole world. He wasn't sure that he wanted it back in his life – the thought of all it enclosed frightened him – and yet the same exhilarating shudder passed through his skin when he touched it, as though the book were meant exclusively for him.

For the first time, he believed he truly understood his part in the riddle. He was the sun the book kept referring to: the son of two seasons, Christopher Winters and Juliet Somers, temporarily divided and now reunited again. Individually, they knew parts of Endymion Spring's story – and, together, the whole.

He could hear them now, sitting side by side in the lounge, reliving their Oxford days. They weren't talking as much as he had hoped, but there was a different kind of silence between them: a more hopeful one. Blake was beginning to feel more optimistic about the future.

Everything was working out fine, exactly as the first riddle had told him it would. *The Order of Things will last forever* . . .

Blake glanced down again at the scuffed leather volume. What more could it tell him?

Almost at his bidding, the solitary clasp came undone and the seal of blood disintegrated like red powder before his eyes. The pages began to flicker. Blake's heart leaped with excitement.

Quickly, he checked on his parents, saw that he was not needed and scrambled up the stairs. 'I'm going to bed,' he called out hastily and bolted to his bedroom. He slammed the door behind him.

Then, in the privacy of his own room, face to face with the book, he sat down on his bed and considered the Last Book more carefully. *Endymion Spring*. The name seemed so familiar to him now, like a friend.

Very slowly, he opened the cover . . .

Historical Note

T he book you are now holding took on a life of its own when a good friend asked me an all-important question: 'Who was Endymion Spring?' Until then, Endymion had been 'more of a shadow than an actual person, a whisper rather than a voice'. I decided to scour the stacks of the Bodleian Library to find out. What I learned next amazed me.

In a crumbly old volume from the sixteenth century, I discovered a long-forgotten secret: the true father of the printing press was not Johann Gutenberg, as most people believe, but Laurens Coster, a Dutch woodblock-cutter who chanced upon a magnificent beech tree while walking in a wood near Haarlem. To please his grand-children, he carved some letters from the bark. When he got home, he discovered that the sap from the blocks had bled into the handkerchief they were wrapped in and left a trace of his handmade alphabet behind. The stain gave him an idea: why not print books using movable pieces of wooden type?

Unfortunately, there was a thief in his midst. On Christmas Eve, while Coster attended Mass, someone broke into his workshop, stole his materials, and fled to Mainz, where the felon conspired to set up the 'first' printing press with Johann Gutenberg, a talented gold-smith who chose to cast the type from metal, not wood – a decision that would change the world. The culprit was none other than 'Johann Faust'.

My pulse started racing. Was this true? I quickly turned to another book, which told a different story. No, Johann Fust was not a thief, but a shrewd busi-nessman who invested a large amount of money in Gutenberg's press. He then dissolved his partnership with the inventor just before the Bible could recoup its costs, sued the man for all he was owed, and was awarded the rights to the printer's equipment (as well as the Bible), effectively putting him out of business. Gutenberg disappeared into relative obscurity while Fust and his son-in-law, Peter Schoeffer, spread their names far and wide across Europe . . .

I turned to another, darker volume. No, Fust was actu-ally 'Faust': the German magician who sold his soul to the Devil for all the knowledge and experience in the world. For centuries, the tale inspired many works of literature, including Christopher Marlowe's *The Tragical History of Doctor Faustus* (1588), and led to a false belief that the press had diabolical origins . . .

How could there be so many interpretations of the past, so many cases of theft and deception? I picked up another book – a mouldering volume by an eighteenth-century printer, Prosper Marchand – but it was riddled with footnotes that clarified nothing and I hastily discarded it. Then I came across a compelling account of the printing press by a mysterious man who had hoodwinked London society into believing he was an exile of a far-off country: 'George Psalmanazar'. He even spoke a made-up language. Could his version of events be trusted?

I delved further into the stacks, poring over each shelf, reading books at random. And yet there was a voice deep inside me quietly insisting that there was something I wasn't quite seeing, some secret that would bring all of these stories together. And that's when I noticed the curious hunchbacked figure on the Gutenberg coat of arms, the peculiar yellow-clad figure that no one has ever been able to explain . . . I opened my notebook. I suddenly knew the answer to that crucial question. Almost immediately, as if by magic, words started appearing on a blank sheet of paper.

Acknowledgements

I wish to thank my family and friends for their unwavering belief in Endymion Spring and to express my gratitude to the following people for their kind assistance with the telling of his story: Sharon Hamilton; Sarah Emsley; Catherine Clarke, Jackie Head, and everyone at Felicity Bryan; Rebecca McNally, Elv Moody, Sarah Fergusson, Tom Sanderson, Adele Minchin and the enthusiastic team at Puffin, especially Francesca Dow.

I am also indebted to numerous works for their factual accounts of the early printing press. I based parts of the Dance of Death scene on Albert Kapr's *Johann Gutenberg: The Man and His Invention* (1996); used John Man's *The Gutenberg Revolution: The story of a genius and an invention that changed the world* (2002) to get a better sense of the period; and first spotted the image of the bizarrely clad figure on the Gutenberg coat of arms in Stephan Füssel's *Johann Gutenberg* (2000). Adrian Johns' *The Nature of the Book: Print and Knowledge in the Making* (1998) explains the Johann Fust/Faust conspiracies in detail and was an endless source of wonder and inspiration (including the naming of two of my characters). The 'Book of Sand' was dreamed up by Jorge Luis Borges, who also considered the idea of hiding a leaf in a forest and imagined a fantastic library, while an actual 'Last Book' is currently being developed by the Massachusetts Institute of Technology. As for Leafdragons: it is rumoured that one was spotted in a tree on Woodstock Road in Oxford not so long ago.